CHRISTMAS TAILS OF THE HEART

JOSIE RIVIERA

INTRODUCTION

To keep up on newly released ebooks, paperbacks, Large Print Paperbacks, audiobooks, as well as exclusive sales, sign up for Josie's Newsletter today.

As a thank you, I'll send you a Free PDF ... The Beauty Of ...

Josie's Newsletter

Did you know that according to a Yale University study, people who read books live longer?

Copyright © 2022 by Josie Riviera

All rights reserved.

No part of this book may be reproduced in any form or by any electronic or mechanical means, including information storage and retrieval systems, without written permission from the author, except for the use of brief quotations in a book review.

5 STAR READER REVIEWS

"Josie Riviera has written this book with the sensitivity of the soul of a genuine musician who also has a deep understanding of God's love and His power of restoration in every area of life. She carefully crafts the personalities of her characters so that each one is unique, and the reader can easily identify with one or all of them. Her attention to detail is remarkable as she allows you to see people and places and to become a citizen of Cherish. You will want to stay there! Thanks Josie Riviera for enriching the Christmas season with this inspiring story." - Amazon Reviewer (*A Christmas To Cherish*)

"A nice combination of characters....Max, Sarah and also the message of Christmas. Loving nature, the environment was perfect with the birds and the others of the forest. Toss in a harmonica and a puppy....(who doesn't love a little puppy?) and the scene is set.

Truly a wonderful positive story for this upcoming season. Most highly recommended..." - Amazon Reviewer (*A Christmas Puppy To Cherish*)

"Chiara moved to Virginia three years ago for a guy and then she broke up with him and since she was already in school so she waited and this Christmas is the last time she is away from her family on Christmas. Vance is divorced and determined not to marry again and then he meets his sister's new nurse try as he might he can't get his mind off of her and now he and Gertrude are celebrating Christmas because of Chiara. Pregnant horses, two people who are scarred by love don't believe they can find it again is like watching a Hallmark movie but in actuality reading a Josie Rivera book. Awesome, well written and the characters are amazing." - Amazon Reviewer (*Sweet Peppermint Kisses*)

InD'Tale Magazine Review:
Inspirational Romance
"If one is looking for a sweet, Christian story, Josie Riviera is a go-to. The sweet and innocent

chemistry between the protagonists will make the reader smile. A feel-good story from beginning to end!"

This book is dedicated to all my wonderful readers who have supported me every inch of the way.
THANK YOU!

CONTENTS

A CHRISTMAS PUPPY TO CHERISH

CHRISTMAS TAILS OF THE HEART

A CHRISTMAS TO CHERISH

SWEET PEPPERMINT KISSES

PRAISE AND AWARDS

USA TODAY bestselling author

DEAR FRIENDS

A heartwarming story is the hallmark of a romantic read. Savor the magic of this collection with three sweet, clean and wholesome inspirational holiday romances.

Find out why readers are falling in love with **our precious animals** & staying up all night reading!

This collection contains 3 books. Available in ebook, paperback, Hardcover, and Large Print paperback.

Each book and audiobook also sold separately.

A Christmas Puppy To Cherish

You don't need ears to hear God's plan. All you need is an open heart...

Music of both birds and harmonicas fills Max's life, but it's the near-silent forest guide he meets in

Cherish, SC, who captures his attention. Small and slim, pretty Sarah's smiles and graceful hands speak louder than her voice. In fact, she's so quiet, he's not sure he's made much of an impression. But with her, he can imagine making this temporary stopover into something permanent.

Sarah has found a comfortable niche in Cherish, working miracles with plants, arranging flowers for church, and taking in stray animals. In fact, her house is so full, she's not sure she can say yes to the Sheriff's plea to take in one more puppy for Christmas.

Max has definitely captured her interest, and he shares her love of nature. But maybe she should take in that puppy after all, because a ball of fur that needs her will fill the empty space in her heart when Max's research sends him off looking for bluer skies.

A Christmas To Cherish

There's nothing a Christmas kiss won't cure. Except perhaps a shattered heart…

When Emmanuelle Sumter steps off the train in Cherish, South Carolina—a town simply glowing with the promise of Christmas—she finds herself praying God will help her find the broken pieces of her life. Shattered, like her beloved harp. Her dreams. And her trust in men.

Her friend Dorothy told her Cherish is a safe haven. But she never expected Dorothy's brother, Deputy Nicholas Thompson, would relight the one thing she thought she'd lost forever. A spark of hope.

Not long ago, while Nicholas' sister was in rehab, Emmanuelle's voice and smile on his Skype screen held him together. After that, she seemed to disappear, an absence he felt keenly when his ex-fiancée left his faith in God dented but not broken.

Now she's in Cherish, even more stunning in person. Yet she's holding tight to a private pain she refuses to reveal. Nicholas resolves to be patient, vowing that he'll never let anyone hurt her again. Even when her past rears its ugly head to destroy what's left of her heart.

Note: Contains references to verbal and physical abuse.

Sweet Peppermint Kisses

There's no place like home. Until the heart gallops off in an unexpected direction...

After Chiara passes her RN license exam, she plans to leave Virginia and return to her beloved Kansas hometown for good. Except her home health client's handsome brother makes her consider changing her plans.

Between his job, his sister's injury, and his horse ranch, Vance has no time for Christmas. But Chiara's delight in the season makes him willing to do anything to keep the enchanting smile on her face. When it comes down to asking her to stay, can he let go of his painful past, throw his heart over the fence, and follow it toward a future together?

Light and sweet, this romance is full of Christmas cheer. Because the best gifts are hiding right under your heart.

USA TODAY BESTSELLING AUTHOR

JOSIE RIVIERA

PUPPIES
FOR
CHRISTMAS

A Christmas PUPPY TO Cherish

Copyright © 2020 by Josie Riviera

All rights reserved.

No part of this book may be reproduced in any form or by any electronic or mechanical means, including information storage and retrieval systems, without written permission from the author, except for the use of brief quotations in a book review.

PRAISE AND AWARDS

USA TODAY bestselling author

Top 35 Amazon Bestseller Animal Fiction

CHAPTER 1

$\mathcal{M}$axwell Archer gave up. The harmonica wasn't there.

He might as well walk the short distance from his rental home in Cherish, South Carolina, to Musically Yours, the local music store. The store was reputed to be the finest in town. Likewise, it was also the only music store in the small town.

Open suitcases lay on the floor in the compact, plain living room of his rental. Further cluttering the room was a confusion of chirping budgies, oversized birdcages, and a stack of research notes piled beside his computer. He definitely needed some air.

Momentarily diverted by Angel, a silvery green budgie who chattered, "God bless us, every one," over and over, Max shrugged on his olive-green twill jacket, uttered a brief good-bye, and headed out the door.

He'd recited numerous words to his parakeets. The key to teaching a parakeet to talk was repetition, but "God bless us, every one," was the only phrase Angel repeated. She was a rescue bird, and her previous owner had been an elderly woman who apparently had watched Charles Dickens's, *A Christmas Carol*, on television many times.

The other two parakeets—one timid, the other bolder—squawked, chirped, and carried on between themselves.

As Max strolled, a brisk December breeze invigorated him, and he paused to regard the poignantly familiar mom and pop shops. Whitney's, the ice cream store, and Big Brothers Big Sisters, where he'd spent many afternoons after school finishing his homework. The brick building looked the same.

At twelve years old, Max had delivered the *Sunday Sentinel* to all the businesses along Main Street, accompanied by a racing dog his foster family, the Monroes, had owned. He remembered that dog. He loved that dog. A Labrador husky named Tinsel.

He couldn't contain his smile as he reminisced.

The calendar showed December fifth, and downtown was in the process of being transformed into a Yuletide fairyland. Numerous workers scurried past him, draping tiny white lights on bushes and sprinkling artificial snow over miniature pine trees.

Through the years, he'd indulged in visions of settling here in Cherish. He had envisioned a prestigious house on the prosperous outskirts and living out his days wealthy and respected.

Three decades had passed, and he hadn't accumulated wealth in any sense of the word. In fact, his last year's research project had been stalled because of insufficient funding.

And respected? In academic circles, perhaps. He fingered the bow tie beneath his chin—his acknowledgement to the realm of academic nerds, in which he was a charter member.

In any event, his appointment to the ornithology department of a large university in Jacksonville, Florida, began January first.

As he stepped inside the music store, a slim woman with dark hair and striking green eyes greeted him.

"May I help you?" she asked.

He nodded toward the frosted-glass front window decorated with treble clef signs, animated polar bears, and a model train weaving around an ice-covered mountain scene. "Nice." He made a comical face. "The motifs enhance the window with a …"

She raised an eyebrow. "Festive touch?"

"Complete with tiny icicles." He moved inside, toward a shelf crammed with key holders and picked up a key holder shaped like an amplifier. Clever. However, he doubted he was allowed to hammer nails into his temporary rental house.

He sighed and surveyed the tidy store. "Do you sell harmonicas?" he asked.

"Yes. A wide assortment." The woman nodded toward a side wall. "Is this for a Christmas gift?"

"For myself. I lost my harmonica during my move." He rubbed his shoulders and unzipped his jacket. Though his rental was furnished, his limbs ached from lifting heavy bird cages and suitcases. He was an academic, not a body-builder.

In addition, his brain was flooded with information. He'd been embedded in research the entire morning when he should have been unpacking. The hours flew by whenever he examined data and he frequently lost track of time.

"Any particular brand or style?" she was asking.

"Fenders. Key of C."

"I'll show you our bestseller, which comes with a vented plastic case." She wended around numerous aisles, located a gold-edged case on a display shelf, and handed it to him. "Here's our most popular model. A twenty-tone diatonic harmonica in the key of C."

"An exact replacement for the one I lost." He ran his fingers along the case. "Thanks."

A sudden, booming symphony burst through the speakers, and they both jumped.

"Sorry," the woman said. "The background music in the store constantly needs adjustment." With a self-conscious grin, she dashed to the counter and lowered the volume. "Beethoven will do that."

"Do what?

"Startle customers with crashing chords." She darted him a sideways glance. "I haven't seen you before, by the way."

Well, that didn't take long, he thought. A stranger in a small town called for questions from the local shop owner.

"I lived here for a brief spell when I attended junior high school," he said. "I arrived yesterday after an almost three-decade absence."

She didn't press for additional information, and he didn't elaborate.

"Are you here permanently?" she asked.

"Only for December. Then I'm off to my dream job in Florida." Again, he massaged his nape. Was it from the move or stress? "My name is Max, by the way. Maxwell Archer."

"Hi, Max. I'm Dorothy Edwards. My husband, Ryan, and I own this store and we sell music, instruments, and fun novelties. We also offer lessons if you're ever interested."

"Which instruments?"

"Harp, voice, guitar and piano." She hailed an entering customer with a warm smile. "Joanna, are you here for your harp lesson with Ms. Emmanuelle?"

The little girl nodded.

"She's waiting in her studio."

"Thanks. Is the puppy here? Ms. Emmanuelle mentioned that he might be."

"He's in the back."

"Yay!" The girl's face brightened. "Sorry, I'm late." She clutched her music to her chest and hurried past them.

"Joanna attends Big Brothers Big Sisters," Dorothy said. "Are you familiar with the organization?"

"Yes."

Uncertain where the conversation might be leading, Max looked away. The last subject he cared to discuss was the Big Brothers program. He remembered it well. Fond memories surfaced. Some not so fond as well, but those weren't because of the excellent program.

"Scarlett, who is married to Joseph Slater, is

heavily involved," Dorothy went on. "Emmanuelle is providing Joanna with free instruction and a harp. Joseph is a well-known worship singer and songwriter. He's also on our staff when he isn't touring."

"I've never heard of him," Max said.

"Do you listen to contemporary Christian music?"

"Never." Max dismissed her inquiry with a wave. "Does anyone teach harmonica? I play for fun, not professionally, but always appreciate any tips."

"Sorry, we don't. Try YouTube," she joked.

He had. He did. On a shoe-string academic budget, self-taught lessons suited Max perfectly. Learning had little to do with musicality, and more to do with determination, goal-setting, and an appreciation for music.

Dorothy set the harmonica on the counter. "What brings you here, Max?"

"I study budgies and how they mimic birdsongs and music." He smiled and handed her his credit card.

She rang up the order. "The two are related?"

"Absolutely. To quote a noted philosopher, 'birds vocalize conventional scales.'"

"Interesting."

Interesting? The fact was more than interesting.

"You studied birds in college?" she asked.

"Yes. I earned a master's degree from a New York City university affiliated with the Audubon Society."

"Is New York City home for you?"

"I don't have a permanent home. I drove down from New York to Cherish yesterday."

"A ten-hour trip," she commiserated. "My husband travels to Atlanta for opera rehearsals, and the four hours back and forth is exhausting."

"My trip was quite an adventure—to put it mildly, especially with three parakeets, all my possessions stuffed into two suitcases and a canvas backpack." He grimaced as he recalled the harrowing journey through the icy Virginia mountains.

"The birds stayed in their cages?"

"I can't imagine them flying around my van while I drive. I secured their cages with seat belts." Max leaned forward, warming to the conversation. "For safety reasons, I always remove the mirrors, bells, and swings, and placed their wooden perches close to the bottom of their cages. And I keep bottled water handy for refilling their cups."

"Good to know." Dorothy shot him a tongue-in-cheek smile. "Not that I ever plan on purchasing a pet. My brother, Nicholas, owns Molly Belle, an overgrown pup who gets into everything. That dog cured me of owning any animals."

Max chuckled. "In some respects, birds are easier than dogs."

"Nicholas is trying to find a home for a puppy that showed up at the sheriff's station a couple days ago. Are you interested?"

"What type of dog?"

"He's guessing a mixed breed—a toy poodle and Yorkshire Terrier."

"A Yorkipoo."

"Maybe. He's a real cutie, brown with silvery-white markings." She paused. "Wait. I'll be right back."

Dorothy emerged two minutes later clasping a puppy to her chest. She set him down and the puppy bound forward in little jumps, then stuck his nose under the counter. Furiously, he tugged on a pencil that had fallen.

"No, no. He loves to chew." At the sound of Dorothy's voice, the little ball of fur rushed head-long down an aisle, apparently unheeding of her calls. He turned a corner and almost lost his balance. Dorothy scooped him up and brought him over to Max. He licked Max's outstretched fingers as he petted him.

"He's a cute pup, isn't he?" Dorothy asked.

"He's also a bundle of charming, unrestrained energy."

"Any chance—"

"Sorry." Max shook his head. "I'm only in town for a month." Plus, he'd vowed never to own a dog again. He'd missed Tinsel too much after he'd been placed with another foster family.

Dorothy returned the puppy to the back room, then placed Max's harmonica and a complimentary candy cane in a bag. "I'm sorry it's such a short stay, but this town is welcoming, especially during the Christmas season."

Max expected he'd enjoy spending December in Cherish. The lease on his apartment in New York had ended, and he'd preferred to travel in early December rather than January.

"Are you a musician?" she asked, offering an irrepressible grin. "Naturally you are—considering you're in a music store purchasing a harmonica. Ryan and I are—"

"Concert artists."

She handed the bag to him. "I'm a pianist."

"And Ryan is an opera singer."

She tipped her head. "How did you know?"

"My friend Gerry Adams lives in Perrytown. He often shops in your store."

Unlike many of the undergraduate students Max taught his online Joy of Birdwatching class to,

Gerry had been interested and engaged. Most of Max's students selected his course as an easy elective.

Not Gerry. In his fifties, he'd developed an increasing appreciation for Max's expertise that had led to a friendly rapport between the two men. Gerry had become a sort of guru, offering guidance and awareness on another subject that interested Max: music.

"I know him." A smile dawned on Dorothy's face. "Gerry sings in the choir at Memorial Street Church."

No comment on the church part, though Max had recognized the wooden sign mounted above the store's entrance.

Proverbs 19:21.

He once knew the proverb, but could no longer recall the words.

Dorothy cast her gaze heavenward. "'Many are the plans in a person's heart, but it is the Lord's purpose that prevails,'" she recited.

Max kept silent.

Memories of sitting in a stiff pew during Sunday services came back in a blink. He'd tried, but he'd never pleased God as a child. He never pleased God as an adult, either. Where was the path to peace God promised? It remained elusive.

The successes Max had achieved hadn't been

enough. Thus, at the age of twenty-five, he'd given up on religion.

As far as his career, he sometimes wondered if he was on the right path. Was his research nothing more than a "fluffy" elective for uninterested college freshmen? Society seemed to think along those lines, and reports through the academic grapevine whispered that ornithology programs were soon to be scrapped.

Sure, Max was appreciated—which was the reason why he was in hamster-wheel performance mode—to continue proving himself to his colleagues.

"Gerry and I are in a band," he replied, when he realized Dorothy waited for him to say something. "We rehearse online."

"Online?" Her brow furrowed.

"You're a professional, so you expect frequent in-person rehearsals. But our band rehearses virtually every week. Technology is marvelous, isn't it?"

"Not as rewarding as live rehearsals, though."

Max had to agree. "There's a likelihood Gerry and I will perform this month, if we can find a venue."

"Inquire at The Garden Terrace restaurant. The owners book entertainment on Friday evenings. In addition, I'd be delighted to host you here at the store. Do you have any CDs for sale?"

"You're kidding, right?"

"What's the name of your band?"

"The Bearded Elves."

"Hmm. Neither of you sports a beard."

"We change our name with the season."

She grinned. "When February hits, you'll become …"

"The Bearded Valentines. But I won't be here in February. My work takes me all over the US, and I'm headed to Florida in January."

"Well, I look forward to hearing you perform this month."

"Thanks. Gerry encouraged me to rent a place in Cherish. He believes all this down-home goodness is beneficial for me."

"You're on a vacation the entire month?"

"I'm rarely on vacation."

"No wife or children?" Pointedly, she peered at his left hand.

"Neither. You're looking at a forty-year-old bachelor."

She granted a conspiratorial smile. "The right woman will come along and change your mind."

"I doubt it. Women can be … exasperating."

She chuckled. "Will you travel to New York for Christmas?"

"I'll spend Christmas day with Gerry, his wife,

Melissa, and their newborn colicky son. They're first-time parents."

Dorothy rolled her eyes. "So I've heard."

Besides Gerry, there was no one else, Max thought. Unless Max's foster brother, John, who resided in a faraway Portuguese village, counted.

It didn't matter. The season had lost its meaning eons ago. December twenty-fifth was just another day that passed in the flicker of an eye.

Dorothy's fixed smile didn't vacillate. She seemed the sort who put immense emphasis on the holidays.

He shifted. "I'm grateful for the opportunity to hunker down with my research this month."

At Dorothy's quizzical glance, he added, "On birds."

"Along with performing a live gig or two."

"Gerry and I aren't expert musicians like you and your husband, or that Slater worship singer guy. Our specialty is performing at roadside diners for a free meal."

"I well remember those days." She shook her head. "Since you'll be working here for the month, do you need any assistance with your research?"

"Can you recommend someone who could go birding with me tomorrow morning? I'd appreciate a guide."

Dorothy studied him. "I picture you in a forest,

somewhere more suited to your rugged looks, rather than writing papers. You must spend a great deal of time outdoors."

"I try." He pushed a hand through his thick hair. When had he last gotten it cut? "The Carolinas have various bird species I'd like to listen to."

"Your parakeets will truly mimic other birds?"

"Optimistically, although I haven't had much luck with them imitating anything."

Except "God bless us, every one."

"I know the ideal woman," Dorothy said.

"She likes nature?"

"Absolutely, and she's passionate about hiking." A gleam of mischief shone in Dorothy's eyes. "She works at Thumbs Up, a local florist, but might be off tomorrow. I'll text her."

"What's her name?"

"Sarah Hartman." Dorothy snatched a cell phone from beneath the counter. "She dropped out of college to care for her elderly aunt, then went on to pursue a degree in floral design."

"How old is she?"

"Sarah turned thirty last month. She's the type who juggles a half dozen projects, numerous details, and never gets frustrated. And ..." Dorothy paused to accentuate the words. "Her flower arrangements are exquisite."

He'd never purchased store-bought flowers in

his life. The most magnificent blossoms—miniature red roses, deep violets, and pale blue ivy—spilled alongside brooks or grew wild in a field.

A response flew across Dorothy's phone screen. "Sarah confirmed she's not working until tomorrow afternoon," Dorothy read. "She had plans but is happy to change them. What's your address, Max?"

"I rented a house a couple blocks from here. It's 8 Poplar Lane. Tell her I'll bring the hiking essentials."

Dorothy typed into her phone, then delivered the response. "She'll pick you up in the morning."

"A hiker and a florist is an attractive combination."

"Oh, and she's plenty more. Animals love her. The cat at the greenhouse that handles mice won't let anyone near her except Sarah. Likewise, dogs practically grovel at her feet." Dorothy glanced up. "Remember Molly Belle?"

"Your brother's unruly dog?"

Dorothy choked a giggle. "She adores everyone and is beyond energetic, although remarkably calm and obedient around Sarah."

"Does Sarah own any pets?"

"Are you giving away birds?"

"I'd never part with my parakeets. Angel is the

oldest, and she's been with me for several years." He lifted a quizzical brow. "What about Sarah?"

"She owns a few animals."

"Is she married?" He didn't want an irate husband or boyfriend on his tail for going bird-watching with Sarah.

"She's coming off a sorry relationship, but you'll discover she's a stunner."

Another word for mantrap. He understood the type well after dating a flirtatious woman who'd been beautiful enough to be on the cover of *Vogue* but who abruptly ended their month of dating with a cursory text.

From that point forward, he'd avoided any romantic overtures from beautiful women. They were interested in a guy's money and power. As soon as they realized Max had neither, they high-tailed it out of his life.

"You'll learn all about her tomorrow." Dorothy peered at the phone screen, grinned, then snapped it shut. "She drives a yellow pickup truck and said she'll see you at eight."

The following day, Max rose before dawn to wash and dry the parakeets' food bowls and water bottles, then placed a slice of kiwi in their cages. Angel, a female, occupied her own cage, while the two males shared a cage.

"God bless us, every one," Angel chirped.

Max covered three sides of the wrought-iron cage and faced her on the open side. Over and over, he enunciated, "Angel. Angel. Angel."

"God bless us, every one," Angel repeated.

"You can say that entire sentence, but you can't pronounce your own name?" He threw his hands up and surveyed the other two parakeets. The blue-winged roommates perched on their respective swings, then burst into a flurry of activity for no apparent reason, effectively distracting Angel.

And thus, the lesson was over.

Max choked on a laugh. Some things never changed.

Regardless, he was in jovial spirits. Although his new bed was lumpy and the bedspread a musty chenille, he had slept well and left his window open a crack. The whisper of a floral-scented breeze had provided him with a comfortable, peaceful slumber.

He flicked a fatigued glance at his handwritten notes, twenty pages and counting, spread out on the computer desk. His suitcases still sat on the floor, waiting to be unpacked. He'd rummaged through them for a clean pair of jeans, a blue button-down shirt, boots, and his favorite bow tie.

A half hour after he'd showered and passed on shaving because he couldn't find his razor, he heard an engine and peered out the window.

A yellow pickup idled in the driveway. The truck boasted reindeer antlers attached to the windows and a red nose on the front grill.

The woman in the driver's seat caught his stare and waved, her smile bright and pleasant.

Sarah Hartman, he assumed. Punctual at eight o'clock in the morning.

Admirable. They were off to a promising start.

He had filled a thermos with fresh coffee and stuffed thermal cups, peanut-butter banana sandwiches, and his favorite brand of frosted sugar cookies in a bag. Hoisting a backpack over his shoulders, he headed out the door.

He opened the passenger door, smiling in at her. "Sarah, right?" he said. He put the food bag and his backpack in the back seat, then slid onto the passenger seat.

"Correct." She nodded to him. "And you're Max?"

"Indeed. Max Archer." He set his thermos in the truck's oversized cup holder. "And you're driving Rudolph."

She laughed, gentle and musical. "I love Christmas."

"Let me guess, you're a sentimental movie junkie too." He gestured to her glittery pine tree earrings and the white snowflake steering wheel cover.

"Sentimental movies are the best." She tilted her head, studying him with sea-green eyes. "You look exactly the way Dorothy described."

"Not a reindeer covered in snowflakes, I hope?"

She swallowed a chuckle. "No."

"How did Dorothy describe me?"

Sarah stared at his lips. "She said you had dark hair, silvery-gray eyes, wore a bow tie and would probably have a backpack."

"A battered and weathered one." He twisted and

motioned to his backpack, its ripped seam fixed with duct tape. "Today, it's filled with necessities—bottles of water, a first-aid kit, binoculars, and my fully charged phone."

She nodded. "Sounds like you've got everything you need."

"Yes. I've brought my microphone and recorder too. To record birdsongs, I'll demonstrate the setup when we arrive at the mountain."

"Okay."

"Are you carrying a cellphone?" he asked.

"I always carry one for emergencies, but I also use my phone camera to take photos."

"Photos of wildlife?"

"Mostly deer, although I can never get closer than fifteen feet before they bolt."

"Deer aren't always the sweet, docile animals you may imagine. Be careful around them."

"I am."

Those green eyes fringed with thick russet lashes, and her creamy complexion, enhanced by light freckles across her nose, stopped him from responding with anything other than "Good."

She continued to watch him, and he returned her stare.

This beautiful, intelligent woman hadn't been scooped up by a guy?

Wearing a hooded red jacket, gloves, and brown

hiking boots, she was small and slim. He estimated no taller than five feet. He found himself staring at her delicate lips before his gaze wandered down to the silver cross necklace around her slender neck.

Preoccupied with an attraction he hadn't expected, he picked up his thermos. "Another requirement for a morning outing is caffeine. Do you like black coffee?"

She nodded.

"Then we share commonalities—coffee and hiking. I also brought a package of cookies. They're store-bought because I'm not a baker. The cookies, not the coffee." He returned his thermos to the holder. "Juniper Mountain is our first stop."

"There's another?"

"Crandall's Mountain, depending on our time frame."

"Okay. My morning is free," she replied.

"Mine too."

With a quick bob of her head, she backed out of the driveway.

He stretched out his legs. "It will be good to go for a long hike. I arrived in town yesterday, driving down from New York. I'm here for the month, then heading for a job in Florida."

Another nod. She probably already knew that because of chatty Dorothy.

Because he liked to have music playing, he

asked her if he could switch on the radio. She hesitated and then said yes, and he scanned the stations, on a quest for something other than a holiday tune. He settled on Jon Bon Jovi singing "Please Come Home For Christmas." Not typically merry, but more of an expressive classic.

Satisfied, Max drew out his cellphone. "Do you need directions to the mountain?"

She twisted. "Say that again?"

"Directions?" He spoke louder.

"No. I've hiked Juniper for years. It's part of the Carolina state park systems."

"I mapped the distance to Crandall's, because the mountains are within a few miles of each other."

Another glance. He repeated that Juniper and Crandall were near each other.

Each time he talked, she swiveled to look at him. At one point, he almost advised her to watch the road, not him.

He lowered the volume on the radio. Possibly, music distracted her when she drove.

"I brought a knapsack," she said after a few silent minutes. "It's on the back seat."

Don't turn around to show me, Max silently implored.

He didn't initiate any further dialogue,

spending the time glancing sideways at her appealing profile.

After they arrived at Juniper Mountain and she parked, they got out of the truck and he poured two cups of coffee, handing her one. He grabbed a swallow, pleased the coffee was still hot, and scanned their surroundings.

Today might provide a breakthrough in his research, an ultimate realization of success. That is, if his parakeets cooperated and actually repeated the birdsongs.

He gazed at the gorgeous woman beside him, leaning against her truck, and smiled. Surely, Sarah would bring good fortune.

When they finished their coffees, they detoured to the visitor center and procured a map. Sarah lingered at a Christmas ornament display, sputtering in disbelief when the park ranger stated that the store was sold out of a particular ornament featuring a bear, hiker boots and the inscription, "Take a hike."

She pointed to an exhibit on the wall. "The ornament is hanging right there and will go perfect on my holiday tree."

"Those are display items only and can't be sold," the ranger responded. "More should arrive by the end of the month. Check back."

She stuffed her gloves in her pockets and

tapped her fingers on the counter. "By then, Christmas will be over."

Eager to lighten the mood, Max steered her out the exit to a wooden bench. "Let's study the map. There are eleven trails." He beckoned her to sit and settled beside her, indicating a twisty pathway. "The Maple Tree route is strenuous with rocky terrain and unsuitable for beginners."

"Fortunately, I'm not a beginner," she replied matter-of-factly.

"Neither am I."

"Maple Tree isn't difficult, but I recommend ..." She ran her finger along a trail marked Oak. "This one passes through Walnut Forest, down to the Nanchee River's edge, up through a meadow, and finishes on a grassy path leading back to the visitor center."

She peered at him for a deciding opinion.

Based on the fact she'd resided in Cherish for many years, Max readily approved.

With her so close, her scent reminded him of an elusive flowery fragrance, similar to the breeze floating through his window last night. Rosewood, perhaps. Peaceful and serene.

He liked that. He liked *her*.

Their gazes merged, and he couldn't stop staring. She was stunning—high cheekbones and a flawless complexion—the type of beauty that prompted people to gape.

"You're the expert in these parts, Sarah." Max thought he spoke, but he wasn't certain, because the world had become unfocused, and she was at the center. He moved his index finger alongside hers, along the map, a light brush of fingertips.

And the attraction. His heart did a backflip.

He forced himself to concentrate on the map and swallowed. Surely, she felt it too.

An easy smile worked its way across her features.

Was she interested in him?

With any luck, she was.

At the same instant his brain shouted no, no, no. He was here for research purposes, and Sarah Hartman was a romantic complication he could ill afford. He had enough conflicts in his life—a stressful job, and no relationship at all with religion. Her necklace signified she was a Christian, and before he knew it, she might be declaring, "'This is the day that the Lord has made.'"

He'd believed that psalm once upon a time. Not anymore.

He pulled his extra pair of binoculars from his backpack and handed them to her, then hung his own around his neck. Next, he retrieved his recording device, a pocket-sized digital recorder and the microphone.

She rose. He automatically stood too.

"Your gear is more sophisticated than I envisioned."

"After years of trial and error, I finally realized my equipment had to be top of the line." He plugged the module into a mini jack cable. "The shotgun microphone has a powering module containing a battery."

She gazed at him with wide eyes and a wider smile. "I'm impressed with you and your work, Max."

"I'm impressed by you too," he replied.

"I haven't done anything remarkable."

He pressed his fingers on her forearm, lightly, to make his point. "There aren't many women who'd change their plans to assist a newcomer in town."

"I'm always happy to help."

He told himself to finish readying the equipment rather than gaze at her lovely, upturned face. He covered the microphone with a wind sock. "This reduces the noise created by the wind."

She acknowledged his description with a nod.

He scanned the sky, checking the angle of the sun. The haze was beginning to clear, gray clouds giving way to shades of pink and lavender. "Sunny days are ideal, but overcast is also fine," he said.

In the wash of the morning light, her complexion glowed. "Birding is a first for me."

"I was under the impression you're an animal lover."

"I am. Usually, I bring my dogs here."

"How many?"

"I have two dogs."

He noted her smile. "Is something amusing, Sarah?"

"I was thinking you're remarkably efficient and obviously an expert in your profession. I admire a man who makes things look easy and effortless."

Her compliment caught him off balance. He uttered a heartfelt, "Birds are my life and my career."

A December breeze rustled the trees and blew her shiny hair across her face. He smoothed an auburn lock from her cheek, and she stepped back out of his range.

"In any case ..." He cleared his throat and passed her a protein bar.

"Is this lunch?"

"I packed sandwiches. This is a snack."

Before he could say anything else, she whispered a prayer, asking God to bless their food, Max's career, and the picturesque day.

Max scratched his neck. Nothing made him feel

more like a fraud than thanking an imagined God. For what? A protein bar? A clear day?

God had never granted any of Max's requests.

Nevertheless, he bent his head and studied the protein bar's wrapper while Sarah prayed.

After finishing with an amen, she said, "I love animals too," as if their conversation hadn't been stalled by prayer.

His response was a dull nod.

She nodded to the knapsack on her shoulders. "Are you interested in what's inside?"

He took a bite of the protein bar. "Sure."

"I have sunscreen and used tea bags."

At his questioning look, she clarified, "Tea bags are a natural alternative to commercial products and will ease the sting of bug bites. Or, for instance, if you walk into a poison ivy plant."

"A person doesn't walk into a poison ivy plant."

"Sure they do. At least, I have."

He grinned. "We're both protected and covered." He surveyed her hooded jacket and jeans. For a petite woman, her legs were long and shapely.

"A slight brush of poison ivy leaves on your skin is all it takes for a rash," she said.

"I'll protect you."

She wrinkled her nose. "From poison ivy?"

"From anything." Protectiveness for her stirred

inside him, an unforeseen response. He'd blurted the words aloud before forming the thought in his mind.

Her dubious gaze leveled on him.

"You don't believe me?" he asked.

"We hardly know each other, and I certainly don't need protecting. In addition, I packed bear repellent."

"I doubt we'll come across any bears."

"Let's hope not, but just in case." She withdrew a soup can from her knapsack and shook it. "It's full of pebbles and makes a handy noisemaker."

"A bear weighs a lot more than we do, and we can't outrun one. Bear that in mind." He chuckled. "Pun intended."

The joke seemed to slide past her. "I've read about bear encounters," she answered. "There are certain rules to remember, such as to speak calmly, not make direct eye contact, and never run."

"If your handy deterrent doesn't scare away a bear, the loud noise will no doubt encourage any birds in the area to take flight."

"That's not a good thing if you're trying to record birdsongs," she replied with a grin.

They burst out laughing, then started down a gravel trail.

He stood on the forest's edge and watched for motion. "Look. Listen. There's a golden-winged warbler in the trees." He raised his binoculars and encouraged Sarah to do the same.

She regarded him blankly.

He held up his microphone and began recording. "The warbler has suffered the steepest decline of any songbird."

"Why?"

"Loss of habitat for breeding."

A sharp *chip* and a melodic *warble* diverted him. He signaled toward a metal-gray and yellow bird hopping between bushes in a cluster of thick ferns.

"You're hearing an adult male Canada warbler," he said.

"Oh."

Oh? *Oh?*

"Some people pish to encourage birdsong." He imitated the sound. "I don't. I've found birds will come out no matter what and I wait for their natural behavior."

As they continued along the path, he was absorbed in recording and figuring out what birds he heard, and Sarah offered no help in identifying any of them. Every few minutes, the hushed air was fragmented by a high-pitched cry, and Max stopped to record.

Well into their walk, an outbreak of wings sounded louder than the crunch of leaves beneath their feet. Before he raised his binoculars, a bird flew out of range and into the brush. Max skimmed the shorter branches to find the bird, disregarding a group of energetic high school students breezing by with their teacher guide.

A second stir of motion in his peripheral vision had Max rushing to record.

Each clue necessitated an intermission, an awaiting, a heeding.

The appeal of ornithology. Search and find.

Max had become engrossed in the study of birds when Mr. Lenny, a foster parent, had brought him birding. He was a kind man with wavy gray hair and tortoise-rimmed eyeglasses. He was the only adult who'd shown a true interest in Max, and they started a tradition of birding every Saturday morning. For a child with precious few traditions, the man was a father figure. Lenny had made a lasting impression, inspiring a young boy who had no real home.

A woodpecker ripping through the brush, accompanied by three cardinals singing *cheer, cheer, cheer,* snapped Max out of his reminiscing. He spun and monitored their calls, tip-toeing through the undergrowth, peering above and below.

Sarah, on the other hand, seemed anxious to move on. She pointed her binoculars skyward and rarely spoke.

That is until they reached the Nanchee River's edge.

"An ideal spot for a picnic." Max nodded to the waterfall beyond and fished in his bag for sandwiches.

The weather had changed, and clouds covered the sky.

"I'll keep my cellphone handy," Sarah remarked, "in case I see a deer."

A crash came from somewhere he couldn't pinpoint. Max whirled around, searching for the source, and glimpsed a large animal emerging from the river.

"I can finally take a close-up photo of a deer," Sarah declared. She stepped toward the river, but slipped on a patch of wet grass and clung to his hand.

It wasn't a deer, Max thought. A deer would shy away.

It was a bear. A wandering yearling male by Max's estimate.

The bear started for them on all fours.

Sarah's breath burst—an inhale, an exhale.

Seconds froze.

"Where's your deterrent?" Max abandoned his equipment and drew her close. She grabbed her knapsack and pulled out the soup can.

The bear came up on hind legs, almost eye

to eye with them, and with one hand, Max flung his peanut butter sandwiches, the cookies, and the protein bars as far as he could. Sarah shook the can, yelled, and tossed it near the bear.

The bear backed away, then turned and ran.

Sarah licked her trembling lips, her eyes damp. "Thank you, God."

Max kept his arm around her tight shoulders and provided a reassuring squeeze. His heartbeat raced, his mouth dry. "We're safe."

"These things happen in books and movies. Not to real people." She attempted a feeble stab at humor.

Despite her ashen complexion, he was impressed she'd lost none of her composure and had reacted quickly. Still, her rounded green eyes shone luminous beneath her russet, delicate eyebrows.

Max didn't have a boatload of experience with women, but he'd lived with enough foster sisters to know when a female was on the brink of tears. Sarah bravely tried to hold them at bay, blinking ferociously.

He wavered between his male instinct to sidestep any prospect of a sobbing woman—or the reasonable desire to offer support.

Her lips parted, her smile sluggish. "Countless

questions are running through my mind," she said quietly.

"Let's begin with the most important. Are you okay?"

"Yes." He heard the quiver in her tone. "We've established we're both fine."

He lifted her chin. "Let's celebrate how grateful we are."

"By prayer?"

"A consideration for a Christian, I assume, but I thought of something more like this." He brought her closer. Unhurried, he kissed her.

Her expressive eyes gazed into his. When she veered, his hands tightened, and his mouth moved more firmly.

"Max."

"Hmm?" he murmured.

The air was hushed, the only sound the babbling river.

She slid her fingers up the collar of his jacket. "Nothing." Hesitant, she returned his kiss.

Max got so caught up in kissing Sarah, a moment went by before boisterous talking penetrated his brain. He lifted his head and glimpsed the same high schoolers from earlier.

With a self-conscious shift, Sarah pulled from his grasp. "I see we have company," she said.

"Right." *And at a most inopportune moment.*

He darted a glance at his watch, retrieved his equipment, and pushed out a sigh. "I suppose we should head back."

As they retraced their steps, Sarah glanced up at him. "Max, I can't believe …"

"I wanted to kiss you as soon as I saw you this morning," he said.

She bit her lip. "Did we do everything right?"

"The kiss was perfect."

A rosy blush tinted her cheeks. "I'm referring to the bear."

He chuckled. "All I remember is throwing food at him."

"Thank you for protecting me."

He hadn't, really. If anything, *she* had protected *him*, protected them *both*, with her bear deterrent.

"Thank *you*." He reached for her hand, soft and delicate, and a rush of emotion made him smile.

In silence, they returned to her truck.

Still dazed by the whirl of emotions between their fear and the resulting kiss, they spoke little on the drive back to Cherish. Max didn't bring up hiking Crandall's Mountain, and he kept the radio off.

When she pulled into the driveway of his home, he didn't encourage her to join him birding again. Nor did he invite her inside—something he had considered along the entire route.

"The sandwiches are gone," he said. "Sorry. No lunch."

"We could have been lunch for the bear."

"Thankfully, we weren't. Besides, he was young and not very aggressive."

"Even when he charged straight for us?"

"He's undoubtedly partying right now, devouring cookies and sandwiches and protein bars with his friends." Max tried a laugh, then sobered. "Sorry you didn't get a picture of a deer."

"I took a rapid sequence of photos with my cellphone."

"Did they come out?"

"I haven't had the opportunity to check yet."

"You had time. I knew we were safe all along," Max declared.

"Uh, huh." She became absorbed in tracing the pattern of snowflakes on her steering wheel. "As long as the bear didn't swat the ground with his front paw."

"Or snort," Max countered.

"Or lunge."

He answered with a smile. She was lovely, amiable, and attractive, and his instinctive reaction was to lean over and kiss her again.

However, other instincts warned to keep his distance. A short-term romance didn't benefit anyone, and Sarah deserved more. With his relentless studies, travel, and limited financial resources, he had little to offer her.

He told himself he was wed to his profession, as a girlfriend from long ago had once accused him.

The mood in the truck became quieter.

Let's face it, he reasoned. Sarah wasn't excited about his profession, anyway. She'd responded to his interest with little more than a few nods. Birding was his passion, and he wanted someone to share his enthusiasm.

Satisfied with his decision, he grabbed his backpack and opened the passenger door. "Thanks for the ride and for being my guide. Have a marvelous afternoon."

Their experience would be remembered as a memorable exploration. A couple hikers who scored a birding, or rather, a bear adventure.

And their kiss? Yes, there was that. Delightful, tender, and exquisite.

Like Sarah.

CHAPTER 3

*A*fter dropping Max off, Sarah stopped by her home to tend to her animals before continuing on to Thumbs Up, the nursery/garden center where she worked.

To her intense relief, the garden center's parking lot was nearly empty. Many customers, particularly older gardeners, preferred to shop for plants in the morning. She blew out a thankful breath. She needed the quiet to revisit her moments with Max.

She'd admired his home when she drove up to the neat and tidy rental, encouraged that he didn't have a bird perched on his shoulder as she'd half imagined.

Dorothy had texted Sarah the previous evening, detailing Max's plans. He didn't intend to stay in Cherish forever—only a month to explore the area for information supporting his research.

December is an unusual month for research, Sarah had texted, *considering the holidays.*

Apparently, any close family is nonexistent, Dorothy replied. *Plus, I asked if he was married and he isn't.*

Sarah could scarcely believe that the brilliant, handsome man, his muscular physique filling out his twill jacket, was so approachable.

On closer range, his eyes, brimming with kindness, shone light silver beneath dark, straight eyebrows. His hair was thick and longish, and she was tempted to brush back the waves that constantly fell across his forehead.

Of course, she didn't. They hardly knew each other.

Besides his intellect (she'd looked up his profile on an ornithology university website), he was amicable, humorous and thoughtful. She made the blunder of staring at him often to hear his words more clearly, and her gaze had been drawn to his firm mouth.

Then the kiss had happened.

Oh my, such a kiss! At first, she'd been tentative and self-conscious at their closeness. His mouth had sought hers with cool expertise, then persistence, then increasing claim. Her heart had responded in rapid, thudding beats.

If the teenagers hadn't entered the scene, would she still be kissing him?

Her cheeks warmed. They must have seen her and Max together.

Almost unwillingly, Max had lifted his head to end the kiss.

A kiss she never should have allowed. What an imprudent, impulsive thing for her to do—in the middle of a public state park.

Yet, his lips had been persuasive and tender.

A part of her insisted she should have ended the kiss first. The other part maintained that she and Max had shared a distressing incident. Subsequently, their mutual fright had drawn them closer.

When the bear came upon them, Max had held her. He'd kept his promise, prepared to protect her.

Once they had begun the hike, Max had been fixated on his work. For her, the birdcalls that excited him had been faint and distant.

Why?

Why couldn't she hear the birds Max was obviously eager to record? He was so in tune with them.

Lately, she'd found that if she didn't watch people's lips while they spoke, she sometimes missed what they said.

Regardless, she appreciated Max's spontaneity, fairly bouncing on his toes as he dashed through the brush. She was accustomed to sitting on the sidelines. Her loud, raucous, older brothers had consistently stolen the spotlight, and her parents often overlooked her.

She fingered the silver cross on her neck.

Max gave the impression of being uncomfortable when she offered a prayer before eating, whereas she was a Christian and faith was important to her. By his quick exit when she'd taken him home, he obviously wasn't interested in her, anyway.

As she always did in moments of confusion, she turned to God to set her course.

The psalmist in Proverbs 4:23 had written, "Above all else, guard your heart, for everything you do flows from it."

She'd had her heart broken by a budding architect. Their relationship had ended quickly, although she'd wept for days. Since then, her emotions were precarious at best.

Nonetheless, she'd vowed to reset her path after that painful experience. Her heart wouldn't be broken a second time. Not even by Max.

Her eyes squeezed shut, and she uttered a prayer. "God, set me free from my reservations and uncertainty. Please show me the way." She always felt better after praying. Her God was a big God, bigger than her hurts and disappointments.

Taking an easy breath, she exited her truck and pushed opened the nursery's heavy steel doors.

"Good afternoon, Sarah." Bonnie Ellerman, a coworker, tapped Sarah on the shoulder. "You're fifteen minutes early. I'm on register today, and you're working the floor. The amaryllis flowers are thriving, and timing the bulbs to bloom for Christmas worked like a charm. No wonder the garden center relies on your expertise. You have a magical green thumb."

"Hardly magical." Sarah tied a blue employee apron around her waist. "If the rest period for the amaryllis begins in late summer, the bulbs will respond. Customers appreciate the extensive blooms, thus it's worth all the planning."

Sarah picked up a warehouse broom to sweep soil off the concrete floor. She tackled the chores she disliked first, before arranging the pink, white, and red poinsettia plants for Memorial Street Church.

An unexpected thickness formed in her throat as she gazed at the tastefully decorated Christmas trees lining an entire side wall. The prospect of returning home to spend another night by herself during the Christmas season … during any season … Well, she yearned for more.

To cheer herself up, she organized a Christmas gift list in her mind. Uncle Gerry, her great-uncle in Perrytown, played guitar. Accordingly, a gift from Musically Yours would be ideal.

An insistent voice in Sarah's ear interrupted her thoughts as Dorothy Edwards came into view.

"Hello," Dorothy said. "I stopped by to purchase a pink poinsettia plant for Musically Yours." Dorothy grinned mischievously, and Sarah knew at once that Dorothy had come into the nursery for more than a poinsettia.

"Who's minding your music store?" Sarah asked with a chuckle.

"Emmanuelle." Dorothy changed the poinsettia from one arm to the other. "So, how was your hike together?"

Sarah quirked an eyebrow. "With …"

"Maxwell Archer."

"Enjoyable."

"That's it?"

"That's it." A wry smile touched Sarah's lips as she navigated the subject back to Dorothy. "Is Ryan in Atlanta?"

"He's preparing for a classical concert there. He's the lead in a chamber choir and singing a sacred text in Latin. The concert will be livestreamed next weekend." Dorothy paused. "You know I love gushing about my husband's accomplishments, but now I want to find out about your date details."

"Hiking a mountain is hardly a date." Sarah attempted to compose her features and disguise her attraction to Max. He was so different from the architect she'd dated, who'd had arrogant qualities and a slight build. Max, on the other hand, exuded strong masculinity. He was also smart, passionate about his work and gentlemanly.

And the kiss.

The sigh-worthy kiss.

Animated chatter from customers swirled nearer, blending with the clink of a clay pot as Bonnie handed Sarah a paperwhite narcissus and requested a price check.

Dorothy trailed Sarah to the stand of blossoming paperwhites. "What are your thoughts regarding Max?"

Sarah focused on Dorothy's mouth in order to lip-read.

She'd been ignoring the polite remarks from friends about having her hearing checked. A woman of thirty was *not* hard of hearing. For the time being, she'd employ all the tools at her disposal, and one was lipreading.

"He seems nice," she replied.

"Nice. Nice?' Dorothy flung a hand to her hip.

"What sort of description is *nice* for a handsome, well-versed man?"

"He's well-versed on birds." Sarah gave Dorothy a good-natured shove. "Period."

Well, no, that should probably be a comma. He was also well-versed on kindness. Similarly, he's sweet and understanding, with a romantic nature she hadn't anticipated.

"I can tell by your reddened cheeks there's more to the story." Dorothy smothered a laugh. "You're attracted to him."

"He's polite and humorous." Sarah's gaze veered to Bonnie, who was frantically signaling another employee over to the narcissus plants.

Sarah's attention swung back to Dorothy.

"Am I right?" Dorothy asked, grinning.

"Maybe."

"I knew it!" Dorothy's expression went from happy to happier.

"My reactions are mixed. He's brilliant, yes—"

"Plus, he's an animal lover, just like you."

"Let's not forget he's taking a position at a Florida university in January."

"Yes, yes." Dorothy moved to the side to allow the employee to pass. "You actually start working here at one, right?"

Sarah nodded.

"So, we have a couple more minutes. Have you

considered adopting the adorable dog that Nicholas and the Cherish sheriff department are caring for? An officer is complaining they are on call 24/7. The dog has a tremendous appetite and eats a lot of puppy chow."

"Have they named him yet?"

"They're waiting for the right person to adopt him. We all agree you are the perfect new owner."

"Who are we?"

"Me, Nicholas, and Emmanuelle."

"I adopted two abandoned dogs, two cats, a goldfish and a hamster," Sarah said. "Plus, my house is a one-story bungalow."

"You'll adore him when you see him."

"I'm touched, and would love to help … but I can't."

Dorothy sighed. "Notify Nicholas if you change your mind. Deal?"

"Deal."

"One more thing." Dorothy glanced at her watch at the same time Sarah did.

"Go on."

Dorothy pulled in a breath. "One of the reasons Max decided to stay in Cherish this month is because he's friends with Gerry."

Sarah stumbled back a step. "My great-uncle Gerry?"

"The men play in a band together. Max told me

when he was in my store yesterday to buy a harmonica."

"Uncle Gerry never discussed Max before. How long have they been friends?"

Dorothy winked. "Ask Max."

With that, Dorothy waltzed to the cash register with her blooming pink poinsettia.

Sarah was left staring at the paperwhite in her hand, trying to remember Bonnie's request. Was the flower supposed to be restocked or bedecked with a ribbon?

No, no. A price check. But another worker had taken care of it.

Sarah stifled a quiet moan. Her focus was fractured. And all because of a man named Maxwell Archer. A sensitive, fascinating and accomplished man.

And then another thought formed.

Perhaps, just perhaps, she could enlist her great-uncle's help to meet Max again.

With a radiant smile and a lively step, Sarah clocked into work at exactly one o'clock.

CHAPTER 4

A week later, Max strode into his living room and ducked as Angel flew by. He allowed the parakeets to fly at least an hour a day and kept the doors and windows closed for their safety. The routine kept them healthy and happy because they needed to explore. He'd limited their time the first week, in order for them to get used to the unfamiliar environment of the rental.

For now, the roommates were back in their cages, which left only Angel perching on a curtain rod. He'd trained the budgies to return to their cages, but Angel sometimes preferred not to.

Earlier, Max had compiled his notes and organized the pages in a computer file. He'd worked eighteen-hour days all week, although emailing his file to the ornithology department in Florida hadn't produced the desired accolades. The university had demanded additional bird recordings—particularly of his budgies repeating the birdsongs.

Except his birds hadn't responded or repeated any of the songs.

After Max received the university's reply, he didn't trust himself to respond. His ideal job. How could the department question him?

Perhaps he was in the wrong profession after all. Published studies demanded reliable facts, and budgies, as well as birds in general, were unpredictable.

Budgies mimicked humans and the sounds of their mates. However, their response to his recordings had brought distress and frustration. They peered around, attempting to establish where the birdsongs came from. When they failed to locate their perceived new friends whom they suspected were close by, they became anxious.

Max contemplated his options.

He wouldn't return to New York City, and the Florida university position didn't seem as appealing anymore, considering the head of the ornithology group wanted Max to work round the clock for little pay.

At any rate, another hike to Juniper Mountain was in Max's forecast. He considered contacting Sarah and asking her to accompany him.

During the past seven days, he'd given the morning they'd spent together deeper consideration. He remembered her face going pale when the bear charged. He also recalled how sweet she was, and how fearless. He admired her beauty, but was more intrigued by her modest and steady presence. She'd bravely held back frightened tears after scaring off the bear.

Society sometimes displayed a cynical indifference to the wonders of nature, but Sarah appreciated the unspoiled forest. He had recognized the romantic interest whenever she gazed at him, and it melted him with surprising tenderness as he recalled their affectionate kiss.

And how did he repay her kindness after she'd given up her morning to hike with him?

Why, he'd departed with a quick, "Thanks for the ride and for being my guide. Have a marvelous afternoon."

Who said such words after sharing a morning with a beautiful woman?

Apparently, he did.

He rubbed a hand over his face. After their tender kiss, what must she think of him? Their hours shouldn't have ended with such finality. He blamed his cool farewell on the fact that he was weary after the lengthy drive, his move, and endless unpacking.

Nevertheless, he needed to rectify any misunderstanding because she fascinated him.

But how?

He lifted a cup of wassail to his lips and swallowed, and a familiar comfort surged through him. Years earlier, Mr. Lenny's wife, Amanda, had mixed homemade wassail using ingredients on hand—apple, orange, and cranberry juice.

Ultimately, Max had come to realize those long-ago times of assembling in Lenny's cheery kitchen drinking wassail with him, his wife, and their son, John, had resulted in Max's fantasy of heart-warming holidays surrounded by loved ones.

That fantasy never materialized. Still, he felt a sense of allegiance and gratitude to Lenny that exceeded every other emotion. Which was why, he supposed, he drank wassail.

A few short months after Max's placement with Lenny and his family, Max had been returned to his birth mother's care until she was hospitalized with liver disease. By then, the water and electricity in their apartment had been shut off. He never learned what happened to his father, who had never been a part of Max's life.

A loud knock on the front door sounded, and Gerry's voice bellowed, "Anyone home?"

"Just me and a bird flying around the living room."

A snicker. "You've been around birds so long you learned to fly?"

"Hang on while I catch Angel."

"Will it take a while?"

"Anywhere from five minutes to an hour, depending on if she cooperates."

A loud guffaw. "The weather is comfortable and I'll wait on the porch. I brought you a housewarming gift. A bottle of blackberry brandy."

"Really? I don't normally drink brandy … but thanks."

From experience, Max knew coaxing Angel to her cage was no easy task. Parakeets were flock animals, and keenly aware of a person's body language. They were, after all, low man on the food chain and had learned to be cautious.

Max chatted quietly and walked nonchalantly, coaxing her down from the curtain rod. After he picked her up, he held his hand lightly over her wings and carried her to her cage.

A half hour later, he and Gerry sat in Max's tiny kitchen drinking cups of wassail. Gerry poured a shot of blackberry brandy into his cup, claiming he needed something to calm his nerves, being a spanking new father and all.

Max declined the brandy. He wanted to keep his wits about him while he engaged with the birds. Tonight, he planned on playing the harmonica—

perhaps a scale followed by a soulful ballade. Maybe they would mimic the musical sounds.

He leaned back in his stool as Gerry brought him up to date on living with a newborn and how he embraced fatherhood in his fifties. Then Gerry poured himself another shot.

Max's initial thought upon seeing his friend in person for the first time in years was that Gerry's hair had turned a bushy stark-white—whiter than it appeared on screen—framing a robust, pink-cheeked face. His glacial-blue eyes were piercing, yet friendly. His once crusty exterior had softened.

By day, Gerry worked in a pet store in Perrytown. By night, his passion was music. Over the course of their Internet jam sessions, Max discovered that Gerry had a powerful bass voice, and his guitar skills were disciplined and focused.

Gerry raised his cup for a toast. "To the Bearded Elves. Forever may we sing."

"Forever may we sing … anywhere?" Max clinked cups.

"An opportunity will present itself."

"Dorothy Edwards suggested The Garden Terrace."

"We'll check it out." Gerry ran his tongue over his lips. "Hey, this is tasty wassail for a bachelor."

"Wassail is my holiday indulgence. I learned how to make it from my foster mother and father."

Max tapped a relaxed fist against his heart. "They were the epitome of kindness."

"I've known you many years, my bird singing comrade. You don't celebrate Christmas. Wassail is Christmas."

Amused, Max drank a final gulp. He too appreciated the irony of savoring wassail, rather than, say, a cold beer. Avoiding answering Gerry, he looked into the living room. The parakeets were busy quibbling with their toys and preening.

Gerry took the hint. "Any luck with the birds repeating your recorded songs?" he asked.

"None, even though I play different tracks for them every day."

"Maybe your birds would respond well if there was another animal around. I hear there is an adorable puppy in need of a home."

"A puppy galloping through my legs every morning, and keeping me up half the night?" Max shook his head. "This house is a rental, and a puppy is known to chew everything in sight. I already bumped up the place when I lugged my suitcases inside."

"My wife and I have discussed pet ownership, but newbie parenting is enough for now." Gerry commiserated with a nod, then gestured to the parakeets. "What do they mimic?"

Max shrugged. "Nothing."

As if on cue, Angel blurted loud and clear, "God bless us, every one."

Gerry swiveled on his stool. "Is that your bird?"

"You're hearing Angel's favorite, and only, sentence."

"Ho, ho, ho. You own a budgie who celebrates the holidays." Gerry chuckled. "Have you seen the Cherish town square transformation?"

"Too busy."

"Those little wooden houses lined up around the ten-foot Christmas tree resemble a Norman Rockwell village when lit at night. There's also a craft fair selling local wares. My wife prefers cranberry-scented candles and pine-smelling soaps."

"It's going to be challenging to shop with a newborn."

Gerry linked his hands behind his head. "Barring the matter that neither of us has slept more than three hours since little Freddie's birth, my answer is yes, it will be. Are you up for any babysitting?"

"Perhaps when he's a little older. He cries a lot?"

"He's colicky." Gerry stared into his cup, then at Max. "I thought you always wanted children."

"Someday. In the meantime, call me when he turns five."

As Gerry rambled about the egalitarian share of chores in his marriage, Max's thoughts gravitated to his research. Should he expand his study to include cardinals? A recent article by a colleague had supported a claim to include natural-history habitats, and cardinals were the state bird in neighboring North Carolina. Perhaps the Jacksonville university would be more attentive if Max's study included additional birds.

He massaged his nape. Shouldn't the ache be gone? He'd moved in a while ago.

Stress, a little voice nudged.

No. An adamant no. Stress is a motivator.

In the meantime, didn't the department head realize Max couldn't *force* his budges to talk?

"Seen the live reindeer at the children's petting zoo?" Gerry asked.

Max's musings gravitated to Sarah. She loved taking photos of deer.

Aware his friend regarded him, Max shook his head. "No time." With a weary sigh, Max picked up their cups and rinsed them in the sink. Then he led Gerry into the living room. "I'll let the birds fly around if that's okay."

"Suits me. I let my cat roam throughout my house."

"Just don't bring your cat to my house when the birds are out."

"You'll meet my new baby before you ever see my cat. I can bring little Freddie over anytime."

"Looking forward to it," Max murmured.

At the far end of the room, beyond a scarred wooden coffee table, stood a cushioned sofa and a side chair. Two large cages were hung at chest level on the opposite wall, situated near the window so the birds could see outside.

Gerry pushed his hands into his jean pockets. "I identified the recordings you sent—a golden-winged warbler and a Canada warbler."

"You're correct. You were always a top-notch student."

Gerry knew his birds. He could have found the information using birding apps, but a conscientious and deliberate Gerry most likely had done his research.

"All the birds were recorded at Juniper Mountain?" he asked.

"Yes. And the setting is superb." With an airy wave of his hand, Max gestured toward the threadbare sofa for his buddy to get comfortable, then opened the doors to the bird cages. "I enlisted the help of a local guide."

"Who?" Gerry took a seat, shooing away a bird that quickly decided to roost there. "A park ranger?"

"A woman named Sarah Hartman. She lives in Cherish and—"

"Sarah Hartman? Sarah is my great-niece."

Max stared in surprise. "You never mentioned that."

"Why would I? Our conversations center on birds and music. So, what's the consensus?" He sounded so matter-of-fact that Max grinned.

"About Sarah?"

"Who else?"

"She's lovely. Absolutely lovely." *Okay, yes, that was an understatement.* His vision of her lustrous hair cascading over her shoulders, the red highlights glistening in the sun, served as a reminder of her beauty. "And plucky. We had a close encounter with a bear and she was magnificent."

"A real live bear?"

"Big and breathing, but Sarah's quick thinking came to our rescue. She's marvelous under pressure."

"Sounds like her. She's a wunderkind with animals."

"I've heard."

Gerry leaned in. "Can I tell you something about her I've noticed lately?"

"Should you betray her confidence?"

"It's more of a speculation shared by me and a number of her friends. We believe she has a hearing deficiency she's denying."

Thoughtfully, Max nodded. That would explain her occasional hesitancy to speak and the way she kept looking at him when she was driving, as if she had trouble hearing him.

He felt a clutching in his heart. He, more than anyone, should understand. Not exactly the same, but Mr. Lenny had worn a hearing aid, saying it helped him listen and communicate—mainly in noisy situations.

Max waited while Gerry went into the kitchen and refilled a fresh cup—all brandy and no wassail.

When he returned, he stopped short and regarded Max for a suspiciously long time. "Well?" he prodded.

"Well, what?"

Gerry took a quick swallow of brandy. "Did you and my divine niece get along?"

Max cleared his throat. "Of course." He turned, a clear sign he wasn't willing to make any small talk when it came to his feelings toward Sarah. Some subjects were personal, and she was special.

"Alrighty then." Gerry's laughter rippled through the room. "Next topic. Church."

"Let's close that topic before you begin." Max flipped open his computer, scanning the files, calculating how successfully he could change the church subject without Gerry asking a thousand questions.

"Let me reword. Not church, necessarily, but the Cherish church *choir*." Gerry hesitated for emphasis, his tone growing insistent as he touched on the real issue. "A strong baritone voice is needed for our cantata. The choir is performing at the six o'clock service on Christmas Eve."

"If you're hinting for me to join, I haven't set foot in a church in years."

He'd attended as a child, since Mr. Lenny had served at the local church as an associate pastor, but Max had gotten away from anything religious once he heard of Mr. Lenny's death. None of his other foster families, nor his birth mother, had favored religion.

"Come once to rehearsal, Max, and see if you're a decent fit. I think you are, though it's your call. The choir members are good people and—"

"No one's refuting their goodness."

"Then help us out." Gerry extended a sheepish smile.

"Isn't Ryan Edwards your main singer?"

"Normally, although he's conducting the choir on Christmas Eve. And right now, he's in Atlanta rehearsing. Another member is stepping in for the next couple of weeks."

Max hesitated, ready to cut off any additional arguments from Gerry with a shake of his head.

"You're here for Christmas, correct?" Gerry asked. "And staying through New Year's."

"I am. However—"

"You'll recognize the traditional hymns: 'Away in a Manger,' etc. You'll catch on quick. You're a fine note-reader."

Max's eyebrows furrowed. His friend knew he wasn't a churchgoer, yet he was asking him to sing in a church choir. He considered Gerry's earnest expression as his mind scrambled for an excuse. At a loss for how to decline, he returned to the computer files.

"Did I mention Sarah is usually at the church when we rehearse?" Gerry added. "She designs and arranges the altar flowers. Sure looks pretty all decked out in red with green velvet ribbons."

"The church or your great-niece?"

Gerry winked. "Both."

Max sprang to his feet. "When are the rehearsals?"

"Thursday evenings at seven o'clock."

"Sarah is usually there?"

"Usually."

"I'll give the choir a try."

"I thought so." Gerry sent Max a knowing grin. "Oh, and bring your harmonica."

"Why?"

"The finale is a rousing rendition of 'We Wish You A Merry Christmas.' I'm playing guitar and a harmonica would be a nice touch."

"What about Joseph Slater? He's a professional guitarist."

"He and his wife, Scarlett, are flying to Australia next week for a worship conference. They asked me to step in."

"No one else plays harmonica in this town?"

"None that I know of. Consider it an honor to be asked. I wanted to add a sixteen-measure solo at the end."

Max digested this and considered reverting to his earlier decision. Singing in the choir was one thing. Playing the harmonica in front of Ryan Edwards, a world-renowned opera singer, was quite another. He opened his mouth, but Gerry interrupted.

"The other day, Sarah mentioned hanging wreaths on all the church windows on Thursday night."

Max chuckled. "I'll bring my harmonica."

Gerry drained his cup. "I knew you wouldn't let the baritone section down."

CHAPTER 5

Harmonica tucked in his pocket, and his favorite bow tie in place, Max arrived at the white-painted Memorial Street Church on Thursday evening. Night had darkened the winter sky, forming a blanket of black velvet, and the steeple soared proud and magnificent against it.

An outdoor nativity scene took center stage. The life-size creche included the Holy Family, two white lambs, kings and shepherds, and a wooden stable.

Gas street lamps were wrapped in fragrant pine boughs, and a trembling wind rustled the tree branches.

Inside, an assemblage of youthful and older men and women were taking their places on the risers, and a small group of women hung wreaths on the arched church windows.

Looking around, he spotted Sarah balanced on the third rung of a stepladder.

He strode over to her and tapped her on the back. "Good evening, Sarah."

She whirled and almost fell into his arms. A burst of delight lit her face, and everything around him—the stained glass depicting Bible scenes, the whiffs of incense and candles, the other people's voices—faded away. The intensity of her gaze did funny things to his insides. Regardless of the way their last time together had ended, she looked pleased to see him.

"Max!" She clung to the sides of the ladder for support. "I chatted with my uncle Gerry this week and he claimed you're singing in the church choir."

"Temporarily," Max corrected.

"You're also in a band with him?"

"The Bearded Elves." Max steadied the ladder as she climbed down.

"The Bearded Elves? That's … different."

"Don't get hung up on the name. It will change soon."

She tilted her head to the side.

"When you're *not* a number one hit band, you're granted some flexibility." He grinned. "Wait until February. You'll see."

But then, he wouldn't be here in February, which left him with a sense of sadness.

She didn't reply, accepting his explanation without question, not even with the prompt of "What happens in February?"

Then again, maybe she hadn't heard him.

"Uncle Gerry raved about your superb baritone voice and perfect pitch," she said instead.

"He's biased since he was an undergrad student in my bird-watching class." Max removed his jacket and placed it on a pew. "Besides, doesn't every choir member sing in tune?"

"I'm not certain. Based on my great-uncle's comments, some don't." Sarah stepped to a side table and gathered red spray roses and luxuriant ivy, creating an elegant bouquet in a green glass vase. "The choir is all volunteer. These folks aren't professional except for Ryan Edwards and a few of the others."

Max turned her to face him. "Are you brave, Sarah?"

She looked startled by his unexpected question. "I try."

"You're the most courageous woman I've ever known."

Her cheeks pinkened. "Thanks."

"I intend to explore Crandall's Mountain next

weekend. Will you join me? I hesitated inviting you, considering our adventure last week."

"You mean, because of the bear?"

"Because of me. I apologize for my rudeness. We didn't part on the finest note."

"You're here now. The present is all that matters."

"Is that a yes?"

Her nod of affirmation was accompanied by a smile of delight. "Let me check my work schedule, but it sounds like fun."

She was full of life. Eager. Forgiving. And stunning. The hiking gear she'd worn the previous weekend hadn't done her justice. She'd looked anything but glamorous in a hooded jacket, snowflake gloves and boots. The woman gazing at him now was entrancing. By the light of numerous church candles, the jeweled sparkle of her emerald eyes mesmerized him.

"For the record, I like hiking more than ever," she said.

Her statement thrilled him, sending a rush of gladness straight to his heart.

Before he could reply, Gerry called him to the choir to begin the warm-up.

Max nodded at Gerry over his shoulder, then curved back to Sarah. "The rehearsal runs an hour. Will you be here when it's finished?"

"Most likely. There are thirty windows in the church."

"I'll see you after rehearsal then?"

She chewed her lip. Glanced away.

He stared at her in eager silence. "Well?"

"Sure. If I'm done beforehand, I'll wait."

The recognizable first notes of 'Joy To The World' led by the sopranos, announced the beginning of choir practice.

Max hurried to the risers and took his appointed place between Gerry and a gray-bearded man. He retrieved a hymnal and thumbed through the selections until he located the correct piece.

The uplifting lyrics and melody, published by Handel in the 1700s, plucked him backward to a tiny church, sitting on a hard wooden pew as he listened to Mr. Lenny's heartfelt sermon.

Max focused on the associate conductor for the most part during the rehearsal.

However, he often stole glances at Sarah. She wore black slacks and a shimmery candy-red sweater, and her slim figure kept drawing his attention.

Whenever she caught his gaze, she quickly looked away. However, she smiled first, and he reciprocated with a responsive grin.

The final selection called for a guitar and harmonica. The "honor" of playing a harmonica solo in front of the other musicians was one that Max would've happily forgone, but when he was done, he was satisfied with his performance.

"What's your decision?" Gerry asked once the rehearsal ended.

Max slid the harmonica into his pocket. "I'll join."

"What was the deciding factor? The beloved hymns, my brilliant persuasion, or my great-niece's presence?"

"The latter," Max assured him.

In a refined southern drawl, an elderly woman introduced herself as Mrs. Marge Addyson. Her gray hair was neatly coiffed, and her rouged cheeks plumped with her smile as she held out a freckled hand. "Your baritone voice is as fine as a sunny winter's day. Welcome to Cherish. I'm the associate pastor."

"Thank you, ma'am. I'm Maxwell Archer." He shook her hand, frail yet sturdy. He was surprised at the callouses.

In a deafening stage whisper that garnered the notice of the remaining choir members, Marge announced, "You're the professor birdman who went hiking with our Sarah."

Our Sarah?

Intent on sidestepping a discussion involving Sarah that might be overheard, Max replied, "I'm affiliated with an ornithology department at a university."

"Birds."

"Ornithology is a branch of zoology," he clarified, "and is a discipline involving the study of birds."

"Impressive, and a distinctive description."

"Animals are important in my life and profession."

He expected Marge to rhapsodize about the significance of pets. She did just that, but offered a particular recommendation.

"Nicholas, the town sheriff, is looking for someone to adopt a cuddly homeless puppy," Marge said. "Considering your animal expertise, you're ideal."

Although both startled and pleased by her consideration of him as a candidate, he replied, "I've already been asked by the woman who owns the music store."

"Dorothy Edwards?"

"Yes, and I declined."

"Aren't you a fan of stray mongrels?"

"I should be, because I'm one myself." He regarded her with an ironic grin. "I used to live in Cherish."

"When?"

"Three decades ago, and for a brief spell. My foster family's last name was Monroe."

"I don't recall a Monroe family, although oftentimes my memory fails me." She pursed her lips. "I'll remember something that happened a decade earlier and forget something that happened a minute ago."

By the looks of Marge Addyson's well-heeled style and demeanor, Max assumed she resided in the wealthy outskirts of town. The Monroe family had occupied the impoverished fringes.

"I'm in no position to take on the responsibility of a dog," he said. "I move around a lot and my three parakeets are a literal handful. In January, I begin my dream job in Florida. I've struggled for ages to be on the faculty of a prestigious university."

"I express the feelings of the entire town when I say I'm overjoyed you're in Cherish." Marge reached for her handbag and tugged on a pair of flowered red gloves. "Regardless of your job, I hope you're here a long, long time."

"I appreciate your hospitality."

It warmed him—this undeniable sense of community, a welcome transition from big city living.

"Our church holds services on Saturday afternoons and Sunday mornings. On Christmas Eve day and evening, we offer several services." She studied him with an astute gaze. "Christmas is an opportune season to honor our Lord."

For a split second, their exchange grew awkward. Max wasn't about to divulge his lack of faith to the elderly associate pastor in the middle of a church.

He opted not to reply, although he recognized the wisdom flowing from her heart.

"You need honest and caring people in your life," she said.

He managed a grim smile.

"Do you serve God?"

Surprised at her bluntness, he answered truthfully. "I tried the religion route when I was younger. It didn't go well. The people in my circle …" He shrugged.

"Perhaps the season has come for a different circle." She squeezed his hand, her intelligent eyes exuding care and friendship. "Press on, Max. We're all here for you in your journey."

Journey to where?

"'Thanks be to God for his indescribable gift,'" she proclaimed.

"Second Corinthians 9:15." At her lifted eyebrows and inquisitive gaze, he avoided eye contact. "My special foster father was a pastor," he said.

"Special?"

"Yes."

"Was?" She grasped her blue tweed coat draped over a music stand.

"Mr. Lenny died many years ago."

She fiddled with the silver bell brooch on her coat's lapel as she studied him. "You miss him."

"Very much." Max glanced toward Gerry, who was collecting choral music.

Gerry picked up his guitar, slicked back his white hair, and approached them. "Hi, Mrs. Addyson."

"Hello, Gerry." Marge smiled up at him. "I just asked our newest choir member if he was interested in adopting the stray pup that wandered into Nicholas's office."

"What was his answer?"

"I'm right here, Gerry." Because they were close friends, Max caught the drollness in Gerry's tone. "As much as I'd love a puppy, I can't commit."

"I refused as well because my plate is full. Sorry." Gerry flashed a guilt-ridden smile. "However, let's all go out for a celebratory drink at The Garden Terrace."

"What are we celebrating?" Max inquired.

"You joined the church choir."

"Don't you have to rush home to your new

baby?" Caught between amusement and confusion, Max and Marge inquired in unison.

Gerry shot them a look filled with emotions—including self-reproach and longing. "My mother-in-law is visiting and insisted on rocking the baby to sleep. She holds the magic touch."

Max grinned. "Therefore, your and your wife's roles aren't egalitarian tonight?"

"Little Freddie giggles from head to toe whenever I make faces at him," Gerry replied. "Or raspberry kisses. I'll do both in the morning."

Mrs. Addyson left shortly afterwards, pleading tiredness, and shaking her head in refusal at the invitation. She reminded them that she was past retirement age and went to bed early.

A bang of the ornately carved doors signaled the last of the choir members filing out.

Max peered around. Sarah was hanging a final wreath on a window.

"Go ahead to the restaurant," he instructed Gerry. "We'll be along shortly."

"We?"

"I'm hoping Sarah will join us."

Gerry clapped a hand on Max's back. "I'm rooting for you, my friend. I'll inquire about a gig at the restaurant while I'm waiting."

"Do you think the management will agree?"

"Simple logic. We order a meal and they'll hire our band."

"Just because we eat there doesn't mean they'll want us to *play* there," Max countered. "Hundreds of customers dine at the restaurant every day."

"It's a start."

"Will we get paid?"

"I was thinking more along the lines of free drinks."

Max bit back a grin at the logic he didn't see at all, pulled on his jacket and hurried to Sarah.

"Perfect timing," he declared.

"For what?"

"You're finished, and I am too."

"I'm *nearly* done." She swerved around him to a table and secured buckthorn berry branches into florist foam, then arranged the branches with a trail of ivy in a copper vase.

He followed her as she set the vase near the altar. "Will you join us?" he asked.

"Where?"

"The Garden Terrace."

"It's after eight o'clock."

"Hardly late."

"There's cleanup here. In addition, I'm scheduled for a double shift tomorrow."

"I'll finish." To Max's relief, a short, heavyset

woman spoke up. "Sarah, you go on and enjoy yourself with this handsome newcomer."

Max turned to her. "How do you know I'm a newcomer?"

"Cherish is a small community." The woman reached for the last two poinsettias. "Word travels fast."

"Thank you, Rosemary." Sarah's shoulders lifted as she turned to Max. "I'd like to, but—"

"Do you have any noteworthy plans on a Thursday night?"

"After I tend to my pets, I planned to catch up on some reading."

He persevered. "Did you drive here?"

"I walked. I don't live far."

"There's a chill in the air, Cinderella. Ride with me, and I guarantee you'll arrive home before midnight. Besides, I don't know where the restaurant is."

She laughed. "I'm certain you can find it without my help." In the flick of a few seconds, her mood had switched from indecision to humor, and it struck him that no matter her disposition, he appreciated her companionship.

"I have it on excellent authority you're the ideal guide," he said.

She gathered a half dozen stemmed red roses

and placed them in a bucket filled with water. "From whom?"

"Me."

With a sideways smile, Sarah retrieved her jacket, then tucked her hand through his arm.

He couldn't help grinning as he escorted her out the wooden doors and down the church steps.

The Garden Terrace wasn't the restaurant Max imagined. Certainly, the Monroes hadn't been able to afford such luxuries as dining out.

He'd pictured a genteel garden, a sparkling fountain, and an abundance of plants. After all, the restaurant's name alluded to a *garden.*

Instead, he and Sarah were welcomed by lively waitresses, a boisterous clatter of dishes, and heavenly whiffs of mesquite smoked chicken. An oversized sign at the entrance stated in bold letters, "The holidays are for barbecue." Multicolored lights were strung from the ceiling and pine cones and faux red berries wound around rustic poles, accentuated by tan burlap. A keyboardist provided a background performance of "Carol of the Bells."

"This restaurant doesn't subscribe to minimalism," he joked.

"They're renowned for sugar-free lemon cake and sweet tea," Sarah told Max as he led her through the crowd and ushered her to a booth Gerry had claimed.

Somehow, Max remembered that about this restaurant. He'd eaten a slice of the cake in his youth and had savored every bite. Another aspect of this appealing town were that things stayed the same. A time machine rewound to an era without the push and shove of big-city living.

"Sugar and sugar-free." Max helped her off with her jacket, tugged off his, and hung both on a coat hanger. "Isn't that a juxtaposition?"

"An oxymoron." Sarah teased him with a nudge. He noticed that she had watched his lips as he spoke. The restaurant was noisy and even he strained to hear their conversation. "Or rather, one cancels out the other. The calories in sugary tea—"

"Is a paradox," Gerry interrupted, indicating the guitar on his seat. He motioned them to sit across from him.

"Wrong," they contradicted him, which produced lots of laughter.

In the minutes between ordering and waiting for their meals—hot chocolate topped with marsh-mallows for Sarah, a slice of the sugar-free lemon cake and tea for Max, and a draft beer and two platters of French fries for Gerry—Max arrived at several important deductions.

First, Gerry wasn't, as Max earlier had presumed, merely a first-rate student, a talented musician, and a newbie father. Gerry was also candid and clever. While he inquired about Max's and Sarah's hiking adventure, he closely observed the way Max draped an arm around her shoulders.

And Sarah, with her delicate features and lilting voice, had a remarkable gift. She was charismatic, and she gave an enthusiastic account of the bear adventure, flavoring it with enough elements to engage Gerry. By doing so, she successfully avoided any reference to the kiss she and Max had shared.

Smiling at her wide-eyed gaze as she described the babbling river, he felt inside him the stirring of a sentiment so remote, so foreign, he gasped in denial.

He was falling for her.

Not in the cards, he told himself. He was leaving in January.

Even so, the sentiment prompted him to curve a lock of shiny hair behind her ear. Her glittery gold star earrings winked back at him.

"You forgot our interruption by the teenagers," he said.

Her eyes glistened with laughter. "If they hadn't approached, we would still be ..."

"Kissing," he whispered in her ear and squeezed her shoulders, a gentle reminder in case she'd forgotten.

Oblivious to the direction of the conversation, Gerry pulled out his cellphone, concentrated on a text and frowned. "My wife," he muttered.

"Is little Freddie sleeping?" Max inquired.

"Almost." Gerry tried for a smile that said all was well, although he didn't entirely convince Max.

After their drinks and food were served, Gerry took a deep pull from his beer and set it down. "Incidentally, my friend, management agreed."

"To what?" Max handed him a bottle of ketchup and watched him smother the fries, then slid the platter to the middle of the table for all to share.

"To us performing here a couple Fridays from now." Gerry broke off a fry and chewed. "The Bearded Elves are back in business."

Max helped himself to an ample portion of fries after scarfing down his cake. He'd forgotten how much he liked lemon. "We weren't ever *in* business. Nonetheless, your news is exciting. Are they paying us?"

"Our gig is doubling as a debut audition and management is requesting familiar holiday tunes." A smile quirked Gerry's mouth. "I'll organize a playlist. We can rehearse separately, then together before our unveiling."

Sarah joined in with a chuckle. "Am I invited?"

"Absolutely. We'll perform in that far corner. There's even a dance floor." With his half-eaten fry, Gerry gestured to where the keyboardist played on a small stage.

Once their table was cleared, Gerry insisted on paying the bill, then peered at his phone and announced, "I'm heading home before my wife and her mother murder me."

"Did the baby wake up?" Max asked.

"The baby never went to sleep."

"No magic touch from your mother-in-law?"

"Our next option is to phone Merlin the Magician. Evidently, little Freddie is offended by the idea of sleeping."

Sarah surged up as quickly as Gerry did. "I should leave too." She peered at the restaurant's rustic wall clock, which showed after nine o'clock.

"Don't rush on my account." Gerry waved toward the dance floor. The keyboardist had begun a jazzy rendition of Ray Charles's "That Spirit of Christmas," and a handful of couples swirled to the rhythm.

Max slid his arm around Sarah and led her to the intimate dance floor. She was so petite, scarcely five feet tall, her head hardly reached his shoulder.

She gazed up at him with a jesting smile. "Are you the type who steps on your dance partner's feet?"

"Exactly." He chuckled, tempted to kiss the edges of her smile. "You?"

"The same, so watch out." Her laughter was mellow and melodic. He loved her ability to laugh at herself, as well as with him.

"Has anyone ever described you as a wonderful, caring man?" she asked.

"I dislike labels."

"I do too, but my intuition tells me you're a good person."

"Never tell a man he's good. Strong, maybe, or marvelous—"

She rested her head against his chest, and he whirled them around and around. Her steps were agile, gliding to the rhythm. Above them, the multi-colored lights sparkled, creating a wondrous, otherworldly effect. Her hair spun with each pivot and twist, and he kissed her forehead, her cheeks, her lips.

"What a wonderful feeling," he sang, adlibbing the lyrics, "to waltz with a precious, vivacious woman who is as sweet as a sugarplum."

As they danced, he reviewed the plan he'd conceived within the past half hour. While he lived in Cherish, he'd see her as often as possible.

Her descriptions of him—good and caring—were poignantly familiar. Mr. Lenny's wife had often called him a "caring little boy." Once, his outlook on life had shone optimistic.

His timeworn thoughts now were shadowed with the awareness that a future with a loving wife hadn't come to pass.

He blew out a labored breath.

He'd gotten over the injustice of being born to birth parents who couldn't focus on anyone except themselves.

Some children were born lucky. Other weren't.

But now he'd met Sarah.

How wonderful they could spend a few weeks together.

How awful they could only spend a few weeks together.

Seeming to sense the dipping of his mood, Sarah muttered she was sorry for stepping on his foot—she hadn't—but her comical expression portrayed her attempt to cheer him and her refreshing humor. But then she added, "I should get home."

With a nod, he maneuvered her off the dance floor and retrieved their jackets. Outside, the streets were dark and quiet. Gas lamps flickered, forming pools of warm light.

"How far do you live from the restaurant?" he asked.

"Three blocks." She turned right. "My house is in the center of town."

"I'll escort you. It'll give me a chance to walk off my fried-food coma."

Plus, it would take longer than a quick drive in his car, and he wanted to enjoy every precious minute with her. He pointed toward the town square as he heard voices rise in harmony. He recognized the "Silent Night" refrain.

"What's going on?" he asked.

Sarah hesitated. "Going on?"

"The singing."

"Oh, singing. It's carol singing," she replied. "The town's Christmas committee sponsors caroling three nights a week in December. Anyone can join. Afterwards, they serve hot apple cider and roasted chestnuts."

Now that she had mentioned it, he recognized the scorching charcoal aroma, rich and nutty, permeating the air, along with the hint of woodsy fireplaces.

Beams of silver fell around them. A full moon graced the sky, and a smattering of stars twinkled in shimmering beauty.

A chilly burst of wind tugged at their jackets.

Sarah bowed her head and closed her eyes to avoid the sting.

His gaze fell to her long, thick eyelashes, an unmistakable reddish-blond. Her copper-colored hair, as smooth as the finest silk, fell loose around her face.

"I recalled Carolina weather being warm all year round," he said, "but my remembrances are from a youngster's perspective."

"How long were you here?"

"Briefly." He shifted the subject, in no mood to upset the fine balance of a pleasant evening by being reminded of his tumultuous upbringing. "I assumed the climate was comparable to Florida."

"Do you like hot weather?"

"In all honesty, no." His reflective pause initiated a jab from his conscience. *Dream job, remember? You're moving.* "How about you?"

"I've lived here my entire life. I know everyone and am comfortable here. Still, I sometimes wish to see other places."

"Like Florida?"

"Are there more palm trees than the Carolinas?"

"Probably."

"You'll receive a pay raise with your new job?"

"Not necessarily, although I'm optimistic my research will resonate with people avid about ornithology. That is, unless my appointment is cancelled. Universities are tightening their proverbial belts, and bird study isn't at the top of their budgets." He shrugged, sighed. "If it happens, it happens."

"You work a lot of hours. It's a considerable workload." She seemed to choose her words carefully.

"Which will become heavier once I take on more responsibility."

"I'm sorry you're not a hot-weather fan."

"I don't particularly like cold weather, either. Nor do I care for synthetic snow, the kind the outdoor fairs manufacture for gala events."

"The Carolinas enjoy four distinct seasons," she replied. "I eagerly wait for snow on Christmas Day. No assurances, though. The weather here is unpredictable."

"I lived up north for years. If it doesn't snow, we're surprised."

She grinned. "In Cherish, if it *does* snow, we're amazed."

Several of the shops' single-paned windows had frosted over, and they peered through the glass, admiring one-of-a-kind gifts—a man's handmade striped red tie, a vintage green and gold pinecone necklace, and jars touting themselves as a "One-Stop Spa." An innovative store advertised a pet-friendly dog bakery, and Sarah commented on the unique toys, ranging from whimsical Merry Christmas bandanas to tail-wagging elf sweaters.

While they strolled, she was more outgoing than the day of their hike, regaling him with hilarious stories of her pets, beginning with what happened when she returned from work each day to a houseful of welcoming animals.

"My two dogs and two cats wait by the door until I arrive," she described. "Even if I leave for ten minutes to get the mail at the post office, they're under the impression I've been gone for hours, and the greeting parade begins anew."

She grew more gorgeous by the second. Her cheeks had grown rosy from the cold, her wide-set eyes sparkling a deep emerald. When she chuckled, tiny puffs of her breathing filled the air. He couldn't look away.

"My budgies are happy," he said. "They spend their days singing or talking."

"Uncle Gerry told me they haven't mimicked the birdsongs you recorded."

"Nothing yet."

Max went over the endless hours he'd spent with his birds. Why wouldn't they mimic other birdsongs or harmonica music? He reined in his frustration and focused on Sarah. "My budgies have individual temperaments. One male is timid, the other bolder, and the third, a female, speaks her mind."

"Hurray for the female. What does she say?"

Max pushed out an exasperated breath. "'God bless us, every one.'"

"From *A Christmas Carol*? Tiny Tim?"

"Exactly. She's a rescue bird. An elderly woman owned her."

"What's her name?"

"Angel." He resisted the urge to laugh. "Don't be fooled. She's the most unangelic bird of the three."

"Is unangelic a word?"

"It is now."

"We all have distinctive personalities, because God created variety and uniqueness."

"You're saying He knew what to do."

"Exactly."

"But how, Sarah? I'm not at peace with all this religious jargon."

"Don't search for peace." Her tone softened, and he felt his expression grow less rigid. "You already are at peace. God is inside you."

She expressed herself with her body, gestures, and expressions rather than a deluge of words.

He had appreciated her artistic flower arrangements at church and he knew she was hard working and industrious. Her faith in God was clear, and he sensed she possessed what Mr. Lenny had called "a new creature in Christ." Combined, these attributes contributed to her magnetic personality.

In the sparkle of twinkling lights dancing from nearby homes, the sadness in his heart diminished. Sarah carried the same unique gift—to enhance the world around her merely by her presence. She was an extraordinary, special woman.

Soon, they reached the gaily decorated Musically Yours. Although the music store was closed, they paused to admire the window display of the polar bears, treble clef signs, and model train.

How many hours, Sarah mused aloud, had it taken Dorothy and Ryan to dress up the window with such flair?

"Maybe they had help," Max said.

"From who? A polar bear?"

"Maybe Beethoven himself." Max curled his fingers around hers. Happiness lifted his spirits, and, judging by Sarah's contented sigh, the holiday atmosphere of the winsome town affected them both.

"Cherish Hills Inn also has particularly noticeable decorations. The inn is located farther up the street." Sarah gestured with her chin. "The innkeeper, Tom Canning, is a long-time resident, and strict about who he rents to."

"I tried to get a room there, but Tom wasn't keen on renting to me and my birds for the entire month of December."

"Not surprising. The inn is posh and unconducive for pets."

"Ah. That explains Tom's half-hearted response."

"What did he say?"

Max grabbed a mouthful of air and shouted, "No."

"That's why Tom doesn't have anyone currently staying at his inn. He's choosey and a stickler for elegance."

"Thank you." Max picked her up and twirled her around.

"What for?" She giggled. Wriggled.

"For sticking up for me."

"I did?"

"Yes. You stuck up for me instead of Tom."

"I'm getting dizzy. Put me down."

He continued to spin, but slower this time, holding her close. "Not until you guarantee me something."

"You expect an assurance after that?"

"Promise me you'll never change." He gazed at her amazing face, trying to ignore the flip in his pulse.

She met his stare. "Our lives, our paths, take many forms, Max."

He spoke clearly and deliberately, as he had done all evening. "Not with us."

He set her down and reached for her hand, whistling the entire last block to her house. It was set back from the road and surrounded by bare-branched trees. The front door was painted gray and bedecked with shiny pink ornaments and a garland heavy with silver tinsel.

"You're a true holiday-lover," he remarked. "I hope the porch doesn't collapse under the sheer mass of the decorations."

At her doorstep, with barking dogs and loud meows in the background, he slipped his arms around her. So close their foreheads touched, he tipped up her chin and kissed her.

She stood on her tiptoes and yielded to his hungry mouth. Her lips were plump and inviting, fitting together with his, two pieces of an intricate puzzle matching perfectly. Her hands reached up and her slim fingers tangled behind his neck.

Her enticing sweetness obliterated his concerns —an uncertain job market, his research, his turbulent past—and he savored every second of their kiss. The promise of December, creamy hot chocolate and tart lemon cake—he'd hit the jackpot when he met Sarah.

He was filled with anticipation and gladness.

And a spark that completely surprised him.

A spark of love.

CHAPTER 7

The following day, Sarah clocked in at the greenhouse at ten o'clock in the morning. Fragrant whiffs of lush evergreens never failed to bring thoughts of sparkly white lights and an array of gaily wrapped gifts.

That morning, she'd secured her flyaway hair with a green headband because it always frizzed after shampooing, even when she used her favorite rosewood shampoo. Then, she'd tugged on a cream-colored cable-knit sweater, jeans, and snowman dangle earrings.

After a wave at Bonnie, who had positioned herself at the cash register, Sarah sorted Christmas cactus. She lavished care on each showy red and white flower. Many had been overwatered, which led to root and stem rot.

97

While she tended to the first plant, she tried to ignore the butterflies in her chest as memories of her previous evening with Max kept surfacing.

His animated features when he chatted about his birds, his quick-witted banter, his musicality, were all part of his personality. He was bold yet vulnerable; humorous yet sensitive.

And she loved every minute she spent with him.

He'd dismissed his upcoming Florida job with a casual "if it happens, it happens" as he rubbed the dark stubble of his beard. Nonetheless, his dismissal had only confirmed that he cared about the prestigious position more than he let on.

The plants, she reminded herself. The plants.

She tended to the next one and again, her mind meandered.

The mouth-watering food and drink at The Garden Terrace, her intimate dance with Max, their leisurely stroll ending in an earth-shattering kiss—all those memories came back in a rush. Rational thought had a way of abandoning her whenever she was within two feet of him.

She pressed a finger to her lips. Was last night a first date? After all, he'd invited her to a restaurant. Or was it a second if she counted their hike on Juniper Mountain?

"Do you have any noteworthy plans on a Thursday night?" he'd asked her.

Um, no, unless scrubbing the kitchen floor and vacuuming were considered noteworthy. In any event, she was glad she'd accepted his invitation.

At the end of the evening, he'd requested her phone number and had promised to text, phone, and see her often.

He was a man, he assured her, who never reneged on his promises. True to his word, he'd texted a few minutes later, telling her how much he'd enjoyed their hours together. That text had resulted in an hour's worth of conversation.

Was his kiss the beginning of something extraordinary, something lasting?

As quickly as it came, she released the thought.

He was in Cherish for one month. He'd made that fact abundantly clear.

Nevertheless, his affectionate words and tender actions were sincere.

Weren't they? What if he didn't call or text again?

A favorite passage from the Bible, Matthew 6:34, reassured her: "Do not be anxious for tomorrow, for tomorrow will be anxious for itself."

She wondered about Max's past, because Marge Addyson had left a voice mail for Sarah that morning when Sarah was in the shower.

"I scoured the Big Brothers Big Sisters files," Marge said. "I believe I've found a photo of your

Max, probably taken close to thirty years ago when he lived in Cherish with his foster family. You'll want to see it, I'm sure. I'll stop by your home … I'm assuming after six o'clock? Call me if that's not okay."

Her Max.

Sarah's heartbeat had drummed at Marge's reference, and she scarcely paid attention to the rest of Marge's words.

Wait.

Big Brothers Big Sisters.

Despite Max's brilliant mind and academic demeanor, his background apparently wasn't silver-spoon. She considered him handsome, but there was a blunt masculinity to his square jaw and muscled physique. Had he been the type of boy who'd been in many brawls?

She knew he wasn't afraid of anything.

Not even a charging bear.

By the river, his strong, chiseled arms had held her tight.

Images of a Christmas spent with him brought comfort to her lonely world, a breathlessness whenever she recalled the glimmer of interest in his gray eyes. His dark hair, a tad too long, curled at the nape, and she'd wanted to smooth the adorable cleft on his chin.

By far, he was the handsomest man to set foot in Cherish.

He's leaving, her sensible side was quick to remind. *Do you honestly want to get hurt again?*

A jarring announcement over the store's loudspeaker called for a price check. Quickly yanked back to the present, Sarah surveyed the rows of cacti, trying to recall which plants she'd tended. White blooms or red?

The nursery door opened, and a blast of wintry air hit her.

Nicholas, the town sheriff, accompanied by Molly Belle, his rambunctious golden retriever, strode toward her. Molly Belle's leash didn't prevent her from romping away from him. She knocked over a bunch of plants in her hurry to chase … nothing.

"Stop." Nicholas tugged on the leash and peered at the spilled soil on the concrete floor. "Sorry, Sarah."

"It's a fast clean-up." Sarah grinned at Molly Belle. "Are those doggy obedience classes helping?"

Nicholas shoved a hand through his blond hair. "The instructor recommended she get lots of exercise. What an understatement." His moan was part sigh, part frustration. "We take her out often, although she's easily distracted."

The dog beamed up at them with expectant

black eyes, then went back to lapping the water spilled from the plants.

"Here, Molly Belle." Sarah grabbed a water bottle, foraged for an empty container, and poured water into it. "You'll find this is tastier."

Nicholas crossed his arms and turned to face her. "You're one of only a handful of people Molly Belle will listen to."

Sarah appreciated that aspect of living in a small community. Folks were now using strong, clear voices when talking to her. Needless to say, it wasn't because she had a hearing impairment, despite what her friends hinted. They merely needed to speak louder, especially when she was in a crowded place with many voices.

Perhaps another reason why Dorothy had recommended Sarah as Max's hiking companion was because she knew that Sarah preferred the quiet solitude of nature.

"Molly Belle isn't obeying your commands?" she teasingly asked Nicholas.

"Once in a while. Once in a *great* while."

Sarah laughed, wiped her hands on her employee apron, and grabbed a broom. "Are you purchasing anything in particular today?"

"I'm here for two reasons. First, my wife wants a live wreath for the front door, rather than the fake one I purchased at the grocery store."

"The wreaths are all hung outside. You passed them when you entered." Sarah swept the soil into the dustpan and discarded it. "What's the second reason?"

"I hoped to discuss the puppy who wandered into the sheriff's office—"

"We discussed the subject. My answer is no."

"Sarah, you're the ideal choice."

"I can't, Nicholas. My house is overrun with pets."

He kneaded the back of his neck. "You have two cats and a hamster."

"Plus two dogs."

"Your dogs are friendly."

"You didn't remember I owned dogs until a second ago. My Shih Tzu is ten years old and set in her ways, and the other dog is a cocker spaniel who thinks she owns me rather than the other way around. I'm confident someone will welcome the puppy as the perfect addition to their family."

"Who?" Nicholas muttered, half to himself. He tugged his phone from his pocket, scrolled through it, then drew her attention to a tiny puppy with fuzzy silver-colored fur. "Do you agree he needs a loving home for Christmas?"

"Absolutely." She scrutinized the photo. "He?"

"Yup." Nicholas eyed Molly Belle, who had secured a place on the concrete floor in a spot of sunshine. "He lacks a safe, loving environment. Here's some videos. Doesn't he look like he's ready to take on the world?"

A bouncy puppy filled the screen, a roll of fat evident under his chin. In the second video, he chased Nicholas and nipped at his pant legs. This was followed by a short bark as the puppy rolled onto his back and stared into the camera with sweet doggy eyes.

"We've had him vet checked and he's healthy. Plus, he's handled daily and exhibits a devoted personality." Nicholas pointed to the screen. "Look at that shiny coat."

"That puppy is in constant motion. Wagging his tail and wriggling all over the place."

"He's a gem, right? The vet estimated he's eight weeks old, and vaccinated him for the first series of shots."

Sarah smiled and leaned in. "Nicholas, you're persuasive, but—"

A tap on the shoulder caused her to whirl.

"Hi, Sarah." Max stepped within a foot of her. He smiled at her and scowled at Nicholas. "Am I interrupting something?"

"Max." She touched her fingers to her throat. "I didn't expect to see you today."

He shoved his hands in his pockets. His lips pressed together. "I wanted to say hello and—"

He looked sinfully handsome, and the thought crossed her mind that Nicholas might book Max, because it had to be illegal to be that good-looking. He wore black jeans that accented his toned legs and a chambray shirt. His familiar bow tie peeked beneath the olive-green twill jacket.

The time showed mid-morning—the hours when Max normally pored over research.

Yet, he was here, and her heart did a slow flip.

Max's scowl stayed on Nicholas.

"You're not interrupting a thing." Nicholas clicked his phone shut and shoved it back in his pocket.

Sarah flinched, sensing an unmistakable hostility between the two men.

"I'm glad you stopped by the store, Max." She gave an uneasy laugh and swallowed. "Let me introduce you to the Cherish town sheriff. Nicholas Thompson, meet Maxwell Archer."

At the same height, six feet tall, both men's features were similar—sharp and athletic and wary.

They shook hands, although Max treated Nicholas with chilly courtesy. He bent to pet Molly Belle. She responded with a gleeful tail wag.

"I'm Dorothy Edwards's brother," Nicholas clarified as Max straightened. "My wife, Emmanuelle, teaches harp lessons at Dorothy's store."

Max's expression eased. "You're off duty today,

sheriff?" He sized up Nicholas' casual attire of khakis and a sweater, then positioned himself between Sarah and Nicholas, bracing a hand on a pole above her head. Although the men's verbal volley might have ended, Max was sending Nicholas a clear message.

He was interested in Sarah.

Because he was jealous. Jealous of *her.* The knowledge brought a wry smile.

"Nice bow tie," Nicholas said flatly.

"Thanks."

Okay, so it was unusual to wear a bow tie into a garden center, but Max was unique. The tie made him unforgettable, offering an air of distinguished academia. Although, considering his disheveled hair, he reminded her of an absent-minded professor.

"Today is my day off." Nicholas offered a scarcely disguised smirk. "You don't, by any wild chance, break the law, Max, do you?"

"Never, sheriff. I'm new in town, and my rental is begging for a little holiday cheer." His gaze rested on Sarah. "I'm here to purchase flowers. Can you help me, Sarah?"

"Definitely."

"Dorothy mentioned our little town had acquired another fine musician," Nicholas said. "The other day, a man stopped by her store to buy a harmonica. I assume that was you?"

"I'm an average musician and a temporary resident," Max corrected.

Nicholas narrowed his gaze. "So, you're here *temporarily*."

"Yes."

Nicholas glanced at the pole where Max still braced his arm. "You won't want to get too familiar with folks, then, if you're leaving them soon." With a crisp nod, he turned toward the entrance. "Well, I'm off to grab a wreath. C'mon, Molly Belle."

The dog didn't move and stared up at Nicholas with a kindly expression.

"Come." Gently, Nicholas pulled the leash.

Again, no response.

"Up, Molly Belle." Sarah ducked beneath Max's arm and stepped over to the sunny spot where the dog sat. "Up Molly Belle. Obey your master."

Molly Belle immediately stood. Her tail wagged with so much enthusiasm her entire body shook.

"You do have a way with animals, Sarah." Nicholas extended a rueful laugh, then regarded Max. "Don't forget that she's an exceptional woman, and well-loved by everyone in this town."

Max gave Sarah a teasing wink. "I've already discovered she's extraordinary, and she's hands down the bravest woman I've ever known."

Sarah felt her cheeks flush pink. She blamed it on the heat and sun in the garden center.

As Nicholas and Molly Belle headed out the door, she set down the broom she hadn't realized she still held. "What types of plants are you looking for, Max?"

"My birds are happiest around dazzling flowers."

"The poinsettias this year are brilliant." She signaled for him to follow her. "Any particular shade?"

After he selected two vibrant red poinsettias and a purple cyclamen with upswept flowers and silver foliage, he said, "A bike was left in my rental and I rode it here. Any chance you can bring the plants by my house when you get off work?"

"I'm done at six o'clock."

He nodded. "Excellent. I'll prepare dinner for us."

"I can't." She bent to pick up Molly Belle's water dish. "I haven't decorated the inside of my house for Christmas and I planned to start hauling decorations down from the attic tonight. Although I don't know why I do both inside and outside decorating. The cats think the artificial tree is a scratching post, and the dogs chew the ornaments. And don't get me started on holiday baking. Why, the dogs will eat everything in sight and ..."

She was babbling, and Max was grinning.

"Can decorating wait one more day?" he asked.

Something in his tone prompted her to study him.

A couple of customers wandered over, asking how to care for a Christmas cactus.

"My specialty," Sarah exclaimed. She cut her conversation with Max short and bustled over to show them the array of cacti. When they had chosen one and carried it to the register, Max was standing exactly where she'd left him.

She intended to refuse his invitation, but an entirely different answer emerged from her lips. "I need to stop home first."

"No problem. Say, seven o'clock?" His expression had softened. He looked pleased.

"You cook?"

"No. Fortunately, The Garden Terrace offers a delicious barbecue takeout."

"If you drive to the restaurant, you can easily swing to the nursery for your plants."

"Hmm." He shuffled his feet.

"Hmm?"

His gaze leveled on hers, the teasing evident. "I'll grant that your idea makes sense, although it ruins my excuse."

"Which is?"

"To see you tonight."

A giggle escaped her. "It would be a true calamity if your excuse was ruined."

"Is your answer a yes?"

"I'd love to have dinner with you."

Her spirits soared madly beneath the brilliance of his ready smile.

CHAPTER 8

Another December night had fallen in the Carolinas, and stars emerged in the sky one by one.

When Max ushered Sarah inside his slightly messy bungalow, she immediately noticed the three colorful blue, white and green budgies near the window—two sharing one cage, the other alone in a separate cage. Mounds of scientific and bird magazines were stacked on a desk, the floor, and various shelves.

He kissed her tenderly on the cheek, thanked her for delivering the flowers, and rushed to take her coat. "Come. Sit on the sofa. It's comfortable. I made chip and dip."

Although he set the poinsettias and cyclamen

on a tall pedestal table, she felt his probing silver gaze drift over her.

"I bought sandwiches, slaw, and a gingerbread cake for dessert." He gestured to the kitchen beyond. "Homemade wassail is simmering in the crock pot."

The cinnamon and apple aroma of the wassail made her mouth water. She grabbed a chip.

"I assumed you didn't cook," she said.

"I don't, but this is an easy family recipe."

Ah, so he had a family. When the subject had come up while they'd texted the night before, he'd veered to other topics—the weather, his research, his birds.

"Well, it smells delicious." She skimmed her fingers across her brown leather tote bag, which contained a precious manila envelope. When she'd stopped home after work to feed her animals and change into dark-wash jeans and a red striped sweater, Marge Addyson had met her at the door.

"Here is the photo from Big Brothers Big Sisters. Max looks young." Marge pressed the sealed manila envelope into Sarah's hands with excessive care. "He's very sweet and that worries me."

"Then or now?"

"Both. That sweet boy has become a charming, caring man."

"Why are you worried?"

"At choir rehearsal I stood across from him, and he could hardly keep his eyes off you. I wasn't sure the interest was mutual, but then I saw your return smiles. He cares for you a great deal."

"We've been friends only a short time," Sarah reminded Marge.

"But long enough. I know you, Sarah, and there's not a mean bone in your body. Do you believe in love at first sight?"

"Is there such a thing?"

"Certainly." Marge paused. "Max tries to hide it, but he's wearing his heart on his sleeve. I was at The Garden Terrace this afternoon for a bit of tea and cake, and he was there, ordering dinner for the two of you. He drove everyone crazy, asking about your favorite foods, obsessing about creating a splendid meal. It was almost as if the queen of England was coming to dine. He insisted on an exceptional holiday dessert."

"Lemon cake?"

"Gingerbread."

"He is very sweet." Sarah offered an affable grin, the kind that pacified fussy customers. Nonetheless, Marge wasn't easily placated.

"And?" Marge asked.

"I care for him a great deal too," Sarah replied. "However, he's leaving in January."

"Is he?"

"A promising career opportunity awaits him in Jacksonville. He's looking forward to it."

"Uh huh." Marge nodded perceptively. "Remember the Bible verse from Corinthians? 13:13?"

Sarah recited along with Marge. "And now these three remain: faith, hope, and love. But the greatest of these is love."

Now, standing in Max's living room, Sarah adjusted her leather tote bag.

"I finished another page of my research paper a few minutes ago," he was saying "This timing worked out well. Dinner at seven is an ideal fit for me."

"Me too."

"Do you often eat alone?" he asked.

"More often than not. You?"

"It depends." He exhaled. "Who am I kidding? I always eat alone." He ran his thumb and forefinger along the edge of a laptop computer, then firmly closed it. "Would you like to meet my uncooperative birds?"

She chuckled. "Sure."

"I want to tell you, Sarah, I'm thrilled you're here."

The question in his persuasive gray eyes was well-defined. *Do you feel the same?*

Slightly, she bobbed her head, a silent response he immediately understood.

He took her in his arms and kissed her. Long and sweet. Her eyes closed, and her breath came in a sigh. He kissed her again and again. Deeply, exquisitely, and soundly.

After the kisses, with her head against his chest, Sarah smiled. Things were so good.

But only for now.

She lived in Cherish, worked at a job she enjoyed, and embraced her church, family and friends. He was off to a promising career opportunity in Jacksonville.

She was a Christian.

He was not.

She loved Christmas.

He tolerated Christmas.

Therefore, she must steel herself for their imminent separation.

She pulled out of his arms, brushed a hand over her hair, which she'd secured in a French braid, and approached the bird cages.

The parakeets squawked as she peered inside.

"Hello, pretty birds," she said.

All three began chirping at once. Vibrant birdsongs flooded the room.

Max came beside her, looping an arm around her. "Fascinating," he said, staring at the birds.

"What's fascinating?"

"The birds. Their reaction to you. I've never seen such behavior from them before."

LATER, they dined in his tiny kitchen on scrumptious barbecue served on his finest white ceramic plates, drinking bottled water. When dinner was finished, he ushered her into the living room and switched on the overhead pendant light.

"Would you like a mug of my homemade wassail with our dessert?" he asked. "The gingerbread is from the restaurant."

"You didn't make the gingerbread too?" she joked.

"My contribution to a festive meal is wassail." He retreated to the kitchen, then returned with two steaming mugs of wassail and slices of gingerbread on a tray. The consummate host. He set the tray on the coffee table, handed her a mug, and took the other for himself. He tapped a seat beside him on the sofa, waited for her to sit, then settled so close their legs touched.

She sniffed appreciatively. Fruity, spicy aromas rising from the mug conjured images of Christmas. The perfect warm drink for a brisk winter night.

She happily sipped and nibbled. The gingerbread tasted fresh out of the oven—sugary, buttery, and delectable. She expressed her compliments aloud, then added, "You touched on the fact that wassail is a family recipe."

Max smiled, but it was distant and distracted. His forehead tensed, and he gave the impression of wrestling with her statement.

Into the beat of an uncomfortable silence, she said, "I have a surprise for you from Big Brothers Big Sisters. Marge Addyson came by my house." Sarah drew the envelope from her tote bag. "She brought this."

Max frowned and pushed his plate of half-eaten gingerbread to the side. "Which is?"

She noted the hesitation in his voice and dipped her head toward the envelope. "A photo of you when you lived in Cherish. You were … maybe twelve years old?"

He faltered. "Close enough."

"You attended Big Brothers, correct?"

"Every afternoon after school when the Monroes worked late." He managed a sardonic laugh. "Or rather, when they forgot about me, which was often."

Knowing she might be placing him in an awkward situation, she handed him the envelope with the same care as Marge had handed it to her.

"You don't have to open it if you don't want to," Sarah said.

"I'd like to." Yet he flinched, as if gearing for a disappointment.

He shoved out a breath, then withdrew a black-and-white glossy photograph.

Sarah peered over his shoulder. "Is that you?"

He nodded. The dark-haired boy staring back at them held a stoic expression. His fingers grasped the collar of an enormous dog who stood by his side.

Her heart turned over at the boy's brave demeanor, despite the uncertainty in his eyes. She wanted to hug the photo to her chest, hug the young boy and never let him go.

"Your features haven't changed." Emotions welled inside her, although she managed to keep her tone even. "I'd recognize you anywhere with that determined expression. It's been what, over thirty years?"

Max sipped his wassail, a deceptively casual gesture. "I remember when this was taken, right around Christmas."

"Is that your dog?"

"Not mine. The Monroes." His gaze swung to the parakeets, who perched silently on their swings. "I missed that dog more than anything when I was moved to another foster family. More than I missed the Monroes. Much more."

Sarah swallowed the lump in her throat. "What type of breed was the dog?"

"A Labrador husky." Max rubbed his eyes with his forefinger.

She waited for him to continue, but he showed every sign of being lost in troubled reflections. He stared at the photo, then looked away.

"What was the dog's name?"

"Tinsel."

She studied the photo. A young Max stood outside Big Brothers Big Sisters. His jeans were five inches too short for his long legs. He looked thin, almost undernourished. But his eyes were warm. Max's eyes.

"Want me to refresh your wassail?" he asked.

"I'm good, thanks." She held a hand over her mug. "Did you want to discuss the photo?"

"Nope. I'm a foster kid, Sarah. I moved around a lot. I had some good foster parents, and some not so good." He choked on the words. "The Monroes were not so good."

"And the family where you learned to make wassail?"

"Mr. Lenny's family."

"Where are they now?"

"He and his wife died. My foster brother, John, lives in Portugal. A few years ago, I gave up trying to stay in touch with him."

"Why?"

"What's the point? He lives so far away." Max didn't move a muscle. He cleared his throat. "Do you suppose it's in a man's best interest to suppress unhappy events, to keep them hidden from the woman he's falling in love with?"

Sarah's cheeks warmed. *Max was talking about her.* "The question is, how can that woman help a man repair those inner hurts?"

"I don't know. Sometimes I want relief from all the past pain." His face was expressionless. "My heritage, or rather, lack of heritage."

Now she understood where his resolve to make something of himself had been formed. It had started with the photo.

Or perhaps years earlier. Perhaps in other photos, in different towns with different families. Perhaps with different pets. And every single heartbreaking situation had strengthened Max with the fortitude to break free and make something of himself.

"Try prayer," she said softly.

"Been there." He linked his hands behind his head and peered at the ceiling pendant. "Done that."

"Try again."

His memories, unwelcome and agonizing,

would continue to haunt him until he released them.

He dragged in a breath. "Years ago, I prayed to God to grant my foster brother a successful surgery."

"Go on."

"John only got one shot at a basketball scholarship. I knew how much it meant to Mr. Lenny."

She measured her words. "What happened?"

"God didn't listen. A week before Christmas, John's last surgery left him with a distinct limp and one leg shorter than the other."

"A physical disability." Sarah slid her fingers through Max's. The appeal, the warmth of his hand … this attraction only grew stronger each time they were together. "A handicap."

"Handicap? Ask John how much of a handicap. He didn't attend college. Now he lives in a faraway village, and I haven't seen him in years."

"How did Mr. Lenny react after the failed surgery? You obviously hold him in high esteem."

"He didn't share my anger and frustration at God. He was a pastor—a virtuous and noble man. After listening to my ranting, he reminded me that John was alive and healthy, which was all that mattered."

"Lenny was right."

"At what cost?" Max tore his hand from hers.

"Why were the other athletes on John's team strong and whole? He had a promising pro basketball future."

"Lenny was a man of faith."

Max stared straight ahead. He didn't seem aware any longer that she sat beside him. "Lenny declared that John had God on his side and God was all he needed."

"You don't agree?"

"I can't shake my resentment toward a God who plays favorites."

"Try again. Try prayer," she repeated.

"Prayer will make the hurt go away?"

"God will. Reflect on the healing truths of His words every day."

Max lifted his arms and surveyed the room. "I don't see God anywhere."

"Just because you don't see Him, doesn't mean He isn't here."

His expression gradually relaxed, and her chest still ached for him. He had erected a barrier around his heart. A barrier that was impossible to breach until he put aside his resentment and anger.

Pushing up from the sofa, he carried himself stiffly as he walked to the computer.

A moment later, birdsongs floated through the room, the same songs he'd recorded during their hike.

She came to stand close and motioned to the parakeets. "They aren't repeating anything?"

"Nothing. Not even when I play my harmonica."

The single green and white budgie in a wrought iron cage flapped her elegant feathers. In a clear, bell-like voice, she said, "God bless us, everyone."

CHAPTER 9

A few hours later, Sarah headed home.

Max sat on his living room's threadbare carpet and leaned against the sofa.

She was exceptional, fascinating, and extraordinary. More than extraordinary.

The Big Brothers photo had transported him back to the land of unfulfilled dreams. Life with the Monroes had been intolerable, specifically during Max's difficult adolescence.

He wasn't certain why Marge Addyson had gone to the trouble to find that photo and then give it to Sarah. A woman of well-meaning honesty, she may have wanted him to confront past issues in order to move forward.

But he'd done that already, hadn't he? He was accomplished. He'd succeeded in establishing a noteworthy career. Besides, life-altering injustices could never be forgiven.

He shook his head, a rueful smile. His thoughts harbored the very bitterness he thought he'd overcome.

Days ago, Sarah had encouraged him to reflect on the truths of God's word.

"Start with Psalms," she had advised. "The verses will promote healing, comfort and well-being."

"All that?" he questioned.

"All that," she echoed an assurance.

He'd heeded her advice about reading the Bible, although he hadn't told her. It wasn't a subject that came up in daily conversation. Although he could have told her tonight …

Sarah. Sarah. Sarah. They were friends, and there were times when she kept him at arms-length. But there were other times when an electrical current, a snap of lightning, flowed between them. Even when they were a few feet apart, it seemed as if they touched.

He unfolded himself and straightened. He embraced the tranquility he felt when he was with her, and their evening had passed in a blur of laughs and kisses and a hint of rosewood perfume from her fragrant hair.

Peace was indeed a part of her, a serenity and

contentment he attributed to more than her excitement for the upcoming Christmas season. It was her Christian faith. This woman, this town, was a shift for him, when his daily life was filled with more duties than he could accomplish.

He mentioned as much to Gerry when they met a few days later for an impromptu jam session at Musically Yours. Dorothy had afforded them an after-hours studio, and the men had gratefully accepted.

A grin on his weather-beaten features, his fuzzy eyebrows raised in a tickled question, Gerry responded by saying, "So, you're in love?"

Max pulled back, disconcerted. "Who said that?"

"You did."

"When?"

"By your eyes, words and actions."

Max navigated to safer ground. "You sure you don't mind meeting here to rehearse? The drive from Perrytown is a haul for you."

"You and I share a passion for music, and rehearsing in person is a blessing."

Max tugged out his harmonica. "I assume your wife is understanding about the hours away from little Freddie?"

"Totally. As long as I'm home by ten o'clock." Gerry set an amp on the floor, then searched for an outlet. He plugged one end of a cable into the amp, the other into the guitar. Snaps and shrill bangs followed, and Gerry switched the volume down.

Because Max lived a few blocks from the store, he had walked, admiring the decorations on the way over, likening them to a Christmas postcard.

The temperature had dropped in the past few days, and blades of grass peeked through a frost of white. Holly bushes were in vibrant red-berry bloom, and blinking red, green, and white lights were everywhere.

He passed a busy coffee shop with folks bustling in and emerging with large cups of hot chocolate topped with creamy whipped cream. Aromas of fresh brewed coffee and toasty choco-late brought scents of the season to mind. A vendor on the corner peddled roasted chestnuts in paper cones. Giggling youngsters ran by him, their laughter high-spirited over the chatter of adults. On side streets, flickering candles gleamed from residences, and vibrant lights from their evergreen trees shone from the windows.

Max never remembered decorating a pine tree, except for the year with Lenny and his family. The snapshot of that one perfect tree, the one perfect Christmas, lived forever in his mind.

When he reached Musically Yours, he was im-mediately immersed in the harmonies of guitar music sounding from the speakers, the cozy overhead lights, and the warmth of an excellent heating system. After greeting Gerry, who was already there, he asked what they were listening to.

"Joseph Slater's newest worship song, a contemporary Christian arrangement," Gerry noted. "He slowed the tempo, kept the instrumentals simple, and let his voice do the heavy lifting. He's an awesome vocalist."

"Awesome, indeed." Max tilted his head, and allowed the poignant lyrics to wash over him.

"'Mary Did You Know?' is one of my favorite pieces," Gerry said. "Are you aware that the composer took seven years to complete it?"

"Good things are worth the wait, time, and effort," Max replied. "And when you find something good?"

"Never let her go."

Max regarded Gerry. "I'm assuming you mean Sarah?" he asked, and then went on to talk about her in such a way that Gerry told him he was in love.

Gerry brought on a grin and didn't reply.

Focus on the music, Max told himself as Gerry finished tuning his guitar.

They decided on a playlist for their upcoming performance—a medley of carols that included, "O Christmas Tree," "Santa Claus Is Coming To

Town," and the finale, "The Twelve Days of Christmas."

"A fun holiday singalong," Gerry said. "For the encore, we'll perform "All Is Well," which is uplifting and inspirational."

"You're certain we'll get enough applause for an encore?"

"Stranger things have happened," Gerry mused while he plucked his guitar. "On another note, my wife and baby are attending. My mother-in-law too."

"How's little Freddie lately?"

"I anticipate my wife's hasty exit after our first song."

"Hopefully, we won't sound that bad."

"We're fairly decent. Besides, my wife deserves a night out."

"With little Freddie," Max reminded with a grin. He pointed to an autographed album hanging on a wall, the cover depicting Joseph Slater and an acoustic guitar. "Musically Yours sure promotes this guy."

"He's a big-name artist who lives in Cherish."

"Joseph settled here," Max mused, arching a single eyebrow.

"Same goes for Ryan Edwards. Love is like a fairy-tale, at least that's what my wife parrots. Joseph met Scarlett when he was here for a music promotion. He decided to put down roots after all those years of touring and married her last year."

"Because of Scarlett, he gave up his career?"

"Hardly. Life is a compromise, my friend, and you're clearly smitten too. Are you still coming to my house on Christmas Day for dinner?"

"Unless you're having second thoughts."

"On the contrary, I'm thinking about inviting my great-niece to join us."

Max beamed. "A tremendous idea."

"I suspected you'd be receptive." Gerry smirked, then leaned back in a wooden chair he'd snagged from the student waiting area. "Now let's rock-and-roll to some favorite Christmas carols."

ON THE FRIDAY evening of The Bearded Elves' debut, Sarah grabbed a seat at a round table near the band, along with Dorothy, Ryan, Gerry's wife and son and mother-in-law, Nicholas, and Emmanuelle.

She'd dressed with care for the evening—a fit and flare lace dress, strappy-leopard print heels she already wanted to kick off, and sparkly gumdrop-red earrings. She'd topped her outfit with the fine royal blue wool coat she wore on special occasions.

During the past two weeks, lighthearted conversations and dinners with Max at The Garden

Terrace, their stolen kisses, their bantering texts, had become routine. Max invited her on another hike, and she'd happily accepted.

Each time they parted, he promised to see or text her the following day.

And he always did.

She should have been joyful. She was. But a heaviness weighed on her spirit because the days flew too quickly. Soon, January would arrive.

Refreshed by endless glasses of sugar-free lemonade, she sang along to the familiar carols with the others, especially during Ryan's sidesplitting rendition of "The Twelve Days Of Christmas."

As he reached the final, "And a partridge in a pear tree," his operatic voice swelled through the restaurant.

Max confirmed his ability as an excellent harmonica player. He'd been too modest, she thought. Whenever he hit an imagined wrong note, he glanced at her with a chagrined smile. The keen, honed bite of blues he produced on such an inexpensive instrument proved him a man of many talents, and pride flowed through her.

Can you believe the tunes a person can produce from such a modest instrument? he had texted a few days earlier. *Wood, two pieces of metal and minute brass reeds.*

The only thing I can play is the radio, she'd texted

back in jest, despite his assurances that he would teach her how to read music.

When? she'd wanted to ask. However, she remained silent.

Wait till you hear our encore, he'd responded.

What's the name of the song?

It's an inspirational piece. It'll bring tears to your eyes.

She was seeing a side of him she hadn't envisioned beneath his polka-dotted tie, chambray shirt, and jeans—a look she'd catalogued as distinctly Max.

During each fifteen-minute break between sets, he'd made it a point to sit next to her. He drew her close, his arm draped around her shoulders in a gesture that seemed possessive, but delighted Sarah immeasurably.

After the band's first set, Melissa, the baby, and her mother left. Little Freddie had been fairly well-behaved, and Melissa and her mother had taken turns walking around the restaurant to soothe the baby.

Sarah surprised herself by offering to help. She'd never been an active participant in group situations, and had felt increasingly uncomfortable in even small crowds now—reticent to speak in case she'd misheard someone, and hesitant to ask people to repeat themselves.

In any case, she wasn't used to these feelings—the attention from Max, the joy of being among a welcoming, friendly group. This was camaraderie, sharing jubilant hours with friends and family who cared.

After the rousing rendition of "The Twelve Days of Christmas," Gerry and Max grinned and bowed to enthusiastic applause. As calls for an encore rose, Max stepped down from the small stage. Dorothy stopped him, saying something to him. Sarah couldn't see Dorothy's face, but she could see Max's, and she couldn't resist eavesdropping by reading his lips.

"January first," he seemed to be saying, "I'm eager to leave for Florida and head up an ornithology department."

January. Leave. Eager.

Sarah's stomach tightened.

She half rose in her seat. But no, she shouldn't be surprised. He'd repeatedly cited his new Jacksonville job. His time in Cherish was temporary.

Unexpectedly weak, she braced her hands on the arms of her chair. She'd been a fool for falling for him. Hoping against hope, while knowing the romance would come to an end in January.

Questions surfaced with no answers. He was a man of his word and had accepted the university position months ago.

Nevertheless, confronting the pain of his departure brought unexpected heartache. They'd never actually discussed him leaving. It was a point in the future neither had chosen to broach.

No matter. She'd slip into the background again, a pattern she'd honed over the years. Loneliness encroached so swiftly she couldn't react, save for tugging on her shoes and scouting out the quickest path to the exit.

She'd been unmoored by the attentions of a stranger. She'd only known him a few weeks. *A few enchanted weeks.*

She swallowed hard and stood to leave as soon as Max and Gerry returned to the stage to more applause. The diners had awarded the men a standing ovation, and the enthusiastic applause soon quieted.

Max angled a glance at her with a broad smile. *Success*, he seemed to say. *Thank you for supporting me and my music.*

She grabbed her coat and turned away, then rounded to glimpse him one last time. His chin drew in, perplexed, as he lifted the harmonica to his lips.

Dorothy caught her hand. "You're leaving? What about the last song?"

"It's later than I thought." Sarah made a show of peering at her watch, aware of how quiet everyone at her table had become. However, she couldn't face another conversation with Max.

From the onset, he'd spoken the truth. Nonetheless, truth was difficult to confront, especially when it waylaid you at the happiest moment of your life.

Nicholas stood and excused himself from the others. "Sarah, I'll walk you to the door."

"Thanks. I can manage." She veered left, away from him, struggling to keep her emotions in check.

"It's no bother. I have an ulterior motive."

They passed straggling diners, plates of food being cleared from empty tables by tired-looking waitresses, while Max's bluesy harmonica accompanied Gerry's vocals.

"'All is well all is well, … Sing Alleluia.'"

"It'll bring tears to your eyes," Max had said.

And it did.

The lyrics were hopeful and encouraging, and Max harmonized with Gerry, his baritone voice complementing the uplifting words.

A Christian song. Max was singing a Christian song.

"What's your motive?" she asked Nicholas when they reached the entry. "The abandoned puppy?"

"Yep. And if I don't find a home for him, he'll

end up in an animal shelter. It's a no-kill shelter, but still ..." His words trailed off.

She opened her mouth. Closed it. She was about to refuse when she paused. A darling puppy would be the ideal distraction for her hurt heart.

"I'll take him," she burst out.

"Sarah, thank you! Why did you change your mind?"

"I can't let a lovable puppy spend the holidays in a shelter."

"I'll bring him over to your house in a couple days." Clearly, Nicholas was uncertain whether he'd understood her. "I realize Christmas Eve is almost here ..."

"No worries. The puppy has spent too many nights alone already."

CHAPTER 10

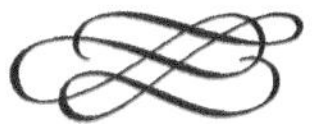

On Christmas Eve, Sarah sat alone.

Only for tonight. Tomorrow, she would drive to Perrytown to dine with her great-uncle, his wife, and little Freddie. He'd phoned her, and she'd gratefully accepted the invitation. In years past, she'd spent Christmas Day with her parents and brothers, traveling to their homes in the Carolina mountains. They'd moved away from Cherish, and she was the only one who had remained.

This year, she'd elected to stay home with her growing number of animals.

She had already attended the three o'clock church service. She'd done so purposely, in order not to run into Max, who would be singing in the choir at the six o'clock service. Right about now, he would be entering the church to get ready.

She'd returned from the service invigorated and encouraged. The sermon had touched on how God didn't free people from traumatic situations, but rather, He was there walking with them every step of the way.

Yes, she'd experienced troubles and challenges. However, any expectations fixed on the Messiah to grant a person's peace came from within. God didn't promise an easy life, and Sarah couldn't experience peace when she had been anticipating a textbook Christmas with the man she loved.

Her mind traveled back to the loving way Max had regarded her—by the river, at the restaurant, in his home. His tenderness when he kissed her.

No. She couldn't allow him into her thoughts anymore. He belonged to the huge, widespread world of birds and his research, not the microscopic town of Cherish.

Yet she'd felt loved and protected when his lips pressed against hers—his strong arms shielding her when they'd encountered that bear.

She hadn't wanted to lose that, the sense of being cherished and safeguarded.

But Max's love was never hers to begin with.

She peered at the roly-poly puppy nestled in his crate. Already, he'd created a wealth of joy in a short period of time.

He was beginning to eat solids, and she'd continued the transition of soaking the food in warm water, then blending it to the texture of gruel. A fresh supply of water was ever present.

The past couple days, she'd brought his toys into her home first for the other animals to sniff. When the puppy arrived, the dogs ignored him except for an occasional sniff. She'd rewarded their unaggressive behavior with upbeat praise, and had placed the resident dogs' toys and food bowls in a separate location.

Likewise, the cats wandered over for a sniff, then dismissed the puppy.

Sarah's goal was to allow the animals to learn to trust each other. So far, so good.

She switched on a holiday radio station, and The Mormon Tabernacle choir sang "Adeste Fideles" in Latin.

Max would've appreciated the arrangement. He was so musical.

Sighing, she looked at the framed photo on her side table. When she had finally scrolled through the photos she'd taken with her cell phone the day of their hike, she found a wonderful one of Max. It was a profile picture. His face had been near the camera, and every handsome quality was evident—the dark stubble of his beard, his silver-gray eyes, his determined demeanor.

She'd also gotten a surprisingly good photo of

the bear. She'd auto-merged them into a silly collage, the bear and Max staring at each other, eye to eye.

She'd planned to gift him the photo and had bought a wooden frame depicting the great outdoors with the words Into the Woods on it. She'd captioned the photo, "I knew we were safe all along."

Max's words.

She would never hear his voice again. She squeezed her eyes shut and took a deep breath. "I love you, Max," she murmured, vowing to rely on time and faith to heal her broken heart.

She slid the photo into a bag and placed it in a drawer in the side table.

As Max looked around the church on Christmas Eve from his vantage point on the top riser, his heart dropped. He scanned the pews—the exquisitely appointed windows and altars bedecked with the brilliant display of flowers that Sarah had arranged. But Sarah was not there.

"Surely, she'll attend church," he muttered to Gerry, as the men took their places in the baritone section.

Marge Addyson, standing near the altar, turned. "She attended the earlier service," she said.

She did? Why?

Two days ago, Sarah had left The Garden Terrace before The Bearded Elves' performance was over and without a farewell. Thereafter, Max's phone calls and voice mails had gone unanswered.

The previous morning, he'd stopped by the nursery. Her coworker, Bonnie, declared that Sarah was in the greenhouse dealing with seedlings and couldn't be disturbed.

The service ended with the cantata and Max's harmonica solo. When the service was over, he exited the church with his heart touched and his spirits lifted. The sermon had delivered a message of optimistic goodwill.

"God's son appeared in the least likely situation and to humble people," the pastor had addressed the congregation. "Forgive and let your resentments go. What will prevent your happiness is to strive for perfection in yourself and others."

Hadn't Max always sought excellence? Blame it on his upbringing, but he'd endeavored to become top-notch in his profession. But what good was that perfection without someone to love?

Unwilling to accept the end of their relationship, he strode from the church to Sarah's house. In a short time, he'd become accustomed to small-town living, where most places were within a few blocks' walking distance. He'd purchased a special present for her and held the package securely under his arm.

When he reached her house, he stood silently on her front porch. Although he didn't move, wild barking sounded from inside before he could even knock.

Then the barking ceased.

He knocked, hesitant to ring her doorbell. Okay, maybe he shouldn't have dropped by unannounced, but what else could he do when she kept slipping away from him?

Suppose she was sleeping?

At eight o'clock on a clear and cold Christmas Eve? Sarah? Unless she wasn't home … But where …

Tiny yelps sounded. A yipping.

The door opened a crack, and a wobbly puppy shoved his nose through the opening, wagging a fluffy white tail.

Sarah scooped up the puppy, then gasped as she stood in the doorway. "Max?"

"Merry Christmas."

"How long were you standing on the porch?"

He shrugged. "A while."

"What were you doing?"

"Praying."

"Praying? What are you praying for? An extraordinary gift on Christmas Eve?"

"I'm praying for the most extraordinary of gifts. You."

Her striking green eyes glistened with tears, her features a flood of emotions. "Merry Christmas."

"May I come in?" She couldn't just stand at the door holding a puppy.

"Yes. Please."

He stepped inside and brushed a kiss across her temple. She cuddled the tiny Yorkipoo to her chest. He grinned at the pom-pom tail, the paws reminding him of a hedgehog, and the molten-brown eyes peeking beneath half-closed lids. Perhaps he wasn't a Yorkipoo …

"Apparently, Sheriff Nicholas convinced you?" Max asked as he stroked the puppy's velvety fur.

"Careful," she warned. "His teeth are like little needles." She set the puppy inside a blanketed crate. The two older dogs settled. The cats walked away.

And Sarah walked into Max's embrace.

He drew her closer, pressing his lips to hers, fearful to break the hold for fear she might disappear.

When the kiss ended, she rubbed her cheek against his jacket. "I'm glad you're here."

Her home wasn't decorated for the holidays, which surprised him, considering her festive porch.

"My fake tree and ornaments are in the attic." She seemed to read his mind. "I haven't had time."

Or rather, had she felt like him, and didn't have the heart to decorate?

She was gorgeous in a crimson cashmere sweater and form-fitting black pants. Her figure was trim with curves, a wreath of dark russet curls framed her perfect face.

"I do have appropriate holiday cookies and eggnog, if you're interested," she said. "And both were bought from the grocery store."

They shared another commonality besides coffee and hiking and a love for animals. They appreciated store-bought items when homemade wasn't an option. Or, he supposed, even if it was.

He smiled, removed his jacket, and adjusted his bow tie. For the Christmas Eve service, he'd elected to wear black dress pants and a crisp white shirt.

"Can I be direct?" he asked, after she'd taken a jug out of the refrigerator, poured him a glass of eggnog, and set out a platter of frosted vanilla sugar cookies in the shape of snowmen.

"I wouldn't expect anything else."

He placed his gift on the coffee table. He'd wrapped it in plain brown paper tied with twine, topped with a green and white parakeet ornament.

"Why did you leave the restaurant without saying good-bye?" His hand slid up her arm in a caress. "Furthermore, why were you avoiding me? Is my singing that bad?"

She smiled. "No."

"I'd like to continue seeing you."

She fixed her gaze on a point beyond him. "I can't deal with a long-distance relationship and you're leaving for Jacksonville in a week."

He heard the hurt in her tone. His gaze stayed on her.

He invited her to sit on the sofa in the living room and he settled beside her. "Who said I was moving to Jacksonville?"

"You've mentioned little else since you arrived in Cherish. The other night at The Garden Terrace when you spoke with Dorothy, you declared your eagerness to leave for Florida in January and head an ornithology department."

And then it hit him. Sarah cared about him. Deeply. So deeply, she couldn't face him leaving.

And he was delighted.

He pulled her nearer. "I said I was eager to greet the new head of the ornithology department in Florida in January."

She blinked. "I don't understand."

"I declined the position. The latest candidate is a colleague from my New York university days who's done amazing research on zebra finches. She's a workaholic and will be an excellent fit."

"So much for my lip-reading abilities. And eavesdropping." Sarah sat straighter. "You didn't accept the position?"

"No."

"I made an appointment with an audiologist to test my hearing. I've read that I won't be as fatigued at the end of the day if I haven't had to struggle with the effort of listening."

"If you indeed have a hearing loss, it should be addressed." Max smoothed his lips over her hair. "I should've been clearer about my feelings. I would've been if you hadn't vanished."

"I haven't gone anywhere."

"This project has involved numerous researchers working around the world. My bit with budgies is only a small part of the larger study on birdsongs."

"And?"

"The paper will take a couple years to complete, especially as current research sends scientists in different directions. Which means I'm not going anywhere. I can continue my research here and will receive a full-time salary."

"You're staying in Cherish?"

"I renewed my lease on 8 Poplar Lane."

"Does this mean more hiking adventures?"

"Weekly." He grinned. "This place, and you, have allowed me to slow down and reflect. However, I will have to travel to Jacksonville twice a semester to meet with other members of the department. I'm hoping you'll accompany me."

"I'd love to."

"I'd also like to visit the university I attended in New York."

"I've never seen a big city."

"New York is filled with diversity, culture, and excitement. I'll take you to see the famous landmarks."

"I'd like that," she said softly.

"And I have a brother in Portugal."

"Yes."

"I need to reach out to him again. If he invites us to travel to Portugal to visit him, will you accompany me?"

She nodded. "Happily."

"Good." He peered upward. "Where's your attic?"

"You're looking in the right direction."

"I've only decorated a Christmas tree once in my life—with Lenny and his family."

"Is that a hint?"

"A broad hint. But first." He nodded to his gift.

Glancing at him, she unraveled the twine. In the box was an ornament—a bear, hiker boots and the inscription, "Take a hike."

She smiled, smoothed her fingers over the words, then curled near him. "You remembered?"

"Of course. After numerous phone requests to the ranger, a shipment finally arrived."

"Thank you." She slid open a drawer in the table beside her and handed him a bag. "I'm sorry it isn't wrapped. By the time the order arrived, I assumed I'd never see you again."

"Yet here I am." He pulled the frame out of the bag and read aloud her caption. "I knew we were safe all along."

"Because we'll do life together."

For a long while, he held her. "I missed you at church tonight. Mrs. Addyson remarked on the preacher's outstanding sermon."

"Yes. I thought so too."

"I played the harmonica. The choir was beautiful."

"I'm sure they were. I'm sure you were awesome."

"You'll hear me play and sing again because I joined the choir." He tipped back his head, as if he were gazing toward heaven. "I was distracted—by my bitterness, and by life. I'm starting to realize that God is for me, not against me. My perspective was messed up, but finally, at forty, I'm seeing more clearly."

"God has always been your champion. He is never against you."

She whispered a word of praise, and Max joined in.

"Gerry declared that dinner tomorrow is at two o'clock, give or take a few hours," she said.

He returned her smile. "He told me the same. I guess it depends on little Freddie's schedule."

She hesitated. "I didn't realize you were dining there too."

"He didn't mention it?" Max chuckled. "He must've forgotten when he phoned you."

"You knew he called?"

"I stood next to him when he made the phone call."

"So, you figured between tonight and tomorrow, we'd see each other?"

"That's one of the things I love about Christmas. All this togetherness." He reached for his jacket and pulled out a handful of wildflowers from his pocket—intense violets and pale blue ivy. "These grow at the edge of town. I'm impressed that plants bloom here in the winter. I'd forgotten. In any event, I picked them for you. Sorry they're wilted."

"They're not. They're beautiful."

He muffled her protest with a deep kiss and

drew her into his arms. "I can't give you much, but I'll give you my love."

"I love you too."

The puppy whimpered, and Sarah freed him from his crate and nestled him in her arms. When Max extended his hands, she placed the tiny bundle in his lap.

"What's his name?" he asked.

"Tiny Tim."

Max swallowed the thickness in his throat, the emotions overcoming him.

He drew Sarah near. She was all he needed, all he'd been searching for. The woman he loved by his side, a reverence for a God who was no longer elusive, and a significant, heartwarming Christmas.

"Merry Christmas, Max," Sarah whispered. "And God bless us, every one."

The End

AMANDA'S EASY WASSAIL

Ingredients:

2 cups apple juice
2 cups orange juice
2 cups cranberry juice
2 cinnamon sticks

Add everything to a crockpot, mix, and warm until the desired temperature is reached.

For a larger batch: (almost a gallon)

5 cups apple juice
    5 cups orange juice
    5 cups cranberry juice
    3 or 4 cinnamon sticks, as desired
    Enjoy!

A NOTE FROM JOSIE

Thank you for reading my holiday romance, A Christmas Puppy To Cherish. I hope you enjoyed this heartwarming, inspirational story. This is the fourth book in my contemporary "Cherish" series.

You don't need ears to hear God's plan. All you need is an open heart...

This story is set in the charming fictional small town of Cherish, South Carolina. The book follows A Love Song To Cherish, A Christmas To Cherish, and A Valentine To Cherish.

In A Christmas Puppy To Cherish, I introduce two new characters to our beloved mix of familiar heroes and heroines. Many of you may know that music is an important part of my life, and many of the characters are musicians.

I also researched the hero, Maxwell's, fascinating profession of ornithology. (The study of birds.)

And the heroine, Sarah, with her kind heart, is the perfect match for him.

If you loved this story as much as I loved writing it, please help *other people find it by posting your review.*

A Christmas Puppy To Cherish is available in ebook, Paperback, Hardcover, Large Print Paperback, and Audiobook.

My Spotify List for A Christmas Puppy To Cherish is here.

CHRISTMAS TAILS OF
THE HEART

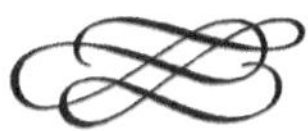

USA TODAY BESTSELLING AUTHOR
JOSIE RIVIERA
a Christmas to Cherish
A SWEET AND WHOLESOME HOLIDAY NOVELLA

Copyright © 2018 by Josie Riviera

All rights reserved.

No part of this book may be reproduced in any form or by any electronic or mechanical means, including information storage and retrieval systems, without written permission from the author, except for the use of brief quotations in a book review.

PRAISE AND AWARDS

USA TODAY bestselling author
#1 Bestseller Women's Religious Fiction
#1 Bestseller Contemporary Religious Fiction
#1 Bestseller Inspirational Religious Fiction
#2 Bestseller Inspirational Prayer

CHAPTER 1

*E*mmanuelle Sumter surveyed the picturesque town of Cherish, South Carolina, brightly lit in crimson and green holiday decor. The town looked as if it had emerged from a Christmas card. Glittering frost framed bare tree branches, and local artists were setting up their canvases for an art walk. The coldness in the air was soundless and serene, comforting in its own way.

She exited the Cherish Central train station, zippered her cobalt-blue puffer coat to her chin, and stepped onto the curb.

Who believed an actual, breathing town could resemble a holiday snow globe?

Evidently, her friend Dorothy did, considering

her enthusiasm whenever she described her idyllic South Carolina town.

Emmanuelle stood on the curb and shoved her hands in her pockets. A cold December gust slapped her cheeks, sharp streams of frigid air. She swept a wisp of hair from her cheek and searched for Nicholas, Dorothy's older brother. He was supposed to pick her up. People were shouting greetings, kissing, cooing over babies. A teeming mass of humanity.

But no Nicholas.

A taxi's horn spiked. Emmanuelle jumped, an involuntary nervous reaction.

Take a deep breath. Relax. Dorothy had assured her Cherish was a safe haven, a harbor in a storm.

Repeating her mantra, Emmanuelle hailed the black-bearded taxi driver parked at the curb. She still didn't see any sign of Nicholas, so she'd take the cab.

She handed the driver her suitcase, then slid into the backseat and gave the address of Dorothy's music store, Musically Yours.

They passed charming shops decorated in glittering lights, and a sign advertising a historic home tour. A few minutes later, the driver pointed at the Musically Yours lighted outdoor sign and idled at the corner of Myrtle and Magnolia Streets.

"The store's two hoots and a holler away,

ma'am." He hoisted her suitcase from the trunk and set it on the sidewalk. "We've reached your destination."

Destination. Was this where her journey ended after a year filled with pain and abuse? Did hope and encouragement wait for her in this little town?

A new life. With perseverance, she could start fresh.

"Thanks." She climbed from the taxi, paid the driver and grabbed her suitcase.

Daylight faded as dusk crept in, and she tipped her head to take in Evergreen Street. Family-owned businesses had switched on their store-front lights, transforming the town into a fairy-tale sparkle of miniature white lights. The tantalizing scent of honey roasted almonds wafted through the air. Boughs of fragrant holly tied with red velvet bows hung cheerily from tall solitary lampposts. Bright-faced children skipped by, lifting their faces skyward to catch a sprinkling of snow. Their conscientious parents followed close behind.

"Emmanuelle! You arrived right on time!" Dorothy flung open the door of the music store and pressed a welcoming kiss to Emmanuelle's cheek. Dorothy's brown hair was swept up in a French braid, her creamy complexion glowing with an enthusiasm Emmanuelle didn't recall from their days working as struggling musicians in New York.

Dorothy had lived there before moving back to Cherish, her hometown, and marrying her high school crush, Ryan Edwards. He had been an opera star in the making and had given up his touring career to settle in Cherish. They were newlyweds. They were in love.

Love. The beginning was always so alluring. It was the end Emmanuelle feared.

Dorothy regarded the departing taxi. "Apparently Nicholas didn't pick you up?"

"I didn't see him so I took a cab."

Emmanuelle turned from Dorothy and admired Musically Yours' frosty window display, bedecked in an infinite array of treble clef signs. A pine wreath, embellished in antique ornaments—tiny pianos, violins, and harps—adorned the front door.

"It's wonderful," she said. "You've worked so hard to set this up."

"Thanks. Ryan and I are still learning the business, and we're inspired by anything musical."

Emmanuelle smiled, but then shivered. "It's colder here than I expected. At least the blizzard that threatened to shut down New York never came."

"The storm hit after you left," Dorothy replied. "You escaped the worst of it."

Did she? She couldn't answer at first, finally whispering, "Hopefully."

Dorothy raised a delicate eyebrow, but Emmanuelle didn't elaborate. Sure, she'd escaped the snowstorm. An escape from George, her ex, was yet to be determined.

Please God, be with me now in my dark season, when I'm so out of place. The world around me is glowing with the promise of Christmas and I feel dark and empty inside.

She leaned forward to admire two animated polar bears sitting amidst the treble clef signs in the shop's window. Beneath a starry sky, the bears tapped drums to the tune of "Jingle Bells."

"Very clever." She couldn't help a grin. "Thanks for the invite to Cherish."

"We're thrilled you agreed to join us for Christmas." Dorothy grabbed her hands for a reassuring squeeze. She was so pleasant and gracious, Emmanuelle thought. So jovial.

On the other hand, Emmanuelle felt the opposite. All she had become in twenty-five years—a dependable, straightforward woman as well as an esteemed harpist—she'd lost in six months to George.

She'd once been like Dorothy, resilient, independent and a woman of God.

Her ex had taken it all away.

Deep in her coat pocket, her fingers worried an angel ornament she'd purchased at the New York airport. For her, the ornament symbolized the sacred Christmas season, its optimism, dreams, and promise.

She hadn't taken it out of her pocket yet.

"You've been difficult to reach these past few months." Dorothy studiously appraised Emmanuelle. "You hardly ever answered your phone."

"I've been busy with concert engagements." Emmanuelle forced her features to remain blank. "You know, musician stuff." It was a lie, and with the lie came heaviness, a wide band of disapproval. Where had her sense of decency gone?

She tightened her paisley scarf around her neck. Although the violent purple and yellow bruises had faded, she still felt self-conscious.

Dorothy guided her into the music store. "My brother will blame his forgetfulness on his new job, or that gigantic puppy he adopted at the animal shelter. You'd think he'd know better at thirty years old."

"He's a good guy," Emmanuelle said. "Nicholas and I Skyped every night for months when you were in rehab."

"Thanks to you both, I'm better." Dorothy smiled. "And most important, thanks to God."

Once, Emmanuelle would have readily agreed.

God was her salvation, her refuge. Now she didn't know how to answer because her faith had wavered.

Truly I tell you, if you have faith as small as a mustard seed, you can say to this mountain, "Move from here to there," and it will move. The verse from Matthew 17:20 came to her mind, a reminder of her strength. All she had to do was reach for it, if she was brave enough.

Inside the store, Dorothy ran a finger along one of the shelves, grinning when she was assured it was dust free. "Ryan and I purchased a cottage-style bungalow four blocks from here and there's an extra bedroom."

"This is your first Christmas as a married couple." Emmanuelle set her suitcase out of the way of a passing customer. "Please celebrate the holiday without me in the middle."

"I insist you stay with us."

"For an entire month?" Emmanuelle shook her head. "Insist all you want. I booked a room at the Cherish Hills Inn. You raved about the inn's accommodations being top-quality when you returned to Cherish for your brother's wedding last year."

"The wedding that didn't happen." Ruefully, Dorothy sighed. "Nicholas is still healing from the embarrassment and heartbreak."

The ending stages of love. Dreams shattered.

Without warning, the front door burst open. Instinctively, Emmanuelle held up a hand, shielding herself from view.

A heavy-set woman, her hair helmeted in a tight gray bun, ambled inside. She called out a jovial hello to Dorothy.

"Be with you in a minute, Mrs. McManus." Dorothy gave a flap of her hands, and then turned back to Emmanuelle. "Sorry. What were we discussing?"

Emmanuelle blew out a breath. This uneasiness, this fear of being followed, had to stop.

Still shaken, she kept her focus on a Mozart statue topped with a red plush Santa hat sitting on the counter.

"We were discussing the wedding that didn't happen," she replied. "Whenever Nicholas and I talked when you were in rehab, he always reminded me we should place our trust in God."

"Sadly, people change, beliefs change." Worry replaced Dorothy's earlier smile. "Hard knocks can shake the faith of the most devout. I pray he'll go to church again because he's faltered since the breakup."

Suggesting Emmanuelle put her suitcase behind the front counter, Dorothy led her past a display table. As Dorothy paused to rearrange two pairs of oboe earrings so they lined up side by side, she said, "God had other plans for him and for me. I believe things work out for the best."

Emmanuelle frowned and nodded, aborting both actions.

For Dorothy, perhaps. For Ryan. For anyone in this idyllic snow globe town. But not for me. And apparently not for Nicholas.

Her cell phone buzzed. She retrieved it from her tote bag and scanned the screen. *Unknown caller.* Her heart stopped. A telemarketer? A wrong number?

"Who is it?"

Looking up, she saw Dorothy was studying her with keen interest.

"No one." Fumbling, Emmanuelle tucked the phone back into her faux leather tote. "You're right. People change for many reasons." And she'd changed most of all. She'd been a competent, successful woman. Now a chill crept up her spine when a door opened into a harmless music store.

"Are you okay?" Dorothy asked.

"I'm fine, just tired from traveling." Emmanuelle's eyes welled with tears, and she averted her gaze. She'd applied makeup, the first time in months, attempting to conceal her sleep deprivation. The endless worrying and crying had taken a toll.

"We're organizing a concert in the town square the weekend before Christmas," Dorothy was saying. "I meant to ask you to bring your harp—"

"My harp weighs nearly eighty pounds." She picked up a pair of piano earrings and fingered the tiny keyboard. "It's in New York."

Broken. She wouldn't reveal how George had destroyed her harp in one of his lightning-fast rages. The memory caused a block of ice to form in her stomach, a block that she knew would be slow to thaw. She hated the thought of her beloved instrument, splintered into pieces, lying on a New York curb under a pile of snow.

Better the harp than you splintered into pieces.

But his shouted insults and rough slaps had been her fault. She'd provoked him.

No, no, no. Her inner voice took on a sharp edge. That was the old Emmanuelle talking. The new Emmanuelle knew she wasn't a dishtowel to be thrown around on a whim. In hindsight, she should have known George was abusive. The warning signs were there.

She blew out a breath. She'd resolved to find peace and comfort in this holiday … in this town … somewhere … and find her footing again.

"Enough about me." She set down the earrings and dismissed herself with a flutter of her fingers. "Where's Ryan?"

"He's rehearsing in nearby Stanley Valley today and will arrive this evening. He'll be singing 'O Holy Night' for a Christmas Cantata service. He gives so freely of his talent." Dorothy's smile was as radiant as a Merry Christmas bouquet. "He's featured throughout the Carolinas in many guest appearances. Plus, the Atlanta opera house asked him to perform the role of Zoroastro in Handel's opera, *Orlando*. I'm incredibly proud of him."

"You should be." Dorothy's smile was contagious, and Emmanuelle managed a warm grin. "He's famous and extremely talented."

"And you? Any upcoming concerts?"

"None." She answered in a firm tone that she expected would discourage her friend from probing. Judging by the way Dorothy's eyebrows drew together, she'd succeeded.

Fortunately, an acoustic guitar arrangement of "Lo, How a Rose Is Blooming" piped in the background, the ideal holiday music to smooth a lull in the conversation.

"I'm sure you're keen to check in." Dorothy broke the silence. "I'll deal with these last few customers, close the store, and give you a lift. Unless you'd rather walk the three blocks to the inn?"

"No, no. I'll wait for you."

She'd never walk alone again. Not in New York, not

in Cherish. Not anywhere, because she'd never feel safe again.

Dorothy gestured toward the front of the store. "If you care to browse, the Christmas music section is on your left. There's a lovely harp arrangement of *The Nutcracker*."

"Thanks. Your store is a music-lover's dream."

Intrigued, Emmanuelle stepped past a buyer laden with music bookmarks and made her way to the sheet music. She thumbed through endless arrangements of Christmas solos, wondering what madness had brought her to this town. She didn't belong here among all this gaiety. Her sadness was a burden refusing to go away.

Disheartened, she stared, trancelike, at the display window. A whimsical model train circled the polar bears, and the sight was enchanting.

Beyond, past the cheery town, past the exuberant children and the enormous Christmas tree illuminating the town square, a darkened sky had followed dusk.

CHAPTER 2

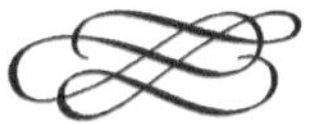

As he entered his apartment, Nicholas Thompson pulled off his deputy badge and set it on a table in the foyer. Except for one traffic violation, a minor fender bender and endless meetings, the day had been relatively calm for a newbie deputy.

He looked forward to relaxing in front of the TV with a good cup of coffee and a chocolate-glazed doughnut. Ever since he'd become a deputy, he'd acquired a taste for both.

All fifty pounds of his six-month-old golden retriever greeted him with an energetic stretch. He'd purchased the dog from an animal shelter in Stanley, two weeks to the day after his fiancée, Alice, had broken up with him. The dog surveyed

Nicholas with expectant black eyes and a fiercely wagging tail.

"No, Molly Belle, I'm not taking you for a—"

The dog ran in circles around him and barked.

Nicholas groaned. He'd no sooner walked in and he was forced to turn around and walk out again. "All right, take a tater and wait a sec." He weaved around a mountain of laundry and strode to his bedroom. His bed was unmade, an old sweatshirt tossed over a side chair. He removed the gun from his holster and locked it in his bedroom closet's safe. Then he loosened his tie and changed out of uniform—white shirt and khaki pants—dragging on jeans, a long-sleeved T-shirt, and work boots. Pausing, he ran a critical survey of his apartment, particularly the coffee table piled with remote controls and junk mail and old catalogues. The large sofa begged for a skilled reupholster, and his sister, Dorothy, had admonished him countless times to hang curtains on his bare windows.

He darted a glance at the motorcycle calendar propped on a shelf. Today was December first, and Christmas was less than a month away. At the very least, the season merited a Christmas tree in the corner and a wreath on his apartment door.

Nope. Not this year.

Despite Molly Belle lightening his days, Nicholas didn't have the heart for celebrations and feasts. What other man in the state of South Carolina had experienced the humiliation of his fiancée leaving him on their wedding day? And by text, no less. Not even in person.

The dog's impertinent barking prompted him to grab the leash, button his navy pea coat and open the front door. With an eager yelp, Molly Belle ran ahead, down his short flight of stairs and onto the sidewalk.

"Slower, girl." The dog, as usual, didn't obey and tugged harder on the leash. Nicholas made a mental note to sign her up for obedience classes.

His cell phone buzzed. He hoped it wasn't a call to drive back to the police station. Relieved to see Dorothy's caller ID, he clicked on.

"Nicholas, are you through with work?" she asked.

"Yes, I just got in." He restrained the dog from sniffing every blade of glass in a neighbor's garden. "I'm taking Molly Belle for a walk."

"Emmanuelle arrived an hour ago. Did you forget?"

He sighed and slapped a hand to his forehead. He forgot a lot of things lately. "I got sidetracked by last-minute meetings at the police station. Please tell her I'm sorry."

"You can tell her yourself. We're at the Cherish Hills Inn and she's unpacking. Meet us here, then join us at Frank's Pizzeria for a slice. It's your favorite restaurant."

His first response was *no* before he thought better of it. He should extend a polite apology, considering he'd forgotten to pick up the woman. He'd swing by and make his amends and then leave.

As he and Molly Belle neared the inn, it was all he could do not to reverse direction and head back to his apartment.

He could work. He could take care of his spirited dog. But he didn't relish small talk with a woman, especially a woman he'd grown close to during their many phone conversations. What would he say to her after all these months?

"Oh, by the way, Emmanuelle, do you remember me talking nonstop about Alice, my fiancée? She left me the day of our wedding."

Molly Belle ignored his command to walk slower, nearly choking on the leash as she lunged forward.

CHAPTER 3

$\mathcal{B}$attling for control of the leash, Nicholas strode into the Cherish Hills Inn's lobby. Briefly, he admired the boxwood wreath hanging on the wooden door, the lighted village scene on a round cherry tabletop in the foyer. He greeted the white-haired innkeeper, Tom Canning, with an apologetic shrug and lifted the dog's leash.

Tom scowled. Crevices grooved the sides of his mouth. "No animals."

"Just this once—for someone you've known your entire life?" Nicholas asked. "For a man who upholds the law in our town?"

Tom sighed, unbending a bit, and peered at Nicholas above the cheaters perched on the bridge of his nose. "Go ahead, deputy." He rewarded

Nicholas with a brief nod, but raised his index finger to issue a one-minute warning.

"Thanks." Nicholas strode across the wide plank floors to the parlor where a fire blazed in the stacked rock fireplace, so large an ox could stand upright inside it. On the center of the mantel sat a handsomely carved Nativity set in burnished wood. Artistically arranged seasonal fruit—oranges and apples and pears—were loaded high in a wide pewter bowl on a side table.

He directed his gaze toward Dorothy, who stood near the fireplace, and that was the last thing he remembered.

The undeniably beautiful woman who stood beside Dorothy, clad in a white lace sweater dress, resembled a dainty, sweet confection. Her complexion was pink, her dark lashes slightly lowered, her lips plush and generous. A puffy blue jacket was slung over her shoulders, and she held a tote bag close to her side.

His mind reeled with memories.

Emmanuelle Sumter. They'd Skyped many times, so he'd known she was attractive, but in person she was positively breathtaking. Silky blonde hair rioted around her face in impossibly tight curls, and her huge blue eyes acknowledged a tentative welcome.

"I assume you remember me." He fumbled with

Molly Belle's leash as the dog sniffed the rug incessantly. "You look … different in person." *Better*, he amended to himself. *She looked better. More than better.* He extended his free hand. "Please accept my apologies for forgetting you."

"Apology accepted." She placed her small hand in his large one. "How could I forget our nightly conversations? You guided Dorothy through a challenging season in her life."

Emmanuelle's features were so petite, her fingers so fragile. "And you were the friend she counted on." He tightened his grip and vigorously shook her hand.

"You were the person who prayed with her every day." She pulled away, politely, decisively. "You encouraged her."

"Hold on you two, I'm right here!" Dorothy laughingly stepped between them. "Are you competing in a compliment contest I'm not aware of?"

Emmanuelle's dimples winked in a slight smile. "Your brother's the winner."

"Please don't boost his ego, or he'll expect you to treat for pizza." Dorothy chuckled. "Frank's Pizza is within walking distance. They advertise the best pizza in town."

"Because they're the only pizzeria in town." Nicholas helped Emmanuelle on with her coat, then swung Molly Belle's leash up and down. "Unfortunately they don't allow animals and I won't be able to go."

Molly Belle responded with a defiant stare and Emmanuelle leaned down to pet her. "Aww, your dog is so friendly." Soon, the dog was lying on the rug legs up, outstretched in doggy ecstasy while Emmanuelle crouched to rub her stomach.

"You said you'd just gotten home from work," Dorothy said as she encouraged Emmanuelle and the dog to stand, then steered the threesome to the doorway. "Have you eaten dinner, Nicholas?"

"I'll whip up something." He couldn't imagine what although there was a slight possibility a frozen pizza sat in his freezer behind a carton of peanut butter ice cream.

Molly Belle had different ideas, having decided Emmanuelle was her new best friend. With a wiggle of glee, she changed direction and hurled straight into her.

Emmanuelle fell back and Nicholas let go of the leash to stop her fall. Freed from her leash, the dog shot in another direction and knocked over a crystal vase filled with red roses. The vase shattered on the floor.

Tom, eye-glass cheaters in hand, tore into the parlor. His face colored to a beet-red as he tapped his watch. "Your one-minute dog visit was up five minutes ago, Nicholas."

"Sorry. We were just leaving." Nicholas righted Emmanuelle as Dorothy picked up the roses, then he dashed forward to retrieve the leash.

"Shoo, all of you!" Tom said. "I'll clean up the mess."

The women followed Nicholas. They exited to a whip of icy wind that blew Emmanuelle's curls around her face. Nicholas lifted his hand, an automatic response to protect her from another gust. She flinched, tightened the pink paisley scarf around her neck, and moved a step away.

He tossed an inquiring glance toward her. She ignored him.

As if by mutual agreement to cover up Emmanuelle's skittish behavior, Dorothy began talking about every holiday event scheduled in three counties between Christmas and New Year's.

"Frank's boasts an outdoor enclosed eating area," Dorothy continued, talking in a loud voice to drown out the quiet. She stopped briefly to commend the florist shop's front window decorated in scarlet-red poinsettias and twine wreaths. "I'm sure Frank's will allow Molly Belle inside, Nicholas. She's leashed and we'll take an out-of-the-way table."

Before Nicholas could comment, Dorothy's cell phone pinged. She grabbed it from her tote bag, read the text, then extended an unapologetic grin.

"Ryan returned early from Stanley. A few weeks ago, he bought a cookbook called *Southern Charms* at a fundraiser for encouraging women empowerment, and he's been learning to cook gourmet. He's preparing a romantic dinner of rosemary chicken and pasta salad and he wants me to come home now. He has a surprise for me."

"I applaud your husband for buying a cookbook and supporting a beneficial cause." Despite his words, Nicholas sent his sister an exasperated glance. "So, you invited me to join you for dinner and now you're leaving?"

If she was trying to fix him up with Emmanuelle, he refused to go along with it. From what Dorothy had revealed, Emmanuelle had accepted his sister's offer to visit Cherish for the holidays primarily to get away from New York. The result of breaking up with a man. It was always because of a man, he thought, reflecting on his cheating fiancée and her new boyfriend.

He wanted to extend a sympathetic ear, for surely Emmanuelle wanted to talk at length about the break-up, although he wasn't in the proper frame of mind to attend to anyone's problems other than his own.

Yes, he'd gotten along well with her. They had talked nightly for months because of their shared interest in Dorothy's welfare, plus their unshakeable faith in God. But his life was different now. His faith teetered. If he had to define it, he'd say his faith was lukewarm.

He tuned back in when he heard Emmanuelle say, "Don't disappoint Ryan." She put her hand on Dorothy's arm, then flashed a look at Nicholas. "I'll double back and finish unpacking if you don't mind walking me."

This was his out. A polite response and he'd be sitting in his recliner watching television within fifteen minutes flat. Instead, he found himself saying, "We're almost at the restaurant so we might as well enjoy dinner."

Besides pizza, the restaurant had good coffee.

"Perfect! You two go on without me. I'm sure there's a lot to catch up on since you haven't talked in a year." Dorothy tucked her brown hair under the black wool cap she produced from her handbag. With a satisfied wave, she swung in the opposite direction.

"This way." Nicholas touched Emmanuelle's arm. She sidestepped him and ran a hand over the zipper of her jacket. Although she appeared to be an elegant and poised woman, she was as edgy as a newborn fawn.

Perhaps there was nothing left to discuss? Dorothy, their commonality, no longer required their help, and he obviously wasn't interesting enough for pretty and popular Emmanuelle. The thought left him maintaining a chilly and reserved silence as they walked toward the restaurant.

His gaze landed on two tow-headed toddlers running ahead of them. They pointed to the fairyland of Christmas lights in the town square and the sight made Nicholas smile. He loved children, although now he'd never have any. He'd never subject his heart to another battering. He'd successfully barricaded himself behind a solid, protective shell.

Lonely? Sometimes.

Safe? Definitely.

He headed Emmanuelle and Molly Belle toward the next block.

Molly Belle had a mind of her own, though, wanting nothing more than to loll on the sidewalk and hug the ground. He encouraged the dog with an assurance of a treat, and Emmanuelle added a "C'mon girl."

When they resumed walking, he asked, "Are you still the principal harpist for … I forgot the name of the symphony. It was in a town somewhere outside New York."

"No, I'm not playing the harp anymore. It's gone." Stillness reigned for several beats after her self-deprecating laugh. He recognized the defeat in her shining blue eyes, and sympathy flickered in his hardened heart.

"What about you?" The audible stress in her tone made him hesitate. "I remember you were studying for an important exam."

"The police academy. I passed and I'm a deputy."

Her eyes widened. "A—a deputy ..." She blanched and missed a step.

"And here I thought congratulations were in order," he half joked.

"Yes, of course." She clutched her tote bag and kept her head down. "Umm, congratulations, Deputy Thompson."

Something had happened to her in New York. Something bad, although he couldn't offer any support because he was empty. The woman whom he'd thought had loved him had left him flat. He'd been a blind fool while she'd deceived him for months, but he'd learned a painful lesson and he'd learned it well. Relationships with women were well off his radar, especially when a woman clearly had a hang-up about men.

Bachelorhood was serene. Naught to fear, because nothing—no hearts, no feeling, no plans—would be broken. Besides, a dog was excellent company.

Despite himself, his gaze lingered on Emmanuelle's profile, her slim figure she kept well-hidden beneath her winter jacket and high boots.

Molly Belle barked a little too enthusiastically, prompting Emmanuelle to jump when a black lab trotted past.

"She's high-spirited," Nicholas offered as an explanation.

"Who's in control here?" she asked him. "I used to work around dogs. They were a big part of my life." She patted Molly Belle's head, then smiled when the dog put a wet nose in her hand.

"I'm considering dog obedience classes. Do you think it's a good idea?"

Emmanuelle opened her mouth, closed it again, grinned. "Yes, it's an excellent idea. In the meantime, begin with simple commands like *sit* and *wait*. Can you do that?"

"Certainly. I'm the master."

An irreverent chuckle burst from her lips and he fought the insane impulse to kiss her.

He knew her through those lengthy phone conversations, and every night he'd looked forward to their discussions about God, and their everyday lives, and their pasts. Their comfortable hour-long chats had become easy and familiar. If he hadn't been engaged to his fiancée at the time, he might have admitted the attraction he'd felt for Emmanuelle.

This stiffness between them was foreign. She had frequently sought his advice, the comfort of his faith coinciding with her hard-won beliefs. She'd been orphaned when she was in her teens, but she had persevered, studied hard, and become a virtuoso harpist.

They walked the last block to the restaurant at a quick pace. Her knee-length dress glided along her legs and her suede boots fit high above her knee. Nicholas kept stealing glances at her. The self-sufficient woman he'd known had evaporated. She'd become breakable, her voice soft, her movements hesitant.

They walked up the steps to the pizzeria's entrance, and he reached around to open the door.

"I'm ordering Frank's deluxe-meat lovers special," he said. "Are you the salad type?"

"Salad? Salad is for vegetarians." She walked past him into the restaurant, her expression amused. "I'm the barbecue and corn fritters type."

CHAPTER 4

The next day was Saturday, and Nicholas worked a half day. The morning had started with an arrest for drunk driving and ended in the police station with multiple copies of blank forms to fill out. He loved his job, but he could do without the written procedures and minute details.

When he returned home at noon, he changed out of his uniform and into jeans and a shirt, a white pullover hoodie, and running shoes. He dashed off a reminder note to price affordable curtains over the weekend, then leashed Molly Belle for a quick jog.

Ryan's surprise for Dorothy the previous night had been tickets to a tuba Christmas concert in Stanley, and Dorothy had given Nicholas the not-so-subtle hint that Emmanuelle would be spending the day alone. Despite telling himself a firm *no*, he found himself veering toward the Cherish Hills Inn.

Their dinner at the pizzeria had ended abruptly when Emmanuelle had pleaded tiredness soon after he began telling her about his job as deputy sheriff. He'd started off by regaling her with amusing tales of some of the absurd arrests he'd made. One had been for drunk and disorderly conduct when a spectator ran onto the field of a high school football game declaring he was the sixth offensive lineman. On another occasion, he'd walked an eighteen-year-old home to face his parents after a keg party had gotten out of control, only to have the boy get sick on their front lawn.

As he talked, Emmanuelle's shoulders had tightened and her hand quivered as she'd pushed the barbecue around her plate. Her fear was tangible, stretching across the red-checkered tablecloth, and the pizza set neatly in the center of the table.

He got the hint and stopped talking about his profession altogether, carrying on instead a reasonably normal conversation, albeit one-sided, observing the average winter temperature in South Carolina and New York.

The inn neared, and he closed the distance to the porch steps in five long strides.

He leaned forward to catch his breath and wipe

his brow on the sleeve of his hoodie. Wide-slatted rocking chairs were assembled on the expansive front porch and evergreen garland and holly berries were strung across each window.

Although he normally would simply walk into the inn, after the mishap the day before, he thought it best if he knocked first.

Pushing his cheaters down his nose, Tom Canning peered through the entry's side glass, glowered, and flung open the door. "No dogs allowed inside, Deputy Thompson." He tried to sound polite, but there was no mistaking that he was issuing an order. "No exceptions."

"I'm sorry about yesterday, Mr. Canning, and I'll be happy to pay for any damages."

"Good. I'll write up a bill for you."

"No hurry. I mean, please do." Nicholas kept a sneakered foot in the door as the innkeeper attempted to shut him out. "Will you let Emmanuelle know I'm here?"

Tom took off his cheaters and polished them. "Is she expecting you?"

"Probably not."

"Hi Nicholas." Emmanuelle appeared at the bottom of the curved staircase, looking bewitchingly beautiful. Her blonde hair was piled high at the crown, her ever-present pink scarf around her neck, her puffy blue jacket all zippered.

"I guess she was expecting you." With a conspiratorial half grin toward Nicholas, the owner ushered them outside, then slammed the door, leaving Emmanuelle and Nicholas standing on the porch with Molly Belle.

Annoyed, Nicholas fixed his gaze on the door. "I thought everyone loved animals. Apparently, Tom doesn't like dogs."

"His reasons are excellent." She didn't withhold her chuckle. "That vase of roses spilled water across his rug and cost him thirty minutes of clean-up, not to mention the cost of the vase and flowers."

"I offered to pay for the damages." Nicholas inspected her trim, shapely form. Today, black jeans and high boots accentuated her long legs. A green sweater peeked from beneath her winter jacket. "Were you ... expecting me?"

The color on her cheekbones rose to a flattering blush against her creamy complexion. The afternoon sun gilded her blonde hair to streaks of platinum, and he favored her with an unabashed smile. She was stunning.

She stretched on a pair of pink knit gloves that matched her scarf. "Dorothy mentioned you might stop by."

"Several local booths in the town square are selling Christmas items. Are you up for some last-minute shopping?" He was prepared for her to refuse. However, he didn't expect the wariness on her face, the absolutely motionless air between them.

"I have no reason to shop. I'm not buying any Christmas gifts this year." She focused a pained stare on the mixed greenery placed around the white rocking chairs.

An unexpected fury flowed through his veins at whoever had hurt her. When? Where?

"Surely there's something you'd like." He grinned, an attempt to disarm her. "The locals sell handmade jewelry and artwork and leather goods. And I have it on excellent authority that one of my friends, who owns a restaurant called The Grill Room, set up early this morning and is smoking South Carolina barbecue as we speak."

She considered her watch. "It's a little late for lunch."

"It's just shy of two o'clock. We'll call it an early dinner." He hooked his thumbs in the back pockets of his jeans and felt the leash go slack. In an instant, his dog had raced off the porch in a mad chase after a squirrel.

"Molly Belle!"

What happened next occurred in slow motion.

The dog ran into the road. Brakes squealed. A sickening thud.

"No!" Unmindful of traffic, Nicholas dashed for his dog, seeing only Molly Belle's limp body lying helpless in the middle of the road. Blood seeped from her stomach, matting her glossy golden fur. He sank down, right there with his dog, and did something he hadn't done since he was a child.

He cried.

CHAPTER 5

Emmanuelle sat in the passenger seat of the innkeeper's lime-green Volkswagen and held the dog in her lap while Nicholas drove. She controlled her voice as she rubbed Molly Belle gently behind her ears. She'd secured a makeshift muzzle using the dog's leash, assuring Nicholas even Molly Belle, a sweet dog, could lash out when she was in pain.

"Looks like a surface wound," she said. Carefully, she lifted the dog's lip, murmuring about capillary refill time. When Nicholas didn't seem to hear her, she added, "Fortunately, the driver stopped in time."

Everything had happened in a blur. Visibly distraught, the driver had burst from his car in a frenzy and groped for the words to apologize. Tom

Canning rushed out and offered Nicholas his car, and then dashed to the inn. He was back almost instantly with sterile gauze and a yellow crocheted blanket an instant later. A bystander stopped traffic, which allowed Nicholas and Tom to use the blanket as a sling and carry the dog to the car. Emmanuelle placed gauze over the dog's stomach and applied pressure, murmuring relief when the blood didn't soak through.

Nicholas drove quickly and silently to Cherish Animal Hospital. She took in his granite profile, his short blond hair shoved back from his forehead. He hunched behind the wheel stuffed into a car not made to fit his six-foot frame.

"She doesn't appear to be in shock." She kept her voice quiet and upbeat.

His dog might not be in shock, but Nicholas was. He had taken immediate action, though, and had phoned the animal hospital to tell them they were on their way.

"You don't know that," he finally responded.

"Yes, I do. I've been around plenty of sick dogs."

When they arrived at the hospital, Nicholas parked near the entrance. Once more using the blanket as a sling, they carried the dog past a red-haired receptionist who announced that her name was Scarlett Evans.

Dr. Judson Troutman, the veterinarian, waited

for them in the examining room. Nicholas had mentioned to Emmanuelle that Dr. Troutman had been widowed two years earlier.

Slim, serious, and sandy-haired, the vet was casually dressed in khaki pants, a button-down shirt, and a white lab coat. After brief introductions, he checked Molly Belle's lungs with his stethoscope and confirmed Emmanuelle's evaluation. The dog wasn't in shock.

"My father was a veterinarian," Emmanuelle said. Reverently, she ran a hand along the stethoscope after the vet had laid it to one side.

"You learned well, Emmanuelle." His deep-brown eyes were kind, his demeanor innately gentle. He angled toward Nicholas. "I'm going to give Molly Belle all the time she needs, Deputy Thompson. After her fluids are stabilized and the diagnostics run, I'll give you an update. For now, there's nothing else to do except sit and wait."

Scarlett ushered them into the reception area. A nervous-looking woman in her fifties cradling a quivering black dachshund bobbed a brief hello.

Emmanuelle slid onto a thinly padded chair and nudged aside a half-finished cup of coffee set on a corner table. She rubbed her arms and then dropped her head into her open hands. Now that her adrenaline had settled, she felt chilled and kept her jacket and scarf over her shoulders.

Nicholas paced the hallway for several minutes before coming to sit beside her. "I don't know why I wasn't paying attention and didn't hold onto her leash tighter. If only I had …" He stared down at his hands.

She scanned his clenched fists, the skin bunching at his eyes. "Molly Belle is blessed with the ability to love life. You're the most important part and not to blame. She's always on a leash and you do all you can to keep her safe."

Her quiet reassurances seemed to help, for he sat straighter.

"Still, I was lax. Will she ever forgive me?"

"Of course."

She didn't know where to put her hands, so she rested them on her lap.

Scarlett ushered the nervous woman cradling the dachshund down the long hallway. A door banged shut.

"The accident should never have taken place." Nicholas scrubbed his fingers over his face. "I can't make sense of it. Lately, I can't make sense of anything that's happened to me."

"Everything in our lives is a result of God's favor."

"Favor? What favor? My cycle of believing has been broken."

"So was mine. Whenever I think about the

person I became these past few months, it makes me sad."

"What happened, Emmanuelle?" He studied her expression. "When we last spoke on the phone you were so upbeat."

She chewed her bottom lip. "A lot happens in a year. Don't ask me about the in-between because I'm not ready to talk about it." Mentally reliving George's abuse, a heavy despair settled in her gut. Whenever he'd banged her body into a wall, he screamed that they belonged together, and he was trying to teach her who was the master. No one had ever hit her before. She'd come from a kind and loving home.

"You were only meant for me, Emmanuelle."

The psychological, and then physical, abuse was always worse after George drank. The sharp smell of whiskey on his breath predicted the flashes of unpredictable anger sure to follow. A familiar sweat of panic slid down her neck. On a jerk, she swung her gaze from Nicholas and locked the terrifying remembrances in a safe compartment in her mind.

"Emmanuelle?"

She faltered, found her axis and drew a fortifying breath. "Dorothy stopped by the inn this morning."

"Why?"

"To talk. And she reminded me I shouldn't rebuke myself for past circumstances. She encouraged me to keep my attention on God and not dwell on myself."

"How can a memory upset you if it already happened?"

"Now there's a question I ask myself. Memories can only upset you if they have your attention. The key is to focus on what really matters." Despite her brave declaration, she couldn't meet his probing stare. Instead, she eyed the white-lighted snowman, accented with sheer purple ribbon, hanging on a far wall.

After breakfasting with Dorothy in the inn's sunny conservatory, Emmanuelle had confessed the beatings she'd suffered while tears had streamed down her cheeks. With every frightening scene she confided, heavy chains had been lifted from her heart.

Dorothy was kindhearted and understanding, a true friend, her intentions always in the right place.

Emmanuelle's rapport with Nicholas was different. He had commended her on her talent and independence, complimenting her on countless occasions. What would his opinion be if he learned she had been foolish enough to allow a man to control her?

She released a sigh and hid her face in her

hands. She carried a shame she couldn't describe, not even to herself.

"Care to discuss what happened to you, Emmanuelle?" Nicholas repeated. "You can trust me."

He stared at her. She stared at the snowman.

She could hear a cell phone ringing in the hallway. She could smell the cold, stale coffee on the corner table.

Yes, she trusted Nicholas, even as she feared his admiration would change to disapproval once he understood her situation.

Why hadn't she left George sooner? She'd asked herself the same question more times than she could count.

"Because, Emmanuelle, you were meant only for me."

She shuddered, recalling his bloodshot gray eyes, as he was liquored up more often than not. When had he changed? He'd been so charming at the outset of their relationship, wooing her with lavish dinners and dark chocolate truffles and evenings at the theater.

"Emmanuelle?"

Despite her resolve to start a new life, she pressed her lips tight and didn't acknowledge him.

"You know," Nicholas went on, "I once was a person of great faith." He inclined his head and spoke softly. "This dejection I've felt ever since Alice—"

Emmanuelle's words came quick with no apology. "Your sister said, "If you despair, you will live in despair.""

"Dorothy is admirable and Ryan has taken her lead. Together their faith is anchored in God. I want to trust in the Lord again, I really do." He lifted his hand and cupped her chin, raising her face to his, forcing her to meet his gaze.

She didn't flinch, knowing that he needed a fresh start, needed her full attention.

"Begin by reaching out in prayer." She took his hand, holding it as he bowed his head and whispered praises to God. Silently, she joined him.

Scarlett strolled over, stacking used coffee cups and folding morning newspapers. "Do you two want anything? There's coffee in the vending machine."

Nicholas looked up at her. "Is it any good?"

"No. It's instant, and cold, and shuts off sometimes. Often, actually." She grinned. "Anyway, I brought in extra junk food from home. You know, candy and cupcakes, bottles of soda. Want anything?"

Emmanuelle smiled. "We're fine, thanks."

"My motto is to embrace life and indulge yourself."

Scarlett's full-figured form, Emmanuelle noticed, was pleasing and curvaceous. She was empathetic and sunny, a person who saw the bright side, even on a bleak afternoon. Upbeat, she finished cleaning up the waiting room and retreated to her desk.

As afternoon slipped into evening, Dr. Troutman emerged from the hallway. He drew up a chair to sit across from them. "Delightful news, Deputy Thompson. Surgery isn't necessary. There's no internal bleeding, organ damage, or broken limbs."

"She's going to be all right?" The guarded hope in Nicholas's voice prompted Emmanuelle to place her hand on his arm.

"Molly Belle will be fine." The vet came to his feet. "You can take her home tonight. Find a comfortable spot and get her settled with some heating pads. Given time, she'll heal with no scars."

"Thank you, doctor."

"Clean the wound and apply an antibiotic cream. I gave her an injection for her discomfort." Dr. Troutman rooted in his lab coat for a pad and pen. "I'm prescribing an anti-inflammatory and I recommend not leaving her alone for extended periods of time."

Nicholas's face paled. "For how long? A week?"

"Recovery time varies. She's a young bouncy dog, and I predict she'll be fit in a few weeks or less. Incidentally, she might be a mixed breed. Although she's mostly a golden, I'm thinking there's a bit of yellow lab mixed in." He scribbled the prescription and handed it to Nicholas. "I'll ask Scarlett to schedule Molly Belle for a check-up next Saturday."

"Are you sure I can properly care for her at home in the meantime?" Nicholas hesitated before starting for Scarlett's desk. "If it's safer, please keep her overnight for observation."

"Nothing to observe. You and your girlfriend are quite capable," Dr. Troutman said. "She knows her animals."

"I'm not Nicholas's girlfriend," Emmanuelle clarified, quick to get to her feet. "I learned a tremendous amount when I helped my father. We lived in Remsen, a little town outside of New York. For years, I visited his office every day after school."

From the corner of her eye, she saw Nicholas's thick eyebrows raise as he busied himself with paying the bill.

"How far outside of New York is your father's office?" the vet inquired.

The memories flickered, faded, a million miles away. Once, she'd felt safe and happy, living like other people. How easy it had been when she was a child.

"He died ten years ago when I was sixteen." She spoke carefully, not letting her sense of loss, her free and easy childhood, creep into her voice. "He was a highly regarded veterinarian in our little town. Cherish reminds me of Remsen. Without Remsen's snow."

"I've never been to Remsen," Scarlett chirped. "I bet it's pretty there."

Dr. Troutman gave Scarlett an indulgent smile, then turned back to Emmanuelle. "A small town's down-to-earth values and its focus on what matters most in life … Well, there's not much that can beat that."

"You're absolutely right." Emmanuelle extended her hand. "Thank you."

Over at the reception desk, Nicholas handed Scarlett his credit card, then peered over his shoulder at Emmanuelle. "All those hours we spent on the phone and you never mentioned your animal expertise."

She shrugged. "There were more serious topics to discuss."

Saying he would get Molly Belle, the vet walked down the hallway. He and Nicholas transported a muzzled Molly Belle to the rear seat of the Volkswagen using a large dog crate.

On the drive to Nicholas's apartment, Emmanuelle pondered what to do. Torn between the belief that helping for a week wouldn't matter because she had no other plans, and the fact she'd be immersed in his personal surroundings, she considered how to word her offer before she spoke.

He needed help, especially when he reported to work on Monday. Yet, he hadn't asked for any. A proud, stubborn man, Dorothy had once described her brother when she'd become frustrated at his inability to talk about his hurt after his marriage plans fell apart.

"Once Molly Belle is situated tonight," Emmanuelle began, "I'll stay with her while you fill her prescription."

"I appreciate that."

Guarded, yet so polite.

"Once Monday rolls in, I'll watch her while you're on duty, deputy."

"Wouldn't you rather kill time checking out the Christmas markets and visiting Dorothy and Ryan?"

"I'd rather kill time being of some use."

"All day nursing a sick dog isn't a vacation." His expression indicated his willingness to accept her offer, although he kept his tone carefully non-committal.

"Who said my visit is about a vacation? Christmas is the season for giving."

What else could she say that was a reasonable justification for offering to help? She simply *wanted* to because Nicholas and Molly Belle had become important to her, but she certainly couldn't say that. "I have experience tending to sick animals."

"I'll pay you." He offered a quick, grateful smile. "Do you cook?"

"Do frozen pizzas count?"

"You're describing the extent of my cooking skills as well." She grinned. "Fortunately, Ryan is learning gourmet cooking so I'll throw out some hints. Or better yet, I'll borrow his *Southern Charms* cookbook."

CHAPTER 6

With Molly Belle settled on a blanket near the recliner in the living room, Nicholas went off to get her prescription. Emmanuelle applied a heating pad to the dog's belly, where it seemed she had the most pain. When she was assured the dog rested comfortably, she removed the heating pad and waited for Nicholas to come back with the prescription.

Dr. Troutman's injection had made Molly Belle drowsy. Her brownish-black nose pressed upon the blanket, and her sides rose and fell as she dropped into a deep, sound sleep.

In the solitude of the quiet room, Emmanuelle set to work tidying the coffee table. She boxed up old magazines and catalogues that lay scattered in a mismatched pile beside five remote controls. Why did a man need so many remotes for one television set?

When Nicholas returned, he hung his hoodie by the door and crossed the room. Crouching, he stared at his sleeping dog.

"She's asleep and not in pain," Emmanuelle assured him. "See? Her tail is twitching. She's probably dreaming about chasing purple pigeons or flopping in the grass at the Cherish Hills Inn. When she wakes up, we'll give her the medicine."

Nicholas nodded. "And I have bad news and good news." He rolled to his feet and handed her a white paper bag. "The bad news is the kiosks were closing. The good news is I managed to plead our upsetting afternoon to my friend from The Grill Room. He was smoking a beef brisket and added coleslaw. I figured you were hungry. I also snagged a couple cups of coffee and two honey-glazed donuts."

She gave an appreciative sniff. "My mouth is watering."

He went to the kitchen and pulled a water from the fridge. "What do you want to drink?"

She followed him and put the kettle on the stove to boil. "Hot tea. Thanks."

He folded his shirtsleeves to his elbows and

draped a dishtowel over his shoulder. "My place is a mess, although I used to be fairly neat."

"I think I have enough tidying here to keep me occupied."

"Yeah, for at least a year." He grinned, then grew solemn. "Since my failed engagement to a woman who—"

"You didn't fail." She reached for a thick mug in the cupboard. "Your fiancée did."

They dished out the smoked barbecue brisket and coleslaw and brought stoneware, napkins, and utensils into the living room. She placed the stoneware on the coffee table, set her napkin on her lap, and took a neat bite of brisket. Chewing, she nodded toward Molly Belle. "After she sleeps, she may be sore. Follow the directions on the pre-scription."

"You'll come … tomorrow?"

She reached for her tea. "I texted Dorothy to let her know what happened. She and Ryan are still in Stanley. She'll stop in tomorrow to see you and the dog."

"And you?"

"I'll be here on Monday morning, as long as you don't mind leaving the dog by herself to come get me."

"The weatherman calls for a pleasant week.

Sunny and highs in the fifties. If you'd prefer to walk—"

"I never walk alone anymore, but will walk with Molly Belle." She gulped her tea and set the mug on the coffee table, and then her napkin alongside it. "However, can you drive me to the inn? It's getting late and I'm sure the innkeeper will be worried. Besides, you have his vehicle."

"I phoned Tom, and he knows Molly Belle is fine. He assured me he isn't leaving the inn tonight." He rested his hand lightly on hers. "Please stay a while longer. You haven't finished your brisket, and I could use the company."

Hesitantly, she replaced her napkin in her lap.

Nicholas relished his meal as if he hadn't eaten in a week although she nibbled and pecked at hers. After they finished, he lifted his water for a last pull while she cupped her mug and stared out the narrow window. A splash of light streaked across the black velvet sky.

"You realize we're in full view of your neighbors." She grinned at him over her mug. "One of them is cruising into their driveway."

"Dorothy has reminded me on a weekly basis about buying curtains."

Still holding her mug, she wandered to the window and considered the quiet night covering the sleepy town. The room stilled to a comfortable silence.

"I've been waiting for a beautiful woman to come along who can help me choose the right ones," he said. "Fortunately, I've known her all along."

She pivoted, catching his wicked grin and look of interest as his gaze focused on her face. Her pulse leapt in a disconcerting combination of anticipation and panic.

"Emmanuelle." His voice grew quiet. "I can hardly kiss you when you're standing on the other side of the room."

"Nicholas, we hardly know each other."

"A year ago, we talked regularly. Our bond was strong. Let's be honest. We both know it still is."

She walked to the couch and set down her mug. He set down his water. Their gazes held, the quiet punctuated by the dog's light snores.

Her thoughts scattered. She rearranged them into a semblance of reason. "A year ago we had a common purpose—ensuring your sister made a full recovery."

"Are things so different?" Gently, his fingers curved around her nape, soothing, stroking. "I'll help you make a full recovery from whatever you're struggling with." He bent his head slowly, and his lips met hers with sweet tenderness.

For a moment, she went rigid.

"I'm attracted to you, Emmanuelle," he murmured. "Always have been. I'm here for you."

Her body reacted in a dizzying sensation of emotions she couldn't explain. She didn't want to respond to him. Or perhaps she did because her reaction felt so natural. Trusting a man, feeling safe and cared for in his arms … She'd thought those feelings happened to other people.

Tentatively, she reached her arms around his neck and returned the kiss.

His mouth deepened as he fit her response to his own. He kissed her fully, insistently, boundlessly, creating a knot of pure awareness in her stomach. The longer his mouth pressed to hers, the more vibrant the sensations became. It was as if a new person had taken the place of the broken Emmanuelle. The new Emmanuelle was sincere and receptive, the former hesitant and uneasy, avoiding any connection with a man.

A sharp woof broke them apart.

Molly Belle lifted her head and regarded them. Before Nicholas could get to her, she laid her head down and went to sleep.

Emmanuelle's lips twitched. "Her injection is wearing off."

He settled on the couch and watched Emmanuelle, his gaze heated. "Shall we continue? We left off at—"

"Your dog may wake up again."

"I'll take my chances." His arms slipped around her, and she reveled in the pleasure of his hard mouth pressed on hers. She kissed him back while his warm hands shifted protectively around her.

Ages later, he lifted his head and cradled her face. Affection smoldered in his hazel eyes. "You came into my life at exactly the right time."

Molly Belle stirred, twitched, woofed to no one in particular, then plunked her nose back on the blanket.

He chuckled. "I think I have a love-hate relationship with that dog." With a sigh, he lowered his hands from Emmanuelle's face. He forked a last bite of coleslaw, leaned against the couch, and stretched out his legs. "Stay a while longer. Please. I'll be sure you make it back to the inn before midnight, Cinderella."

Across the inches of the couch separating them, she met his stare. His striking features were full of hope, almost boyish.

He was an honest man. Genuine and steadfast, his every movement capable, yet easy-going.

"All right, but only because you said 'please,' Prince Charming."

He reached out and gathered her to him. "Remember the night we watched television together when we were Skyping?"

"How did you ever persuade me to stream a documentary about the Hubble telescope when I had a concert to prepare for the next day?"

He threw back his head and laughed. So good-natured, so familiar. "You should thank me because you learned several new outer-space terms. And all the planets—Mercury, Venus, Earth—"

She laid her hand on his arm. "I'm a musician, not an astronaut."

"Where is your harp, by the way? In New York?"

She kept her features blank and tried to make her voice impassive. "My harp is gone."

His expression was thoughtful as he obviously sensed her bleak mood. A beat passed.

"One of my favorite memories," he said, keeping her in his arms, "is the night you played the harp for me. 'Danny Boy.' Remember? I'd had an argument with Alice, and you said music would soothe me, so you lit candles and darkened your apartment. You had told me your harp was accented in twenty-three karat gold. I remember it shimmered in the candlelight each time you plucked a string. Truly, Emmanuelle, you looked like an angel, and it gave me goosebumps." He traced her cheekbone with his forefinger.

"You sang while I played," Emmanuelle said. She'd clung to the memory of those shared times, although she'd known he was engaged and never pressed him for anything other than friendship.

Not long afterward, Dorothy had gotten out of rehab for opiate addiction, and Emmanuelle had met George, the wealthy hotel magnate.

And George had taken away her harp. Her pride. Her life.

Nicholas felt like he danced through the following week, and he wasn't a man who'd ever managed more than a two-step.

Molly Belle improved every day. She had reclaimed her sleeping spot at the foot of his bed, ate regularly, and reveled in her short daily walks with Emmanuelle. She'd even taught the dog to "sit" by holding a treat near the dog's nose. Once Molly Belle was sitting, she'd repeat the command, give the dog the treat, and shower her with affection and praise. She'd repeated the same sequence throughout each day, then demonstrated Molly Belle's progress for Nicholas each evening.

She'd taken Molly Belle to a shop a few doors down from his place and selected a fresh pine wreath, simple and unadorned, that she'd hung on his front door. On another occasion, she purchased curtains in a dazzling shade of lipstick-red and hung them on his bare living room windows. The effect was homey, warm, and Christmassy.

She'd also experimented with cooking new dishes. Thanks to Ryan's *Southern Charms* cookbook, Nicholas never knew quite what to expect for dinner. He only knew an exotic, savory meal waited for him when he got home.

In the evenings, he and Emmanuelle dined in his cozy kitchen, on a wooden table tucked beside a snowy window, polishing off spaghetti carbonara and thick slices of buttery bread accompanied by oven-fried pickles.

"Surprise me," he'd tell her each morning after she'd arrived.

And she did.

He enjoyed her companionship, her considerate nature, the way her dimples flashed whenever she was amused. He hadn't found a word to put to his feelings, especially since he hadn't wanted to become romantically involved with a woman after his breakup with Alice.

With Emmanuelle, though, the word *love* came to mind.

On the last day of the work week, Nicholas issued his customary thank you to her as soon as he strode through his apartment door. Molly Belle wriggled with delight, bounded to his side and greeted him with a continuous train of wet doggy kisses.

He scrubbed a hand along the dog's ears.

Emmanuelle was seated on the couch, intent on studying a page from Ryan's cookbook.

"I've been thinking about dinner all day," he said. He'd been thinking about her too, although he didn't mention that part. For a celebratory end-of-the-week supper, Emmanuelle had declared she was experimenting with a different fix on a traditional Christmas recipe—roasted turkey and sweet potatoes garnished with a fancy topping Nicholas had forgotten the name of.

He slid his gun from his holster, took off his badge. "How was your day?"

"Busy. Despite her size, Molly Belle thinks she's a lap dog." Emmanuelle kept her head down, busy flipping pages. "And Dorothy and Ryan invited us for Christmas dinner so I tried a new dessert recipe tonight too."

He breathed in a lungful of smoky air just as the smoke alarm went off. "Is something burning?"

"Oh, no!" The cookbook fell from her lap as she jumped to her feet. "I forgot to set the timer."

They sprinted toward the kitchen. The dog whined and raced in the opposite direction, scratching at the door to be let out.

"I was testing a fruitcake recipe," Emmanuelle said as he opened a kitchen window to let out the smoke, and then turned off the alarm.

Not a dreaded fruitcake. Since Nicholas was fairly intelligent, he kept the comment to himself as he retrieved the burnt cake from the oven and set it on the counter. He commiserated with Emmanuelle, sighed, and tried to look regretful. He wanted to joke about the fruitcake making a good doorstop and wisely changed his mind.

"The cake can't be salvaged, so I'll phone for pizza delivery," he said. "Sound good?"

"If you stopped to look around, you'd see I cooked a twelve-pound turkey and sweet potatoes. Is pizza your fix for whatever comes your way?"

"There's no such thing as bad pizza. So …yes." He lifted the foil off the potatoes and pointed accusingly. "What's this white stuff on top?"

"Goat cheese and scallions."

"Sounds awful …" He caught her scowl. … "fancy." He congratulated himself for thinking so quickly on his feet. "Sounds awful fancy. Do you think I'll like it?"

"Fifty-fifty."

He suppressed a chuckle. She looked positively intoxicating, even with her heart-shaped mouth twisted into a grimace as she beheld the burnt cake.

He left the kitchen to check on the dog, who'd resumed her place at the foot of his bed.

When he returned to the kitchen, he drew off the hairband she'd used to secure her hair when she cooked, brought her closer, and embraced her for a lengthy kiss. "We're beginning to sound as if we're a couple, and I like the sound of it."

She drew an unsteady breath and dropped her gaze, but not before he noticed the warmth kindling in her vivid blue eyes, the flush of heat tinting her creamy complexion a soft pink.

"We can't be a couple."

"Why not?"

She kept her gaze rooted on his bare wood floor. "Because I won't be a burden to you." She placed her arm between them, an effective wedge.

He'd half expected her reaction.

Anything to do with Molly Belle's care prompted an easy conversation. So did the latest recipe in the cookbook. Or classical music, especially her favorite composer, Beethoven. She responded to his kisses, molding herself to him. But any talk of a serious relationship put her off-balance.

He drew her to the couch and took a seat beside her. In an attempt to lighten the mood, he teasingly bumped her shoulder with his. "Tomorrow is

Molly Belle's vet appointment. I'm hoping you'll go with me."

"Absolutely."

He smiled, relieved. He'd come to rely on her for emotional support.

"Afterward," he went on, "I'd like to buy a Christmas tree. My apartment is begging for a dose of holiday cheer, so are you up for a stop at a tree farm outside of town? In the past I've cut my own tree." He gestured to the dog. "Because she's still recovering, we'll buy a precut tree."

"Perfect." Her smile was luminous and lit his small apartment with merriment.

The attraction sizzled between them. Soon, he thought, when she was ready, she'd tell him her trepidation, and he'd assure her she was safe. Mutually, they'd dismiss her worries. She was in Cherish where life was secure. He'd keep her out of harm's way—whether real or imagined.

Trying to tamp down his eagerness, he reached into his shirt pocket and withdrew a small box wrapped in gold paper with a red satin ribbon. "Thank you, Emmanuelle, for everything you've done for me this week. On my lunch hour today, I stopped at Musically Yours and bought you something." He held the box out to her.

Lightly, she touched her hand to his. "Nicholas,

you didn't have to buy me anything. I wanted to take care of Molly Belle."

His senses buzzed, alive to the brush of her fingertips, the thickened skin where calluses had formed. Once she had told him she was proud of those calluses, a badge for practicing long hours to pursue her dream of becoming a professional harpist.

And she had.

He'd taken her suggestion to give God his attention and had begun praying every night. Lately, he'd lifted a plea that she'd make Cherish her permanent home.

She could build a life here. *They* could build a future together.

He slipped an arm around her waist, delighting in her nearness, staring at her for a long moment. "I wanted to buy you a gift. It was my pleasure."

"Nicholas …" She ran a hand through her unruly blonde curls. Her chin trembled. Although they'd known each other for over a year, she grew unexpectedly shy.

"Please open it." He stilled her hand and kissed her temple. He was giving her what he could. He wanted to give her so much more.

Nodding brightly, she rapidly undid the paper and unlatched a plain gray box. A tiny harp dangling from a solid-gold chain shot emerald green and diamond prisms across his plain white ceiling.

"The harp charm is from Ireland, from Dublin. I wanted an Irish harp fit for the most gifted woman I've ever known." He brushed his knuckles over her flawless cheek, brushed away a stray tear.

"Happy tears," she said.

He nodded. "Our conversation from the other day about the night you played 'Danny Boy' brought back good memories. I want this necklace to do the same."

"It brought back good memories for me too." She fingered the necklace. Her eyes shimmered a soft blue velvet. "I haven't bought a piece of clothing or jewelry for myself in months. Thank you."

"I looked for a twenty-three-karat necklace to match your harp, but this was the best I could afford. My salary as a deputy sheriff isn't much, though I plan to work my way up to a position of management." He drew her to him and she rested her cheek against his chest. "Someday I'll buy you a real harp."

He spoke above her, breathing in her floral perfume, citrus and violets and expectation.

"Money isn't important," she said. "I know this gift is from your heart."

She was splendid. She made him feel alive

again, brought him out of his sadness. After his fiancée had left him, he'd grieved, focusing on his scars. But a new emotion was rising over the scars, allowing him to become again the man he once was—one of faith, free from cynicism, free to open his heart once more.

They avoided eye contact. The moment held too much emotion for her, for him.

"I know how much your harp meant to you," he murmured. "You once let me in on a secret, that your parents surprised you with a harp for your twelfth birthday. They'd saved money for years to buy the best. A Lyon and Healy harp, correct?"

"You remembered." Her tears came hard, sudden, and she let them.

He soothed her, crooning, rocking her. "You're not alone anymore, Emmanuelle."

Any further conversation was forgotten as she wept. When she withdrew, she wiped at her eyes with the handkerchief he provided. "I'm sorry. I mean, crying was uncalled for and I put you in an awkward—"

"Don't apologize. You're the best thing that's ever happened to me." He swept wisps of hair from her nape and secured the delicate gold chain around her throat, then ushered her to the bathroom mirror. "Dorothy assured me you'd fall in love with this necklace."

At first, Emmanuelle kept her gaze downcast before staring at herself. Carefully, she slid a finger along the fine chain and then found the exquisite detailing of the harp. "I haven't worn anything this pretty in many months. Thanks to you, I'm beginning to feel like a woman again. Someone who matters." Her smile sparkled in the mirror reflection.

He stood behind her and rested his hands on her shoulders. "You matter very, very much. More than you can ever imagine."

He stared at her, a vision of beauty with the heirloom-quality necklace shimmering against her creamy skin above her navy-blue cashmere sweater. At that moment he knew. It had returned, his love for a woman.

Only this time it was real.

CHAPTER 8

After Dr. Troutman's nod of approval, Nicholas and Emmanuelle set off for the Christmas tree farm. Molly Belle waited in Nicholas's car while they chose the last fir tree on the lot. The tree wasn't perfectly shaped; in fact, it wasn't shaped at all. Nicholas named the tree Charlie Brown since the branches jutted out in random angles.

"Every underdog needs a loving home," he declared, and Emmanuelle wholeheartedly agreed.

One of the employees at the farm shook the tree to remove any loose needles, then wrapped it for transport. A short drive later, Emmanuelle and Nicholas hoisted the scraggly tree up his flight of stairs and into his apartment.

"The tree looks better already," she said as Nicholas secured the tree in a sturdy metal stand. "It's just begging for lots of care and plenty of water. And we'll trim your whole apartment to resemble an old-fashioned Christmas. Ryan's book features all sorts of inspiring ideas."

Nicholas pushed himself to his feet after pouring water into the base of the tree stand. "I thought it was a cookbook focused on recipes."

"Recipes and decorating tips. And there's a thought-provoking article on empowering women that provides tips on how to keep safe in dangerous circumstances. The entire book is highly motivating."

"Quite the cookbook," he observed.

They referenced a "traditional Christmas" article as a guide and spent the afternoon decorating. Using heavy embroidery floss, they strung popcorn and cranberries. Nicholas found a set of multicolored lights stuffed in his hall closet. He began at the tree trunk and moved upward, wrapping the lights taut by weaving them from side to side.

"There isn't much of a tree to light," he said with a laugh. "The branches are beyond sparse!"

"I'm always drawn to these types of trees." She stepped back to assess the tree. "In the end, it's all about hope, isn't it?"

"True. And few people are as hopeful as Charlie Brown."

"Multicolored lights remind me of happy times with my family in Remsen. Call me nostalgic and old-fashioned."

"Then I'm old-fashioned too. Nothing is better than colored lights on a green pine tree to get you in the mood for Christmas."

"Last year, my ex wanted white lights and neon-blue bulbs on the tree he'd purchased for his swanky condo in a high-rise. I argued for colored lights. He didn't agree, of course, saying white lights were chic and modern. I like modern." She hesitated, combed nervous fingers through her hair. "No that's wrong. I just told him that."

"You lied?"

"I had no choice. He had two switches, calm or angry. I knew better than to disagree and kept my opinion to myself. He'd trained me like we're training Molly Belle—to obey commands." She watched the dog, resting on a blanket in the corner. The dog returned her stare with steady, shining eyes.

"I understand my former situation now," she went on. "It's easier at a distance."

"What's your ex's name?"

She took a moment to adjust her fire-red tunic,

fussing and fidgeting, as if the tunic didn't fit correctly over her jeans. "George."

"That's it? George? George who?"

"Just George." She shrugged, shivered. Slight, but he saw it.

"Where's George now?"

Another shrug. She looked around, rubbed her hands together. "I assume he's in New York."

Her ex had evidently hurt her, and the realization brought anger bubbling to Nicholas's throat. When he found him, *and he would*, he'd silence George with a good stiff jab and a command of his own. *Stay away from Emmanuelle.*

He wrapped an arm around her shoulders and she leaned into him. Each time they were with each other, his need to protect her grew stronger.

He turned to the next page in the book to change the subject. She might get too upset if they continued discussing her ex. "The next round of decorating is to find red and green bulbs for our quirky tree. Do you prefer glass bulbs or—"

"I prefer family vintage bulbs and pinecones and silver tinsel. But ..." She dug in her tote bag and drew out a tiny angel ornament, brandishing it in the air. "I've carried this with me ever since I left New York. The clerk at the airport told me it was a good luck charm. It belongs on your tree."

"*Our* tree," he corrected her, and hung the ornament on a thin lower branch. "All this decorating warrants a celebration, so let's call out for pizza."

"Again? Is pizza your remedy for everything?"

With a laugh, he pulled his phone from his jeans pocket and placed an order for a large cheese and pepperoni pizza, with a side of barbecue for Emmanuelle.

After pocketing his phone, he took her hands. "Let's wait for the delivery on the porch steps. The weather is mild, so we can go outside without jackets." He glanced at Molly Belle, sleeping soundly, then eased open the door.

They sat on the stoop. It was one of those inviting South Carolina evenings, when the sun had warmed everything in its path, including his front porch.

The view of his charming cul-de-sac lit with strings of festive lights, the nearby clip-clop of a horse-drawn carriage, filled him with gratitude. He imagined the residents inside their homes, savoring steaming cups of hot cocoa, sitting beside their cozy fireplaces.

From a few streets away came the last strains of "We Three Kings." Sung, he surmised, by the Cherish Church ladies' caroling group. He grinned, envisioning the women, young and elderly, dressed in their traditional Victorian costumes, complete with big bonnets and hand muffs.

The day had been perfect. Ending the evening with Emmanuelle by his side brought a quiet, joyous peace, and he whispered a prayer of thanksgiving. Tenderly, he pressed a kiss on her palms. "Two weeks from today is the Musically Yours holiday concert," he said. "Ryan is leading the elementary school chorus in a Christmas carol singalong and then singing a couple solos."

She rested her cheek on his shoulder. "Cherish is like a picture out of a Christmas card."

He chuckled and went back to appreciating the street decorations. Several neighbors had run animated light displays in a scalloped pattern along their fences.

Yes, this was the ideal town to live, to work, to raise a family.

He put an arm around her and she snuggled nearer, the warmth of her body reaching out to his. He could get used to this. A delightful woman, her breathing soft and even, whose slight body had grown heavier because she was … sleeping?

He grinned. She'd fallen asleep quickly, even quicker than he usually did. Between taking care of his dog and creating nightly meals fit for a food connoisseur, she was clearly exhausted. He considered her profile, her small turned-up nose, the light sprinkling of freckles on her cheeks. Several times during the past week, he'd caught her staring at her cell phone as it rang. She never answered a call, and a few times her face had turned bone-white when she'd glimpsed the screen.

"Unknown caller," she always said, dropping the phone back into her tote bag. Whenever he pressed for details, she just chewed her bottom lip and stubbornly stayed silent.

He reached into his pocket for his phone and canceled the pizza. No sense in waking her when the delivery person arrived. Surely that frozen pizza was sitting somewhere in his freezer.

From inside the apartment, Molly Belle barked.

Emmanuelle woke with a start and rubbed her eyes. She peered at him, darted a peek at her watch. "Sorry, I didn't realize I dozed. I haven't rested well in several months."

"Because of George?"

A noticeable gap hung in the air as she scanned the street and its bright decorations. Distractedly, she nodded.

He went to brush pine needles from her shoulder and she flinched. He let out a whistled sigh and pulled back his hand. "Don't. You insult me when you do that."

"Do what?"

"Treat me as if I'm your ex. Just because I raise my hand doesn't mean I'm going to hit you." He deliberated, but only for a second. "What's really going on with you?"

"Too much." She eased up, then sat back down. "Nicholas, I can't give you the relationship you want. I'm not the right woman for you."

"How do you know?"

She closed her eyes. Tears escaped. "Because you're a good man and my life is complicated."

"I like complicated."

"No, no, you don't." She opened her eyes, a deep shimmery blue. They stared at each other.

"It's odd," he mused.

"What?"

"The fact you're a harpist and you don't have a harp. Did you sell it?"

"My harp was smashed to pieces." She didn't pause for his sympathy, didn't bury her face in her hands. "George destroyed it."

"Why?"

He hadn't meant to ask the question because he knew the answer. As a law enforcement officer, he'd come across men like George. Domestic violence was the leading cause of injury to women. He'd read the statistics, recognized an abuser's behaviors and characteristics. After the honeymoon phase, they became controlling and jealous, and oftentimes sought to isolate their partner.

"Why?" Emmanuelle repeated. "Why would a

man who supposedly cared for me take away something I loved, something so meaningful? To break me, I suppose." She shook her head; she'd answered her own question. "He knew precisely which buttons to press. He was exceptionally charming and people were attracted to him. Me included."

Nicholas's anger was sharp. He pulled it in. "How did you meet him?"

"His secretary booked me to play the harp for one of his office functions, the grand opening of his tenth boutique hotel in the New York area." Her voice caught. "After we became a couple, he always reminded me I was beneath him and how thankful I should be an important man like him was interested in someone like me ... someone who was little more than a street performer."

"You know that's not true. You're a skilled professional."

She trailed her fingers along the edge of the porch railing and let out a sigh.

"When are you deserting me for New York?" he asked.

"I'm not deserting you. I happen to live there." She smiled and broke off, apparently waiting for his rejoinder. When he didn't offer one, she added, "I don't have a definite date in mind. Dorothy offered me a job at her music conservatory. I've considered finding a place in town and teaching harp lessons." She shrugged and blew out a breath. "Although I know it's better if I keep moving."

The last part of her answer didn't register because he'd fixated on the first part. His heart had leapt when she'd mentioned living in Cherish.

"Is he the reason you came here? Is he the reason you choose to keep running?"

"I have no choice and I'm not running." Her fingers nervously worked the hem of her tunic before she propped her chin in her hands. "Okay, yes, maybe I am. If George O'Donnell finds me, I don't know what he'll do."

George O'Donnell. Piercing rage sliced Nicholas like a knife. "He won't do anything to harm you. I'll make sure of it."

"You don't know him. He's well-off and powerful."

He joined her cold hands with his warm ones. "And I'm in law enforcement."

"That's why I'm afraid. If you go after him, you'll get hurt. He operates in influential circles with big-city types."

"In our quiet town, you'll be safe. You must know I'll always protect you."

"Our town," she repeated.

"Yes. And our life."

"Nicholas?" A smile ghosted her lips as an errant tear streamed down her cheek. "Will you do something for me?"

He gazed at her enchanting face, her over-bright eyes. He would protect her with his life.

"Anything," he said.

"Will you hold me for a minute?"

CHAPTER 9

$\mathscr{I}$n the ensuing two weeks Emmanuelle slept poorly, despite the inn's exquisitely appointed room and her luxurious queen-sized bed. Nightmares chased her and were always the same: the dim outline of a man with flat black eyebrows above dull gray eyes, trailing her every move.

George O'Donnell.

She'd scramble through unnamed woods while the flash of something vicious, and corrupt, and overpowering, followed her. The nightmare always ended the same, with her weeping and running farther and farther away from Cherish.

She'd wake beneath her cozy coverlet, her heart hammering, searching the room for something recognizable. Country-green walls, the hand-stitched quilt draped over a rocking chair, the braided rug covering the wide-plank pine floor, helped steady her breathing.

"Only a nightmare," she'd murmur, wiping her sweaty brow. "Vivid, horrible, and not real."

She'd focus out the window at the sprinkling of stars against the black velvet sky. Then she'd close her eyes and think about Nicholas—his kindness, his easy-going manner, his self-assured confidence. Efficient and calm, whether tidying his home or ministering to Molly Belle, dealing with dangerous circumstances on duty or holding her as if she were a china doll. He was all man, all kindness, all compassion.

"In our quiet town, you'll be safe. You must know I'll always protect you," he'd said.

Only then, imagining his capable arms around her, could she seek the peace of slumber.

* * *

BY THE THIRD week of December, Cherish had become a jubilant fairyland, a kaleidoscope of Yuletide hues. Parades were held every weekend, and quaint mom-and-pop stores were decked out in magical window dressings. Children and adults alike stopped and gaped, mesmerized in child-like fascination.

Illuminated by tiny white lights, Emmanuelle's comfy inn, with its snow-covered roof and wisps of smoke billowing from the chimney, looked like a postcard image of Christmas town, USA.

Tom had taken a liking to Molly Belle and allowed her inside, provided she stayed in the foyer and didn't jump on any of the patrons. Unfortunately, the third day she was allowed in, Molly Belle knocked a teenage boy over when she'd leapt on the boy's legs. Despite Nicholas's explanations that the dog was still a puppy with a playful, silly personality, Tom banished Molly Belle to the porch. Both hands braced on his polished wood desk, he'd leaned forward until his cheaters slid down his nose and declared she wasn't allowed inside until she graduated from dog obedience school. Considering Nicholas had abandoned the idea of obedience school until Molly Belle was fully recovered, Emmanuelle was certain the dog wouldn't be entering the inn anytime soon.

A cold front had brought snow to Cherish, a white dusting that topped off the winter-wonderland. As the snow fell softly, day after day, Emmanuelle's mood became more hopeful. She spent her time at Nicholas's apartment caring for Molly Belle and cooking delectable meals—a flaky crusted chicken pot pie brimming with roasted chicken and baby carrots one night, a sweet winter cornbread with a splash of jalapeno the next. Oftentimes, she'd bake a tray of Christmas cookies, oozing chocolate chips, warm from the oven. As she cooked, she'd tune the radio to a Christian holiday station and hum along to every Christmas carol.

In the middle of the afternoon, she'd leash Molly Belle for a walk. Few things outshone walking a devoted dog who loved going outside for a squirrel-chasing adventure, especially when sunlight warmed Emmanuelle's cheeks and bracing air brought remembrances of Christmas in Remsen.

At Dorothy's prodding, the two women spent an evening shopping. Emmanuelle purchased a pair of shiny gold earrings to complement her harp necklace, plus a rose-tinted lip gloss. There was something so feminine about earrings and lip gloss, Dorothy said, that made a woman feel attractive. Regarding her reflection in the shop's mirror, Emmanuelle agreed. She'd caught her hair at the nape and secured it with a lace bow, the result a messy bun highlighted by escaping corkscrews of blonde hair.

She'd also painted two opposite walls of Nicholas's living room in a golden-yellow and convinced him to reupholster his couch in a deep-chocolate brown. He'd grinned his approval, and she too was pleased with the result. After Christmas, she aimed to tackle his kitchen and paint those walls a cool mint-green.

After Christmas.

Yes, because she'd decided to live in Cherish. She hadn't told Nicholas, not yet. She'd decided to surprise him on Christmas, after they attended a church service with Dorothy and Ryan. She'd accepted Dorothy's offer to give harp lessons at the Musically Yours music conservatory and had begun formulating a plan to buy a new harp. Ryan told her that the nearby city of Stanley boasted an excellent symphony that was actively looking for a principal harpist, and encouraged her to audition. She'd agreed, the idea prompting recollections of how much she enjoyed performing.

On the Saturday of the holiday concert in Cherish, Emmanuelle spent the morning peeling potatoes and carrots for a hearty beef stew she simmered on Nicholas's stove. The weatherman had predicted snow, which had rapidly accumulated to several inches.

Nicholas had had to respond to a domestic-dispute call, and she'd gladly volunteered to stay with Molly Belle. He'd added that one of the other officers, Joseph Hannaford, would be on duty at the concert that evening. Large crowds were expected because of Ryan Edwards's performance.

Done with the stew, she surveyed the living room from the kitchen doorway. The Charlie Brown Christmas tree was delightful, brightly lit and brimming with cheer. Her angel ornament hung from one of the branches, and she laughed out loud, inhaling the scents of pine and promise.

Life was good. Very good. On an even more optimistic note, there'd been no sign of George. After she'd begun watching Molly Belle, every morning she'd received a phone call precisely at eight o'clock, a few minutes after Nicholas left for work.

Whenever she answered, no one spoke.

Once, she'd sworn she'd heard breathing on the other end. Bad connection? Most likely. She rejected her suspicions that it might be George. Merely an over-zealous telemarketer, she'd tell herself.

Still, she told Nicholas, admitting to her uneasiness. He listened thoughtfully before assuring her she was right—a telemarketer had programmed her phone number on speed-dial. After a long, thorough kiss, he assured her there was nothing to worry about.

And then, without warning, the mysterious phone calls had stopped.

As the next few days passed, the realization she

was finally free from George renewed her confidence. With a strong handsome deputy by her side, friends who loved her, and a spirited dog ever near, what was there to fear? Truly, Christmas in Cherish promised a happiness she'd never dreamed.

CHAPTER 10

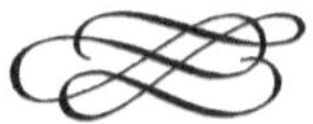

After they'd eaten stew for an early dinner, Nicholas drove Emmanuelle back to the inn to get ready for the evening concert. They passed tree limbs heavy with snow, bushes dusted with a fine white powder.

At the inn, she gifted Tom with a loaf of her crusty bread, prompting him to taste it. He'd chewed with his eyes closed and exclaimed, "Will you marry me, Emmanuelle?"

Before she could reply, Nicholas draped an arm on her shoulders and assured the innkeeper she was spoken for.

She floated to her room where she ran a warm shower, refreshing herself under a stream of multiple jets. The scents of her soap and shampoo—

brown sugar and vanilla—reminded her of hot cinnamon rolls slathered in butter cream frosting.

Her anticipation of the evening rising, she grabbed a fluffy towel for her hair, and wrapped herself in a luxurious white robe. She padded across the wood floor of her room and deliberated on her outfit, ultimately choosing a comfortable pair of colored denims and a red cashmere sweater.

Despite his numerous concert engagements, she'd never heard Ryan perform live, and she was looking forward to the evening.

At 7:00, a light tap on her door signaled Nicholas's arrival.

When she opened the door, he lifted her to her toes and held her. "Emmanuelle Sumter, you look gorgeous and smell like a cinnamon roll." He frequently remarked on her appearance, always complimentary, always causing her to melt, just melt.

She saw the seductive-green passion in his hazel eyes as their lips met.

"And every time I see you," he went on, "I fall more in love with you." He stated his feelings simply, without preamble or fanfare, his mouth brushing against her ear, his warm breath heating her insides.

She ran her fingers over his nape. His blond hair was thick and curled over his collared parka. His lips were smooth, his mouth perfectly shaped. His well-defined jaw and sharp cheekbones brought a chiseled handsomeness to his cover model features.

It's too soon to talk of love, she wanted to say. But it wasn't too soon, because she was falling in love with him too.

She hugged the realization close. This good-looking, conscientious man loved her, and with each heartfelt embrace, each heady kiss, her defenses were thawing. Slowly, she was shaking off her fears and yielding to him.

"Ready for an amazing concert?" he asked.

"I can't wait." She went to her closet and tugged a pink tasseled hat over her hair. "Dorothy said she'd accompany Ryan on keyboard if they can figure out how to run electrical power on stage."

"So far, they haven't," Nicholas said. As she rummaged through the closet, he added that the afternoon sun had melted much of the morning's snow, so the streets were messy tonight.

"Just let me grab my boots. Where's Molly Belle?"

"She's near the porch."

She swiveled. "Alone?"

"She's on her leash. Tom is playing with her in the snow." Nicholas struggled to keep a straight face. "He won't admit he's got a soft spot for dogs, although you and I know he does." He helped her on with her jacket and exaggeratedly hefted her tote bag from the bureau. "What do you carry in this? Lead?"

"Necessities. You know, my cell phone, wallet, loose change ..."

"I wouldn't want to tote this heavy bag around."

"You would if you were a sensible woman." She laughed. "I can't be deprived of my pink lip gloss."

Still bantering, they made their way down the carpeted staircase.

As soon as they strolled onto the porch, Molly Belle scampered around them, feathery tail wagging, as if she hadn't seen them in a month. Nicholas thanked Tom and reached for the leash. Hand in hand, Emmanuelle and Nicholas stepped from the porch.

Although the morning snow had blown in quick and heavy, as Nicholas had said, most had melted under sun-kissed daytime skies. As the evening thermometer plunged, what was left had frozen, causing thin sheets of ice to gloss over the surface of the remaining snow. Tom had shoveled a generous path and covered the steps and sidewalk with rock salt.

"I've never listened to opera," Nicholas said, tucking her hand in the crook of his arm as they started for the town square. "I expect—"

"You've never heard Ryan sing?" Her lips

twitched with amusement. "Your sister is married to one of the most famous opera singers in the world!"

"Once, maybe, when we were teenagers, I overheard him singing an operatic version of Dorothy's favorite top-forty hit. I assumed he was trying to impress her. They used to sit for hours on the side porch of our house." Nicholas's deep voice vibrated with laughter. "But I'm all for the idea of a bonfire and roasting s'mores after the concert."

When they reached the square, Ryan and Dorothy gave an absent-minded wave as they arranged chairs beneath a white canvas tent. A stage had been set up alongside the ten-foot decorated Christmas tree. Various kiosks serving refreshments lined the outer edges of the square, and Nicholas briefly introduced her to his coworker, Joseph Hannaford, the officer on duty. As the crowds thickened, a fine, snowy mist began to fall.

A halcyon town awaiting Christmas, Emmanuelle mused. The entire scene was a miniature version of New York's festive theater district. Cheery memories, she thought, … until … until …

She brought a jittery hand to her forehead.

A few months after she began dating George, she wore her favorite sweater to a theater event, and had left her jacket in the restroom at intermission. When he noticed, he demanded they leave before the show was over. She assumed he was angry because she had been foolish enough to have forgotten her jacket. He was concerned, as the theater was cold, she reasoned.

She was way off the mark. He shouted at her and called her a tramp for strutting around in a clingy sweater that he deemed too provocative.

He was jealous. She got that, and even felt flattered.

At first.

The relationship deepened. She believed she was in love with him, and he was in love with her. However, he began to erupt when she least expected, no matter how fine a line she walked. Scary remembrances of George's viciousness, his narcissistic behavior, his insincere repentance, brought a quake down her spine.

She forced the chilling memories away and glanced at the rugged man standing beside her.

She was being foolish. She was safe, the town was real, this man was real. And this was the picture she needed to carry in order to move forward in her life. The uncommonly large crowd had simply dredged up memories from her uneasy mind.

As if he'd read her thoughts, Nicholas protectively tightened his arm around her waist. "Are you all right?" His hazel gaze locked on hers.

"Yes, I was thinking about how grateful I am to be here. And I'm happy, truly happy."

"So am I." He spoke quietly, tenderly. "I love you, Emmanuelle."

She beamed up at him, this man of faith whom she'd enjoyed endless conversations with, a man who spoke plainly what was on his heart.

"I love you too, Nicholas."

He smiled at her as if she were incredibly beloved.

She sighed with contentment. Finally, her world was coming together, and she whispered a thank you to God for giving her a promising future alongside the man she loved.

As they wove through the tent to find a good seat, she scanned the tent to see where Dorothy and Ryan had gone.

An exuberant Dorothy was arranging the last row of folding chairs. Her simple, classic black sweater dress showed off every curve of her lithe figure. She'd pinned her dark hair into an understated twist at the back of her head, drawing attention to her emerald-green eyes and pearl stud earrings.

Ryan strode over to her, impressively tall with dark, compelling features, his broad shoulders filling out his navy jacket to perfection. He draped a tweed coat around Dorothy. Something she said made him laugh out loud, and he gathered her in his arms and kissed her.

Their delight in each other was so infectious that Nicholas and Emmanuelle shared a grin.

"Well?" he prompted.

"Well what?"

"Well, if everyone is kissing, then where's my kiss?"

"You're impossible. We're not performing in a concert tonight."

"I plan to sing along to every Christmas carol. Does that count?"

She chuckled. "No. Besides, we're not newlyweds."

"Not yet." A slow, roguish smile moved across his face.

She felt her blood heat from her toes to her temple. "You're thinking to kiss me here, with all these people around?" Coyly, she shook her head, teasingly discouraging him. Then with a mischievous smile, she tilted her head back, inviting a kiss.

Dr. Troutman and Scarlett entered the tent carrying two cups of coffee and a bag of chips. They spotted them, waved, and jostled through the crowd. Molly Belle yipped and tugged on her leash in her attempt at a greeting.

Her red hair springy beneath her leopard ear muffs, Scarlett offered a sparkling smile and opened her chips. She offered them to the group, then began munching.

"How's one of my favorite dogs?" Dr. Troutman rubbed Molly Belle's head as she scrabbled her front paws up his legs. He bent and examined her feet. "Just making sure there's no snow trapped in the pads."

"I've been checking," Emmanuelle said.

He sipped his coffee. "Are you two here for the concert?"

"*I* am," Emmanuelle said and then pointed to Nicholas. "He's here for the s'mores."

Dr. Troutman made a dramatic show of choking on his coffee. "Glad to see you're still in Cherish, Emmanuelle. Don't you live in New York?"

Nicholas pressed a light kiss on her forehead. "I'm trying to talk her into moving permanently to Cherish."

"Well, I could use a knowledgeable person in my office. Scarlett is a wonderful receptionist although she's going to be a little busy, now that we're engaged." His hand reached out to cover Scarlett's, but not before Emmanuelle noticed a three-stone diamond ring in a rose-gold setting on Scarlett's ring finger.

"Congratulations," Emmanuelle and Nicholas said simultaneously.

"Thank you." Scarlett's shimmery, ruby earrings swung sideways as she nodded. Enthusiasm glowing in her face, she turned to Dr. Troutman. "I love animals, but I love you more."

Emmanuelle saw the elation in the veterinarian's smile as he swung his attention back toward her. "If you're looking for a job, Emmanuelle, you can work for me anytime."

"My sister beat you to it." Nicholas said, nodding toward Dorothy. "She asked Emmanuelle to teach music lessons at her conservatory. Did you know Emmanuelle is a professional harpist?"

"I'd like to hear you play," Scarlett said.

"Someday." Emmanuelle grimaced. How's that for evasive? she upbraided herself. She was a professional harpist with no harp.

"I'm sorry. I can see from the expression on your face that I troubled you." Scarlett swallowed a chip and snapped up another. "Dorothy mentioned you don't have a harp."

Emmanuelle stopped her grimace and turned it into a smile. "Don't apologize. Look what Nicholas bought me. Isn't it beautiful?" She drew out the harp necklace from beneath her jacket for Scarlett to admire.

"Yes, very beautiful, and very thoughtful." Scarlett eyed the necklace. "An early Christmas gift, Nicholas?"

"Nope." He laughed. "It's my gift to Emmanuelle for coming to Cherish. She's a blessing to me."

Emmanuelle's heart gave a funny lurch. Nicholas offered safety and security and he was more considerate than anyone she'd ever known. Not every man was cruel and intimidating, she reminded herself yet again. Healing from abuse was a slow road, and it took time and infinite perseverance. And she'd walk that road with the man she loved.

New beginnings.

"You make a very striking couple," Scarlett was saying. "Two good-looking blonds."

"I agree with one of your observations." With a mile-wide beam toward Emmanuelle, Nicholas said, "We'd better claim a seat, my good-looking blonde."

As people converged, aromas of chocolate fudge and honey roasted almonds lifted into the air.

"The staid doctor and his perky receptionist are engaged?" Emmanuelle asked.

"Apparently." He grinned. "He must be twice her age."

"They're charming together and I'm delighted for them.

"The vet has lived alone on his alpaca farm since his wife's passing. He's a moral Christian man and I'm glad he met someone he can share his life with."

"I hope Scarlett likes alpacas." Emmanuelle laughed. "Do they bite?"

"Not normally. And she can eat her junk food while Dr. Troutman's alpaca herd munches on green plants and grass."

They settled on seats in the last row, just in case Molly Belle spotted another dog and attempted to dash off for an impromptu romp in the snow.

When the audience quieted, the first half of the concert began with the elementary school's children's chorus. The music teacher conducted, and everyone joined in a heart-lifting rendition of "Silent Night." Before intermission, Ryan led the crowd in the "Hallelujah" chorus from Handel's *Messiah*. As tradition dictated, everyone stood.

"I've always wondered," Nicholas said under his breath, "why are we supposed to stand?"

"There are many theories, the principal one being that King George II was so overwhelmed by the 'Hallelujah' chorus that he stood up. And whenever the king stood, so did everyone else."

After a brief intermission, Ryan came on stage for the second half. His bass voice, rich and finely textured, was exactly as Dorothy had described, and Emmanuelle felt as if she couldn't breathe during his entire a cappella rendition of "Away in a Manger."

When the concert finished to thunderous clapping, whistles, and cheers, Ryan held up a hand to quell the applause and extended congratulations to the children's chorus. The children scampered back on stage, bowed low, and then grinned and waved at the audience.

Emmanuelle rose along with Nicholas and announced she'd ferret out the booths serving roasted almonds and fudge. Her nose could only take so much temptation.

He circled an arm around her shoulders. "What about our s'mores? The mayor is building the bonfire and we'll eat in a few minutes."

"I'm adopting Scarlett's motto—to embrace life and indulge yourself. No worries. I promise I'll eat the fudge and almonds and s'mores." She sighed. "Although I won't be able to fit into the holiday skirt I brought if I keep eating at this rate. Fortunately, I also own a pair of slacks with an elastic waist."

Nicholas didn't appease her with a chuckle. Instead, his fingers tightened on her shoulders. "I'll go with you."

"Why?"

"Those suspicious phone calls you were getting ..." He looked around and nodded at a busload of fans swarming around Ryan. "There're too many people here tonight."

"I'm twenty-five, not five, and I lived in New York, one of the busiest cities in the world. I can certainly navigate a crowd and get my own snacks without an escort. I've gotten over my fear of walking alone." She shook off his arm and grabbed her tote bag. "Besides, Dorothy's headed our way. Please congratulate her for me. I'll shoot ahead of this next horde and catch up with all of you in a few minutes."

He hesitated. "Are you certain you'll be okay?"

"Enough time has passed. I'm better. Really." She walked purposefully toward the food kiosks. Out from under the tent, she saw the night was black—no moon or stars, and the shimmer of snow was now a gray mist.

She wound past the busy fudge and caramel-corn stands. The stand that advertised roasted almonds was farther down, and there was no line. Actually, the stand looked deserted. Had they sold out of almonds already and closed shop?

She paused, debating what to do, and sensed someone walking up behind her. "Emmanuelle," a man said, "can you give me directions to the stage?"

She was so sure she'd imagined the familiar voice, she started walking toward the stand.

"Emmanuelle."

She froze. Her shoulders tightened, her breathing stopped. *Move*, she commanded her feet.

"Turn around, Emmanuelle."

Obediently, she did. George had always had a hold over her.

The sight of him standing so near was enough to unfreeze her. She shifted, one foot stepping back, but his gaze immediately sharpened on her. If only she could make him believe she was standing stock-still while she slowly moved backward.

"How … how did you find me?" She licked her lips and expelled a quick breath. He couldn't be here. He was locked away in a hidden compartment in her mind, in New York, at a theater festival.

"Didn't take long." He grabbed her arm. "A couple of your so-called friends mentioned you'd gone off to some backwater town in South Carolina for the holidays." He laughed derisively. "'Cherish.' I couldn't even find it on a map."

"You don't know any of my friends." She braced her body against a cold wind and tried not to inhale. He smelled of vodka and anger and day-old sweat.

Despite herself, she couldn't control the shiver that rippled through her. He noticed. She saw the satisfaction in his bloodshot gray eyes. He had foreseen this, her cowering, her clumsiness, as she fingered the straps of her tote bag.

"I hired a few musicians for my office party," he said. His fingers tightened on her arm and she flinched. "They were more than willing to help once I offered a large bonus. You starving performers are always looking for handouts."

She swallowed a terrified scream and eyed her isolated surroundings. Several long sprints lay between her and the roasted-almond stand. She could outrun him.

No, argued her practical self. He was a large man. His pace outmatched hers, and he'd overtake her. All he'd have to do was drag her into the nearby woods, and she'd be alone with him.

Adrenaline consumed her, shaping her terror into a soundless rage. She wasn't a weak, passive victim, shrinking into herself just because he spoke.

This was her town, not his.

Mentally, she reviewed the article from the *Southern Charms* cookbook. If a woman was confronted by an attacker, one of her first lines of defense was her handbag.

She lifted her chin, straightened her spine. "Well, now that you've seen for yourself I'm here, go slither back to your swanky place in New York."

Momentarily, his composure slipped, his fingers loosened. "Every day, I think about when your broken harp was hauled away. I felt so bad, I decided to buy you a new one. We'll call it my Christmas gift to you. It's expensive. You'll like it."

"Keep it. I don't want it."

His eyebrows lifted in distracted mockery. "What—"

She couldn't be afraid. She couldn't allow herself to cringe and plead, but needed to prevent her fright from taking over.

Don't back away. Use the element of surprise. He won't expect you to fight.

"I said keep it." She lifted her heavy tote bag as a club and swung directly for his face.

She was too slow. He saw the blow coming and shoved her to the ground. A dull roar filled her ears, pain firing through her body as she hit solid ice. He fell on top of her, and she fought him, biting and kicking, jabbing at his eyes, focusing all her energy on getting away.

A shiny, silver knife sliced the air and came at her throat. "I heard you've been seeing an officer in town, Emmanuelle. Did you forget? You were meant only for me."

She shut her eyes to keep out the light-headedness, seeking the safety of somewhere dark and safe and silent.

Heavy, racing footsteps cut through her dizzying thoughts.

"Drop the knife and keep your hands over your head."

"George O'Donnell, you're under arrest for aggravated assault."

Two men's voices. Nicholas. And another man. Officer Joseph Hannaford.

"Emmanuelle? Are you okay?" Nicholas's steady tone reached through her fogged thoughts. She squinted. The color had drained from his face, and even in the darkness she could see his distress.

Tears welled. "Yes, yes. I'm—I'm fine. He didn't hurt …"

Her brave declaration was diminished by her sobbing. She couldn't contain her tears and reached out to Nicholas for comfort. She wanted to be held, wanted her apprehension quieted, wanted only him. Her legs wobbled as he helped her to her feet, and she sagged against his strong body. His gaze stayed focused on her.

George sneered at her as Officer Hannaford snapped handcuffs on him. "You won't get away with this, Emmanuelle."

She noted that he showed no remorse.

"I already did," she said flatly. "Quit following me and go back to New York. I never want to see you again."

"This one stop-light town is no fun. I was leaving anyway." He didn't look tough or threatening now, not with his hands cuffed behind his back. "Just remember, Emmanuelle. You're an insignificant nobody."

Nicholas tightened his fists. "What did you say, O'Donnell?"

"Nothing, Nicholas," she said quickly. "He can't hurt me anymore."

The slow dance of George's belittlement, his cruelty, had ended. His hurtful comments would no longer snake through her dreams because she refused to carry her resentment anymore. She'd acted with courage, and someday, with God's grace, she'd forgive George. Just not today.

"Mr. O'Donnell," Officer Hannaford said, "we've been monitoring your activities. Lots of illegal narcotics are being siphoned through your hotel deliveries into other states besides New York. Drug trafficking is a felony, a federal one when it's across state lines. And then there's the evidence of money laundering, illegal weapons, and other crimes." His gaze flicked to Emmanuelle, then zeroed in on Nicholas's clenched fists. "Why don't you bring your girl back to your apartment and cool off? I guarantee this guy will be locked away for a good many years."

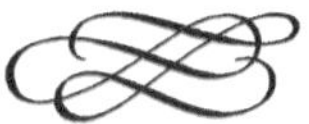

CHAPTER 11

Emmanuelle looked like a dream and cooked like a gourmet chef, Nicholas decided, taking a whiff of something heavenly as he strode into his apartment. He was greeted by Molly Belle's hopeful eyes and madly flapping tail.

He hung his pea coat by the door, took off his deputy badge, and slid the gun from his holster. With the dog on his heels, he locked the gun in his safe.

"No walks, Molly Belle," he said. "Emmanuelle texted me and I know you've been outside twice already."

Molly Belle cocked her silky ears, then followed him into the kitchen.

Nicholas feasted his gaze on Emmanuelle as she blended ingredients for a holiday fruitcake. She was dressed for Christmas Eve in a red velvet top and black pencil skirt that showed off her perfectly toned legs. She'd tied a plaid apron featuring a gingerbread man over her outfit. Her blonde hair tumbled in ringlets around her shoulders.

"Merry Christmas, angel," he said. "You're stunning." He tried not to stare, but she sure had shapely legs. He'd brought home a bouquet of red and white carnations, a festive beginning to the Christmas season, the florist had declared, when she'd snatched his credit card and rung up the sale.

No matter how hard he tried to budget, money seemed to slip out of his fingers faster than water.

"Well, thank you, Deputy Thompson," Emmanuelle said. "You're quite handsome yourself in your deputy uniform." She wiped a hand on her apron and twirled. "I was able to squeeze into this skirt after all, despite the endless barbecue sandwiches I've eaten lately. How do I look?"

"Gorgeous." He grinned approvingly, then held up the flowers.

Her face lit. "For me?"

"For Ryan and Dorothy's house," he amended. "The carnations are a Christmas dinner centerpiece, a thank you gift to them along with your ... fruitcake." He gave himself a silent pat on the back for not grimacing.

He blamed his fruitcake dislike on the media,

for the cake was fodder for endless jokes. His favorite was one by Johnny Carson, "There is only one fruitcake in the entire world, and people keep sending it to each other."

He didn't share that quote with Emmanuelle.

"I'm trying a new recipe," she said. "This one was passed down to Ryan by his nana."

"Yes, you'd mentioned it this morning. No *Southern Charms* recipe?"

"This one is better." Emmanuelle grinned and pressed the mixture into a baking pan. "It's so generous of your sister and Ryan to welcome us into their new home for the holidays."

The air smelled subtly of candied cherries and walnuts and dates, and Nicholas sniffed enthusiastically. Should he give fruitcake another chance? Most likely, Emmanuelle's cake would prove as tasty as all the other delicacies she'd prepared the past few weeks.

He set the bouquet on the table and brought her into his arms for a hello kiss.

"I missed you today." He nuzzled her neck. The splendidness of her, her sweet lips pressed to his, her sylphlike form leaning into him, brought him such happiness.

She wiped her hands on her apron and twined her arms around him. When he didn't release her, she shifted. "The fruitcake," she reminded him.

"Fruitcakes are invincible." He kept her close and rested his chin on her shiny blonde curls.

"Nicholas …" She extracted herself to pop the cake into the oven. "The recipe says the cake takes forty-five minutes to bake, which gives us plenty of time to arrive at Dorothy and Ryan's house by seven for dinner. The church service starts at midnight." She glanced at her watch. "It's five now."

Absently, he rubbed Molly Belle's head and eyeballed Emmanuelle as she pulled off her apron and put the flowers in a vase with water.

"Nicholas, did you hear me?"

"I think so."

"What did I say?"

"Something about Christmas dinner." He'd heard the dinner part and little else. He'd been preoccupied with her gorgeous legs.

"I brewed a pot of coffee. Do you want a cup?"

Before he answered, she brought out two mugs from his glass-front cabinet and poured.

"No donuts?" he teased, rousing her into a smile.

"On Christmas we eat fruitcake for dessert."

He sighed and scratched his head. *How could he forget?* He'd just have to keep hoping for the best.

"Emmanuelle …" From his shirt pocket, he withdrew a neatly wrapped present tied with a white satin bow. "This is a little gift I bought for you."

She looked surprised. "You're very generous, but my wonderful harp necklace is more than enough."

Which, he'd noticed, she wore every day.

"This is another gift because it's Christmas. And because I appreciate you."

Ever since she'd arrived, his apartment had been transformed. Maybe he hadn't paid attention to the dog hair accumulating on his unswept floors before, but he'd sure appreciated it when his wooden floors gleamed.

She smiled. "I bought gifts for you too. They're wrapped and under our Charlie Brown tree. Let's open them now."

With the dog at their side and coffee cups in hand, they wandered into the living room. She clicked on her favorite Christian radio station, then brought a gold-foil-wrapped box from beneath the tree and handed it to him. "Merry Christmas, Nicholas."

They sat together on the floor, backs against the wall, and stretched out their legs. She was barefoot, free from the restrictions of her former lifestyle—one of control and fear. Now, her smile came easy, her movements unrestrained. The subdued colors of the Christmas tree lights warmed her complexion to a healthy rose hue.

Molly Belle settled beside them, patient, good, eyeing them thoughtfully with shiny black eyes.

Nicholas chuckled. He felt like a kid again, filled with the magic of the season. He felt like singing out loud when a new artist's rendition of "O Come All Ye Faithful" lilted from the radio.

"Well? Why are you waiting?" she teased. Expectantly, she watched him open her gift, an electric travel mug. "Do you like it?"

"I love it. Thank you." He shouted with laughter. "This is perfect."

She grinned. "Now that you're a deputy, you're always focused on getting a good cup of coffee. If duty calls and pulls you away from the office, your coffee won't be left cold anymore."

"Thank you. I've become attached to my coffee. And I've become even more attached to you." He pressed a kiss to her temple.

Still grinning, she reached behind the tree and produced another box, this one lighter and wrapped in the same metallic-gold foil paper.

"Two gifts?" he asked. "Why?"

"You bought me two, so now we're even." She placed the box on his lap, her expression growing serious.

He unwrapped the foil paper slowly, revealing a

large jeweler's box. Then he paused, regarding her for a long moment, wondering why she'd lowered her head and seemed suddenly self-conscious. He unhooked the lid, and a silver pendant hanging from a heavy chain shone back at him.

"Read the words on the front," she encouraged. "It's a prayer."

"All right." He read aloud. "'Lord, keep my deputy safe from morning till night, give him strength in your precious light.'" He turned the pendant over. She'd personalized the back with an engraved script: "'I'm proud of you.'"

He wiped at his eyes as the emotion swept over him. He swallowed and held the pendant up to the light to admire it. "Thank you, Emmanuelle."

"You're very welcome."

He nodded toward his gift. "Now it's your turn."

Her fingers moved more slowly. She set the wrapping paper on the floor and gazed at the silver case she'd revealed. Carefully, she unsnapped the lid. A black velvet bed held a solitaire diamond ring in a twist of fourteen-karat white gold.

She drew an unsteady breath. "It's … it's beautiful." Tears welled, falling down her cheeks. She wiped at them, laughed as she brushed the wetness away. "These are happy tears," she clarified, laughing and crying at the same time before she sank her head into his chest and gave in to the weeping.

"I know." He held her until her cry had passed. The same joy had gripped him.

Taking her left hand, he slid the diamond engagement ring onto her finger. "Will you marry me, Emmanuelle?"

She stared at her finger, stared at him. "Read the explanation on the box that came with your pendant first."

He gazed at her and pondered her reply. How had the conversation shifted to *her* gift when she wore *his* gift on her finger? If his feelings weren't in such a tangle because she was sitting so close to him, because it was Christmas, because it was so easy to love life again, he would have noticed how her bright eyes shone with anticipation.

He lifted the box and read the inside flap. "'A deputy's wife's prayer.'" He set the box down. Paused. Reflected. "Wait a minute. A *wife's* prayer?"

"I planned on making my home in Cherish, and wanted to tell you on Christmas Eve." She looked almost sheepish. "Then I decided that if you didn't ask me to marry you, I'd ask you."

"Well, my answer is yes." He smothered a laugh and tipped up her face. "What's your answer?"

"Yes, yes, yes. I love you, Nicholas Thompson."

His mouth descended on hers as she pressed

closer. "I love you so much," he murmured, and then his mouth captured hers again for a breathtakingly long kiss.

When the kiss ended, she stayed in his arms.

"I've been thinking," she began, snuggling closer.

He brushed a kiss against her hair. "About what?"

"About the past few days, going over and over what happened the night of the concert. You obviously knew my relationship with George wasn't over. I didn't. And then I fought back when he attacked me. I shouldn't have."

"He's a dangerous man. You didn't realize how dangerous."

She blew out a breath. "Afterward, when I thought about how deserted it was back there, I chastised myself. I reacted foolishly for edging him on, and then trying to fight him."

"It was a knee-jerk reaction. You were threatened. You didn't realize how serious the situation would become, and so quickly. Officer Hannaford and I had been running a long background check on George O'Donnell ever since you told me his last name, so I was at fault. I knew how dangerous he was and I should never have let you go off alone."

"I only walked across the square to buy almonds." She sighed. "Although I've been blaming myself. I'm good at that."

"Don't." He kissed her again. "If anyone is responsible, it's me. I knew that George was involved in illegal activities."

She nodded. "And then I thought, through the bad came the good. Because of you—because of me—because of us, I've taken my power back. I didn't deserve his violence, and I felt so bitter and resentful when I arrived in Cherish. I've prayed a lot, and I finally realized if I kept feeling that way, that meant he still controlled me. So, I've let go of it. New beginnings, thanks to the grace of God."

Nicholas knuckled a tear from the corner of her eye.

She'd confronted her shame, her anger at herself, and realized God had helped her through the storm.

Love was here, love was now. Love was the magic of the season. They were standing on the edge of Christmas, waiting for the new year and their new life to begin.

For an eternity, they sat together on the floor, his arms enveloping her and holding her close.

* * *

NICHOLAS AWOKE to the sound of Molly Belle's whining as she darted across the living room. The shriek of the smoke alarm had him staring blindly ahead. Smoke rolled out of the kitchen.

"Emmanuelle." He shook her awake. "Are you keeping tabs on the time?"

"Yes, it's—" She gaped at her watch. "It's nearly seven o'clock!"

They raced to the kitchen just in time to extract a burnt fruitcake from the oven.

He shut off the smoke alarm. She winced at the cake.

"Oh no." She blew out a breath. "I hope I have enough ingredients left over to bake another one."

"You mean you're going to try to bake another fruitcake?"

She scanned the counter. "Unfortunately, it's too late tonight."

"Well, there's always tomorrow, although none of the stores will be open on Christmas, so we'll just have to wait."

He tried to sound regretful and knew he didn't.

He opened a kitchen window to let out the smoke and inhaled crisp winter air. A neighbor was inching his car into the driveway, wheels spinning, windshield wipers flapping like a wild bird's wings. Fresh snow was falling to the ground, hugging the landscape in a burst of white potential.

"We may not be going anywhere tonight," Emmanuelle murmured. She stood beside him, peering outside the window.

"What will we eat for Christmas dinner?" he asked.

"Burnt fruitcake and coffee?"

"I'll call Dorothy. Once the roads are plowed, we should be able to get to their house and then attend the midnight church service."

He hugged her. The exquisite feeling of her warm body next to his, made his heart beat stronger. He'd been bitter, just like her. In his bitterness, he hadn't wanted to change. He'd preferred to feed on his own loneliness and feel sorry for himself. And then, God had blessed him with Emmanuelle. He'd brought her into his life at the perfect time.

She was his family now, along with Dorothy and Ryan. And Molly Belle, who'd trotted into the kitchen, plopped beneath the kitchen table and curiously eyed the burnt fruitcake.

By the window, Nicholas kissed Emmanuelle, a kiss full of love and promise. "I love you, Emmanuelle."

Her eyes were wet with tears. "I love you too."

"And I'll take a lifetime to prove it to you, right here in Cherish," he said.

"You don't have to prove anything. I know the man you are, and that's why I love you."

Truly, whatever came their way, they could handle it. His faith had been tested, but these were lessons. He'd bounced back from sadness and adversity. They'd both bounced back.

Because God had them covered. Together and always.

With Emmanuelle in his arms, they were ready to face life's challenges.

And this was a Christmas to cherish.

THE END

A NOTE FROM JOSIE

Dear Friends,

Thank you for reading, *A Christmas To Cherish,* set in the charming fictional town of Cherish, South Carolina.

I've always enjoyed writing about small town life, and Christmas is a special time of year.

Because I am a musician and even played the harp for a while, my heroine, Emmanuelle, is a professional harpist.

The hero, Nicholas, is the heroine's brother in *A Love Song To Cherish,* and I wanted him to have his own happily ever after.

If you loved this romance as much as I loved writing it, please help other people find *A Christmas To Cherish* by posting your review.

A Christmas To Cherish is available in ebook, paperback, Large Print paperback, Hardcover, and audiobook.

My Spotify Play List for A Christmas To Cherish is here.

NANA'S FRUITCAKE RECIPE

Ingredients:

4 eggs
1 cup flour
2 teaspoons baking powder
1 pound candied pineapple
1 pound pitted dates
1 pound candied cherries
8 cups walnuts

Instructions:

Pour flour and baking powder into a large paper bag, shake to mix, then add fruits and nuts. Shake well to coat all pieces with flour.

In a large bowl, beat eggs. Pour the fruits and nuts mixture into the egg mixture and use your hand to mix well. Coat all pieces. Grease a small baking pan and press the mixture firmly into the pan. Bake approximately 45 minutes at 350 degrees or until golden brown.

Enjoy!

USA TODAY BESTSELLING AUTHOR
JOSIE RIVIERA
Sweet
PEPPERMINT
Kisses

Copyright © 2018 by Josie Riviera

All rights reserved.

No part of this book may be reproduced in any form or by any electronic or mechanical means, including information storage and retrieval systems, without written permission from the author, except for the use of brief quotations in a book review.

PRAISE AND AWARDS

USA TODAY bestselling author

CHAPTER 1

*C*hiara Johnson sat on a chair near the chrome table in her kitchen, inhaling the enticing scents of vanilla and almond wafting from the oven as her cookies baked. Sighing, she peered around her modest apartment. Although she categorized the first day of December as the beginning of the holiday season, it didn't feel much like Christmas.

"Sugar cookies," her mother had always said, "were the answer to all life's problems."

Well, maybe they were.

Nostalgic images of baking with her mother and sister brought misty tears. These pangs of nostalgia erupted at the oddest moments, although in December, homesickness was justifiable.

Of course, she would volunteer at the women's

center. Chiara believed in giving back, especially to an organization that had indirectly affected her. Adeline, one of her co-workers, had been homeless for a while until she secured a job. The shelter had enabled her to get back on her feet.

Besides, Chiara thought, volunteering gave her a sense of purpose.

It was just … well … she hadn't imagined herself still living in Turning Point, Virginia after three years.

Sure, she'd made friends. Adeline had even launched a book club that met in town every Friday evening, and the women were a delight to be around. However, with Chiara's work schedule, she had attended only a couple times.

She turned the volume louder on her cell phone as "I'll Be Home For Christmas," the 1943 version sung by Bing Crosby, came on. One of her favorite holiday tunes, she sang along to the last few bars: "If only in my dreams."

Dabbing the tears from her eyes, she stood to check on the sugar cookies.

Her cellphone rang and she answered, recognizing the incoming caller's ID.

"Hi, Emma," she said as she settled back in her chair.

"Are you sure you can't move home by Christmas?" her younger sister asked.

"You read my email? Yes, I'm positive." Chiara cradled the phone to her ear. "I accepted a full-time job for December to help pay off my last tuition bill."

"Couldn't someone else in your nursing agency work instead of you?"

Emma was a typical nine-year-old girl. She had a lot to say about every subject, couldn't see any side of the story except hers, and regarded Chiara as the world's best sister.

Chiara smiled. It was wonderful to feel adored.

"Everyone else in the agency either has a significant other or children or both," she replied. "And they all had holiday plans. I didn't, and I was available. Plus, the agency was scrambling to fill the position on such short notice."

"Mom and Dad said you're an awesome nurse. They say you genuinely care about people."

"Thank goodness parents put us on a pedestal, right?" Chiara laughed. "Between classes and other expenses, I've worked hard to make ends meet. Right now this job is necessary."

Wasn't *that* the understatement of the year?

Obviously, she couldn't ask her parents for money. Due to the recent economic downturn, they struggled financially. The Midwest had been hit particularly hard.

However, Chiara was determined to succeed.

She'd studied nonstop to earn her RN degree at a high-quality Virginia university and planned on securing a stable, well-paying position.

"So, you start your new job right away?" Emma asked. She was chewing on something, presumably a fruit snack. The little girl ate fruit snacks endlessly.

"Monday is my first day, and it's a live-in position, so I'll be saving rent money," Chiara said. "My client is a woman recuperating from a fall and a concussion."

"Did she trip or something?"

Chiara went to the sink to run water into the mixing bowls. "She was riding a horse. The woman lives on a horse ranch."

"Horses? Lucky you! I want a brown and black pony for Christmas."

"Umm, horses are way too big for my liking and can be extremely dangerous. Also, it's not my ranch, and I won't be riding any horses."

"Maybe Santa will bring me a horse from the ranch. Tell him."

"I'll be staying in a guest apartment over the garage, and I probably won't run into Santa."

Chiara wondered if the over-the-garage apartment would be an improvement over her current home. The bland beige walls in the galley kitchen screamed for a colorful face-lift, and the vinyl flooring was outdated. A dose of Christmas decorations should have been on her to-do list. Unfortunately, between her classes and home-nursing appointments, she was beyond exhausted.

"Doesn't Santa come to Virginia?" Emma asked.

"I'm sure he does, although I've never seen Santa ride a horse."

Emma paused. "Do you think you'll see one of his elves?"

"You never know."

"Well, one of his elves riding a horse is almost as good as the real Santa."

"I agree."

"Just in case, I'll tell Santa I want a pony when I see him at the mall."

Chiara chuckled. "You do that." Homesickness welled again. She blew out a breath and kept her voice light. "I'll Skype all of you on Christmas Day, okay?"

She envisioned her parents and Emma attending the festival of lights exhibition in Kansas City. Oh, how her family delighted in the festivities, marking off the four Sundays before Christmas on the Advent calendar, skating every weekend on the city's outdoor rink. Emma would be the first one on the ice, gliding fearlessly, not afraid to fall.

Her chest squeezed. Family togetherness was

the most significant part of the holidays, and she'd once again miss those days with the people she treasured most.

As she listened to Emma's excitement about the cool Harry Potter book she was reading, Chiara opened the oven to an eruption of heat. According to the recipe, the cookies were done. According to her eyes, they weren't. However, the last time she baked cookies, she had burned them until they were unrecognizable.

To be prudent, she removed the raw-looking cookies from the oven and set the trays on the stove. Hopefully, they didn't taste the way they looked.

"Are you still there? Did you hear what I said?" Emma asked.

"Yes. I'm overjoyed you're liking the Harry Potter books." Chiara nodded into the phone. "I'm baking sugar cookies for my agency's holiday party and had to take them out of the oven."

"Remember how we test different recipes for our gingerbread houses?" Emma giggled. "And how they always collapse?"

"We'll experiment with another recipe this year, an easier one." Chiara bit into a cookie before realizing it was burning her tongue. Gingerly, she chewed, swallowed, then groped for a glass of water. "Royal icing will stick the pieces together like cement."

"When? If you're not here, we won't be able to build a gingerbread house."

"I'll be home by New Year's Eve. This nursing gig is only for December."

If she lasted that long. The last wealthy family she'd worked for had treated her poorly. She remembered them well—five people residing in the same home, each settled into their separate spaces and hardly conversing with one another, disregarding her as nothing better than invisible hired help. Defensive, she'd managed her job professionally and kept to herself.

What gave some people the right to be so dismissive to others just because they had money?

She pushed away the memory and finished the cookie. It had hardened already and tasted delicious even without icing and sprinkles.

"Promise?" Emma was asking.

"Absolutely."

"And if you see Santa at the horse ranch—"

"I'll mention your pony request." Chiara glanced at the clock. "I should get ready for the Christmas party, so we'll talk soon. I love you."

"I love you too and I'm giving you a cyber cuddle."

This was Christmas, Chiara wanted to say. She

needed more than a cuddle. She needed to be with people she cherished.

"Be good and tell Mom and Dad I send my love." She returned Emma's blown kisses and then ended the call.

That squeeze in her chest again, an ache of loneliness. Lips pressed tight, she moved to the counter where her laptop sat and switched her computer on. Quickly, she scrolled through the job listings on the nursing agency's website.

There it was. Her one-month gig.

Home Nurse. Temporary live-in position assisting a woman with self-care, companionship and everyday tasks. Immediate opening.

The agency's report stated the patient was recovering from a concussion and broken ankle after missing a vault in a high-stakes horse competition.

Just like Kevin.

Despite her efforts to never think about him, her mind brought up an image of her ex-boyfriend. Of course, his concussion and broken wrist hadn't been the result of a horse show. It had been the result of a bar fight.

Why, why, why were his violent tendencies so clear in hindsight? Fortunately, he'd never hit her. But if only she'd had that knowledge beforehand, had understood that a man's online dating profile didn't necessarily reveal who the man really was.

Despite her parents' reservations, she had left home and relocated to Virginia to be near him. A few months after their relationship began, she realized he wasn't the guy for her and broke it off.

Although she longed for all things Kansas, by that point she'd enrolled in a nursing degree program and secured a full-time job.

So here she was, three years later. Overdrawn on her bank account, in a town she didn't consider home, not so much as a hint of a boyfriend, and celebrating Christmas by herself.

Focus on the future, not the past, her favorite pastor had once preached, and bring your views on life into context. A home was more than a building, more than a place. A home was where she was a participant, not a consumer who followed from the sidelines.

As she contemplated this, a message from V. Thatcher popped into her inbox:

"Miss Johnson, a change in plans. My sister has a late morning doctor's appointment. Please report for your position on Monday afternoon after lunch."

"Is four o'clock okay?" she quickly typed. "It would be better for me and give me more time to pack my things."

She pressed send, then felt her body freeze in place.

Since when did a person who'd just gotten a job tell her employer what hour was best to meet?

An immediate reply appeared.

"Make it five. The front gate will open when you drive up. Thanks. Vance Thatcher."

* * *

ON MONDAY AFTERNOON, Chiara heaved her suitcases into the living room. She tugged on red patent leather boots and buttoned her new cream-colored jacket, which had been an early Christmas gift to herself for completing her degree. Peering into her bathroom mirror, she styled her blonde curls into a side bun and applied natural lip gloss. She wore no other make-up, so there was nothing she could do about the vivid spots of pink on both cheeks. She was eager, she told herself, anticipating her newest job. Or, she realized with a wry grin, she was punch-drunk from exhaustion.

As a result of late-afternoon traffic and bad weather, her trip took longer than expected. She drove her ancient Ford Escort slowly along the rain-slicked roads.

Strings of garland adorned the businesses on Post Avenue, the main street in town. Streetlights added a mellow glow to the silver puddles, and a sign advertised horse-drawn carriage rides.

All this fanfare because the town of only 20,000 inhabitants had been voted one of the most festive in America.

She couldn't contain her smile. The description was so fitting, notably at Christmas.

Sometimes, she marveled at how the towns-people did it. A week earlier, harvest flags and gourds had been everywhere. Now there wasn't a pumpkin in sight.

So why had she never seemed to belong, forever pining for Kansas's flat grasslands, the fields of wheat, the meat-falling-off-the-bone barbecues? The likelihood of a white Christmas in Kansas City was generally assured. In Virginia, December was commonly a rainy month. Turning Point averaged seven inches per year, so snow at Christmas was hit or miss.

If she were honest, she didn't even like snow, except between Christmas Eve and New Year's. Nevertheless, she loved four distinctive seasons, and Virginia had that commonality with Kansas.

Minutes later, her cellphone's map brought her to a street address at the north point of town. Her agency had detailed the property as an equestrian estate and, as she drove past, limitless tracts of farmland looked untouched. As she neared the final turn, she slowed and then stopped at a red light.

Further down, she sighted a gated driveway leading to a luxury log cabin mansion, sitting on acres of land and resembling a wooden lodge. The ranch even had a name—Wellington Acres. And according to the agency's information, the home bordered a pond.

So large. So beautiful. Despite the fluttering in her gut, Chiara dismissed her intimidation. She could do this.

Several horses grazed in pastures, and one tossed its head toward her. Behind the fencing, a white horse with big brown eyes seized a mouthful of grass, then greeted her with a whinny.

Emma would love it here—outside in nature, with all this open pasture to run wild and play. Age-old pine trees lined muddy trails. Whatever else happened, Chiara thought, Wellingon Acres was an extraordinary place to spend the holidays.

Perhaps she'd purchase a miniature evergreen tree for her garage apartment and spruce it up with bright gold tinsel. For Christmas, Emma wanted Judy Blume books, a portable piano keyboard, and a hair straightener for her unruly blonde curls. With part of her salary, Chiara could give Emma a special Christmas, and the items would easily fit into her luggage.

Except for the pony. Chiara grinned. Well, her

sister would need to wait, unless ponies learned how to fly.

She fiddled with the radio while she waited for the light to change. On the other side of the highway, a bright-red Corvette sped toward the light, apparently intending to run the yellow. Despite the rain and swiftly falling darkness, the car had no headlights and was cruising well over the twenty-five mile per hour speed limit. The teenage boy behind the wheel glanced down, undoubtedly studying his cellphone. Then he gestured to another teen boy in the passenger seat.

A drumming sound grabbed Chiara's attention. A large black horse had galloped onto the road. Wildly, she looked around. Where had the horse come from?

The Corvette sped closer. The horse's eyes were wide with fright as it whinnied in terror.

The driver of the Corvette looked up in time and slammed on the brakes. The car fishtailed on the wet road, coming perilously close to the horse. The driver overcompensated, and the car swerved off the road, hurtling through a pasture fence. The horse spun in a circle and loped away.

Noise exploded all around Chiara—horses in the pasture neighing, the boys screaming.

She jerked her car over to the curb, shut off the ignition, and dashed across the road. The sharp cold air seemed to slice through her as she raced to reach the boys.

Clearly shaken, they emerged from the Corvette. One was crying as he wiped at his bleeding forehead. The other was shaking and whimpering. As she pulled her cell phone from her purse, he pleaded for her not to call his parents.

She didn't know his parents' phone number, she thought to reply. Instead, she stayed quiet, and, with disciplined focus, she examined them both for injuries and spoke quietly to calm them. Then, supporting the wounded boy's head in her lap, she punched in 911.

CHAPTER 2

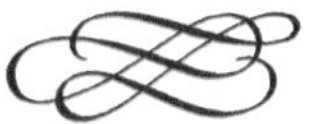

*V*ance Thatcher sat in his favorite wingback chair across from his younger sister, Gertrude, in the living room of their childhood home at Wellington Acres. Between them, the fire crackled and burned cheerfully in the stone fireplace, bringing warmth to a massive room that boasted a twenty-seven-foot-high vaulted ceiling.

"How's the beta phase going for your new computer app?" Gertrude asked.

He could go on and on about how he thought his dating app would revolutionize matchmaking since he was using broader parameters than other dating sites, such as similar tastes in movies, books, and foods, as well as mutual friends.

He didn't say a word, though. Legs outstretched, he settled back in his chair and surveyed the pine-paneled study across the hallway. His thoughts ran together, reflecting on all the responsibilities he had left to accomplish before the day was over.

"If you have to make any business calls ..." Gertrude was indulging in her nightly glass of red wine, set on a table beside her wheelchair.

"My phone calls can wait a while longer." He pushed to his feet and glanced at his watch. "Chiara Johnson should have been here at five o'clock."

"It's only a couple hours past."

"She obviously doesn't need a job if she keeps prospective employers waiting this long. Her credentials are outstanding, her references were verified, and the nursing agency highly recommended her. Apparently, everyone was wrong." He had little patience for people who weren't dependable. If she decided to show up, he was going to tell her all that and more.

Gertrude brushed a strand of hair from her face. She had pulled her long hair into a ponytail, highlighting the startling contrast between her black hair and pallid complexion. Her freckles nearly jumped off her skin.

He studied her, searching for the same bright eyes and flash of adventure in the sister who seemed to have disappeared. Her cheeks were ashen, her eyes dull.

Ever since the accident.

His heart thudded a solemn beat.

A daredevil, Gertrude surely longed to be outside doing what she loved best ... skiing in Colorado, gliding through a canopy of trees on a zip line, riding fearlessly on her favorite horse across the open pastures. All while his warnings stuck in his throat and he ordered his lips to stay sealed. Otherwise, she'd accuse him of over-reacting.

Instead, she was confined to a wheelchair, a result of a broken ankle and a cumbersome cast, and further incapacitated by a concussion.

"Vance, you should get back to your office in town," she said.

He'd thought the same thing about a million times. "I can work from home. I've been able to accomplish just about everything from here."

"'Just about' isn't enough, at least not for you. And then you played hooky from work today to drive me to a doctor's appointment." She went for her wine, sipped, swallowed. Typical Gertrude, his dramatic-pause sister. "I could've rung a taxi."

"Absolutely not. Cognitive testing was scheduled during your neurology examination."

"And it wasn't necessary. My memory and concentration are outstanding. Your start-up business app isn't going to start up by itself."

She was right, but he didn't want to leave her.

He couldn't help himself. It was necessary to ensure she was able to rest, both physically and mentally. In the first couple of days after the accident, she'd been so badly confused, she could barely function.

And that had scared him.

He strode to the large picture window, leaned his shoulder on the frame and gazed outside. Nighttime had gathered, casting the pastures in a dark charcoal hue. Their five-bedroom home afforded panoramic views of the fields, horse barn and bordering pond. He and Gertrude had inherited Wellington Acres from their parents. Along with the property, though, had come unexpected debt.

He studied his parent's wedding portrait over the fireplace mantel, an overly large black-and-white photo. They held themselves straight, staring into the camera, not even holding hands. Had they ever been in love, especially after the debts started rolling in?

Next month would have been their fortieth wedding anniversary.

"Perhaps Mom and Dad didn't know how to handle money," Gertrude said, reading his thoughts. She too gazed at the portrait.

"Perhaps?" He turned to her. "More likely, they completely disregarded a mortgage and property taxes since they were too busy jet-setting."

In his mind, Vance ticked off the chores he intended to discuss with the ranch manager, Joe Brown, before he left for another late night working alongside his computer programmers.

A fence was down in an outlying pasture, a result of all the rain. The horses, he thought ruefully, were the easy part of running a ranch.

His cell phone pinged. Vance glanced at the text from one of his investors. The investor was reminding Vance about their meeting in Turning Point the next morning at ten o'clock. He acknowledged the message with a quick response, then shoved the phone into his pocket. He'd much rather be writing code than talking to business-men, trying to drum up financial support.

"Vance." Gertrude's delicate chin lifted. "I can certainly handle this interview by myself."

"I won't leave you alone until I know there's a nurse in place."

"Amanda's here."

"She's not a nurse, she's a housekeeper, as she has reminded us very politely one hundred times. Besides, at sixty years old, Amanda has enough to do. Suppose you require—"

"Since I got home from the hospital, you've never been more than two steps away from me."

Gertrude's lips trembled as she held back a laugh. "All this hovering is getting on my nerves."

For a moment, he stared at her, too startled to speak. *He was hovering?*

"I can stay, really," he replied.

"No, you can't. Besides, you've accomplished more than enough already when you should've been involved in your app's beta testing phase. Instead, you're in your study paying bills, or making phone calls, or ensuring I'm comfortable—"

"You're making me sound like a helicopter brother."

"That's a term used for parents who are excessively protective of their children, although the description aptly suits you." She grinned, then sobered. "Our ranch is finally productive. I never thanked you, and I should."

"You're welcome." He nodded. "By the way, I fixed the pregnant mare's paddock fencing."

"And how was Peppermint this morning?"

"You know her, the official greeter of the horse world in all her snowy white splendor. Even being six months pregnant, she's as social as ever. She's no bother, and neither are you."

In truth, he wanted to do more for Gertrude. Ten years his junior, she looked so young and frail, so different from the wild, anything-for-a-dare sibling he'd grown up with. If their parents were alive, she undoubtedly would have added to their gray hairs.

Or not. They'd been so busy on their travel adventures, they probably wouldn't have noticed the scrapes their daughter got into. In fact, he couldn't recall when their parents were around for more than a few months at a time.

"Vance, really. Go."

He wavered, peered at the clock, and then went to get his parka hung on a brass rack in the foyer. The December 31 deadline for the official presentation of the app to his investor group was coming fast.

"Amanda can help me get into bed," Gertrude assured him when he returned. "And tomorrow we'll place another Internet ad."

"Miss Johnson should have called, or texted, or—"

"It's the Christmas season." Gertrude checked him in mid-sentence. "People are busy. Just because we don't observe the holidays doesn't mean other families don't."

They'd rarely celebrated Christmas. As a boy, he'd heard vivid descriptions of Santa and his flying reindeer from his classmates, but Santa never rode his sleigh to the Thatcher house. The Thatchers never put up a tree or exchanged presents. If they had, his parents probably would have hired a personal shopper to buy their gifts.

Briefly, Vance closed his eyes and sighed. He'd always liked Christmas—the snippets of traditions he gleaned from his classmates and friends, the endearing movies on television, the beloved music. And church. He remembered attending services with his family when he was young, hearing about Bethlehem and the wise men and the birth of baby Jesus.

But they stopped attending church regularly, then not at all.

When he'd asked his parents why, he never received a clear answer. He'd only been a kid then, and after a few years, it didn't matter. It was just the way things were done in their house.

"When Miss Johnson replied to your email," Gertrude said, "she requested her interview time be changed. Maybe she had family commitments."

From what he'd gathered from her agency's report, she wasn't married, nor had children.

He paused, shuffled his feet, eyed the majestic grandfather clock in the corner.

"My accident wasn't your fault," Gertrude said softly. "Don't keep blaming yourself."

"I should have been there for you."

"Like you could've stopped my fall." She waved

her hand. "Don't be ridiculous, Vance. You can't solve all the world's problems."

"Only half." Grinning, he strode to her and grazed a kiss on her shiny hair. "If Chiara Johnson happens to show, text me. In the meantime, I'll grab a flashlight and take a walk to the stable."

As he was about to leave, Amanda rushed into the room.

"Mr. Thatcher? Miss Johnson has arrived. And she brought someone with her."

Gertrude looked up, her gaze puzzled. "Who?"

Amanda hesitated, catching her breath, tucking strands of silver hair into her bun. "A police officer who wishes to speak with Mr. Thatcher."

"Police? Why?" With a slight shake of his head, Vance wondered again about the audacity of a woman who not only ran two hours late for a new job, but decided to arrive with a police escort.

Gertrude launched her wheelchair forward. "Is the woman hurt?"

"Wait here." Vance placed a hand on her arm to stop her, then draped his parka over the wingback chair. "I'll go see."

"No one's hurt, Miss Thatcher." Amanda clasped her hands together. "Although Licorice broke through the pasture fence and caused a car accident down the road."

CHAPTER 3

"Mr. Thatcher?"

"Call me Vance."

"Vance. I ... I assume we should cancel our meeting." Chiara stared at the dark-haired, slightly bearded man wearing jeans and a heather-gray T-shirt. He and Officer Bennington, the policeman who had accompanied her to the residence after the accident, had spoken privately while she had ducked into the marbled powder room off the foyer to wash her hands and face. Now she faced the man who was supposed to be her employer.

"Why cancel now?" Vance extended his hand. "I presume you're Miss Johnson."

"Please call me Chiara. And yes, of course, you're right. Why cancel now?"

Oh, my. He was so good-looking. She didn't

mean to gawk, but he radiated the casual refinement she recognized in the well-to-do. Just the type she dreaded—supremely confident, prosperous and privileged.

This close, she caught the scent of him—open air and cedar and fine leather.

Feeling totally out of her element, she glanced around. The home reminded her more of a getaway retreat for the Vanderbilts than a real house.

He assessed her in turn, and she imagined what he saw. Wrinkled black slacks, muddy boots, her cream-colored jacket stained with blood.

Entirely self-conscious, she accepted his outstretched hand. His fingers were callused and firm, not the fingers she imagined for a moneyed man who ran an equestrian estate this size. She assumed he sat parked behind a desk all day and issued orders to his employees.

But no, evidently not.

"I apologize for my lateness. There was an accident."

Ridiculous. Of course, he was aware of that. Why couldn't she think straight around self-assured men? She avoided dating guys like Vance because they made her feel like a minion.

"Please. No apologies." His eyes, the color of deep mahogany, held her gaze. "Officer Bennington briefed me, and my manager called to say he's safely secured our runaway horse. Licorice is my sister's horse, actually, and very tame." He glanced at the policeman, then returned his attention to her. "I'm sorry I wasn't notified sooner. I could have helped." His gaze flicked to their hands, still joined.

"Miss Johnson was certainly an asset." Officer Bennington offered her a brief salute. "She knew precisely what to do. Fortunately, the teenage boys weren't hurt—only some surface wounds and scratches. They've been transported to the hospital in town, their car towed, and their parents notified. You're well-trained, miss. Thank you."

"You're welcome." Chiara pulled her hand from Vance's grasp. "I'm glad I could assist." Without warning, tears pooled. She blamed them on the stress of the move, the accident, the pressure of this new job. She drew a hard breath to collect herself and sidestepped the men's gazes. Fortunately, neither seemed to notice her distress as they walked toward the front door. Or, they were well-schooled in the art of politeness.

After ushering the officer out, Vance walked back and openly studied her. "Are you okay?"

She brushed a stray tear on her cheek. "Yes, of course."

"Sorry about your coat. Once you're settled, I'll have it cleaned."

She stared down at the blood stains, and a wave of emotion clogged her throat. "Thank you."

He paused. "Do you have another?"

"Coat? Yes. It's in my suitcase in my car." Along with everything else she owned.

Keep cool. No more tears. No long-winded explanations. He's your employer and doesn't care about your traumatic day.

Besides, she refused to crumble into an embarrassing meltdown in front of him.

She shook out her slacks, straightened her shoulders and held onto her determination.

A grandfather clock in the foyer chimed the hour. Eight o'clock.

"I'd like you to meet my sister, Gertrude," Vance said, "so you two can get to know each other. Afterward, I'll show you to the guest loft above the garage." He guided her to the living room where his sister waited in a wheelchair.

Gertrude was beautiful, with jet-black hair slicked into a ponytail and a sharp sprinkle of freckles across her cheeks. A flicker of a resemblance to Vance shone in her keen brown eyes.

She wore an ankle-length plaid skirt and V-neck yellow sweater.

Chiara smiled and acknowledged a greeting, then scanned the room. The vaulted ceiling added to the enormity of the space, painted in subdued gray tones. A fire burned in the grate, emitting a hint of pine.

And no Christmas decorations anywhere. Certainly not a tree, but not even a wreath over the massive fireplace, nor a grouping of glowing holiday candles on the mahogany buffet table. It was sad. She couldn't think of a room more suited for a joyous tree and shimmering gold-leaf garland.

A shiny-black grand piano was positioned beside the picture window. How Emma would have loved to run her fingers over the keys of such a magnificent instrument, Chiara thought. She'd been teaching herself how to play using YouTube videos.

Turning from the piano, Chiara focused on Gertrude. Once they started talking, she took an instant liking to the younger woman. She had a spark in her smile, a sense of mischievousness that reminded her of Emma.

"This wheelchair is temporary," Gertrude explained. "I had a bad fall from my horse in a riding accident. The doctor said I'll be recovering for a few more weeks, at least until Christmas."

So she said the word *Christmas* although they clearly didn't celebrate. Unless they preferred to wait until Christmas Eve to decorate as lots of people did.

In Kansas, Chiara's parents would have illuminated their house as if they were competing in a Christmas pageant by now. Their decorations went up on Thanksgiving night. A giant tree took up half the area in the narrow den, and their outdoor-lights display beckoned cars to stop and take photos.

Gertrude turned toward Vance. "How is Licorice? Did Joe—"

"Licorice is safely boarded in her stall. And Joe Brown is no concern of yours."

"Don't tell me what to do, big brother." Chiara caught the look of stubbornness on Gertrude's face. "Joe's a remarkable guy. He's responsible and reliable and his affinity to horses matches mine. We share a common bond."

"He's an efficient manager. Too bad you don't share a common age." With an exasperated shake of his head, Vance grabbed his parka and shepherded Chiara out of the room.

"Thanks for taking the position," he said.

She extended a smile. "That was the fastest getting-to-know-you conversation I've ever had."

"I have a business meeting this evening and I'm already late." He tapped his watch. "So we're all set. My sister seems to like you. Officer Bennington likes you." He paused, his gaze softening. "And I like you."

"So, it's okay for me to live in the guest apartment?"

He pulled on his parka. "There's space for a small army on this ranch. It's only Gertrude and I and a household staff of two. Currently I'm tied up, which is why we advertised for extra help while my sister recovers."

"What do you do?" What a question, she scolded herself. Just look around.

She was gazing at him again, like she'd never seen a handsome guy before. But oh, with his sinewy muscles beneath his worn T and his movie-star smile, she couldn't deny the instant magnetism.

"I work." He zippered up his parka, and she regretted the loss of the view of his broad shoulders. "And then I work, work and work."

"And at other times?"

"Probably more work." He grinned, his smile crooked and appealing, and her heart did a flip-flop in her chest.

Chiara followed Vance past her parked car, across the gravel driveway to the garage, then up the exterior stairs to the guest quarters. He unlocked the door, and they entered the loft.

"Here it is." He spread out his hands, indicating curved stucco walls and slate tile flooring. In a whirlwind, he gave her an abridged tour of the eighteen-by-thirty-six-foot space, which was comprised of a bedroom, open-style kitchen, living room, and bathroom with a laundry nook.

"Wow, it's incredible. I never imagined anything as well-appointed." She unbuttoned her coat. "This apartment is the opposite of my former place in town."

"Which was?"

"Umm, in dire need of a thorough repainting for one thing. I considered painting the place myself."

"Well, please don't decide to repaint this apartment. You'll be busy enough keeping my chatty sister company. So here's the key." He set it on the coffee table.

"Thanks, Vance, and I'll say it before you do." She stood in the kitchen and held up a hand. "I'm not in Kansas anymore."

He laughed. "I saw on your application that you're originally from Kansas City."

"Yes, it's my home. That's why I can get away with that *Wizard of Oz* saying."

"That movie is all I know about Kansas. I was envisioning a dark-haired girl in pigtails wearing ruby-red shoes. You're wearing red boots."

"But, my name isn't Dorothy, and I'm a blonde," she countered.

"You know, you're a lot prettier than Dorothy."

His dark eyes glinted as he closed the distance between them. "In fact, you're very beautiful."

She felt her cheeks heat as she gathered her thoughts into a protest.

"And do you want to know a secret?" he continued with a grin.

He was well-polished. A real charmer. She'd give him that.

"Do I have a choice?" she asked.

"I imagined you with curly blonde hair. And wearing a ruffled green blouse that matched your emerald eyes."

She took a step back and regarded him. "How did—"

"Your agency forwarded your profile picture along with your application."

Okay. She'd had the picture taken a year ago, her hair freshly styled, wearing pink lip gloss and her favorite pair of gold hoop earrings. Well, she certainly didn't look anything like that this evening, and, she assumed, he was quite disenchanted.

"Dorothy from Kansas," he said, smiling his heart-tripping grin again. "If you strolled into my foyer carrying a little dog named Toto ..."

She chuckled. "Chiara from Kansas—please."

"Chiara." He focused on her face with disconcerting intensity. "Your dimples turn up whenever you speak of your home. I suspect you miss Kansas?"

"Very much. My parents and sister live there and I'm returning for good after this job." She paused. She'd said too much. "Have you always lived in Virginia?"

He gestured toward the window and fields beyond. "Nowhere else, although my parents traveled all over the world. Nowadays, the ranch and my business keep me occupied." His smile turned grim and then faded altogether. "At any rate, I'm grateful someone can utilize these guest quarters. No one's ever here, unless a displaced cousin happens to call on us."

"Are you expecting guests for the holidays?"

"Considering my cousins haven't visited in years, and last I heard they migrated to Ireland, I safely assume no one will be here except you and me and Gertrude." He checked his watch. He did that a lot. "I'll get your suitcases, then I'm heading to the stable, then straight into town."

He left. Within minutes, he reappeared carrying her suitcases, strode through the apartment and placed them in the bedroom.

It was remarkable, she thought. All her material possessions fit into two suitcases, which was all she needed. All this commercialism at Christmastime, the buy, buy, buy mentality, was disheartening. The true meaning of Christmas could be found in … Well, in Kansas, attending church services, watching holiday movies on TV, and baking cookies with her family.

"The refrigerator and pantry are stocked," he said. "I can phone Amanda to deliver dinner."

"No, I'm fine, really. I'll eat breakfast in the morning."

"What's your cell phone number?" When she told him, he sent her a quick text to confirm his. "Report to the house tomorrow morning at eight. I won't be around much these next few weeks."

"Because of work?"

His dark eyebrows lifted and he grinned. "Work, work, work. If you're missing anything while you're here, text me." He brushed a hand against hers as she walked him to the door.

"Sure. Thanks." Her cheeks warmed at his touch. What was she doing? She wasn't an enamored employee with a crush on her handsome employer. She'd only known him a little over an hour.

You're here one month, remember? And then you're homeward bound.

Yes, yes, she remembered. With a head shake, she shook off her attraction.

After Vance left, she devoted the next hour to unpacking, then showered with her favorite lemon body wash she'd brought with her. All the while, she couldn't stop thinking about Vance. He had touched her hand lightly, a fleeting, spur-of-the-moment gesture. Yet his touch lit a strange sensation inside her.

After slipping into a pair of pink velour lounge pants and a cozy sweatshirt, she inspected her blood-stained coat draped over the chesterfield sofa. She'd forgotten to give it to Vance.

She set a kettle on the stove for tea and opened the container of leftover sugar cookies. She was thankful she'd brought them. After the exhausting day, she needed comfort food and a jolt of pure sugar.

On her first day off she'd drive into town for groceries, and purchase an evergreen tree and wreath to bring Christmas cheer to her cozy loft.

She plugged in her phone and switched on her favorite holiday radio station. A piano arrangement came on playing a buoyant "Jingle Bells."

A crunch of tires on the gravel driveway prompted her to peek out the window. It was a little after ten PM, and Mr. Dreamboat Employer was getting out of his SUV. She hurried to open the door as she heard him climb the outside stairs.

"My coat," she said. "We both forgot. It's on the couch."

He wiped his boots on the mat on the landing. "I'll get it." He walked past her into the apartment, wearing the same parka he'd worn earlier with the addition of scuffed work boots.

"Really, you didn't have to come back to—"

"Never turn down a man offering to help." He got to her coat before she did. From behind, his thick black hair was longer than she'd first realized and curled at his nape. She recognized the scent of fine leather again on his clothes, and the scent was oddly reassuring.

"How is your runaway horse?" she asked.

"Licorice? Spooked, but calm now." He hung her coat on the doorknob, then reached inside his parka and brandished a bottle of sparkling water. "I was in a rush earlier and forgot proper protocol. My apologies. Welcome to Wellington Acres."

"Thank you."

A beat passed.

From the kitchen, the piano arrangement of "Jingle Bells" had morphed into a medley of "We Need A Little Christmas."

He was staring at her. Or rather, she was staring at him. Why hadn't she bothered to brush out her hair after her shower? When her hair dried naturally, it spun into a mass of curls.

He flicked a glance toward the kitchen, then her. "I love jazz piano music," he said.

"Me too. My sister plays piano. Or rather, she wants to learn how to play."

He rested an elbow on the back of the sofa, along the quilted leather upholstery. "I play."

"Piano? Really? I wondered when I saw the gorgeous Steinway in your living room."

This ruggedly handsome man had an artsy side she hadn't expected.

"So, we have something in common," he said. "The piano."

She pondered pointing out how much of a comparison stretch that was. He played a real piano, a glossy nine-foot concert grand. Her sister pretended her desk was a keyboard.

"Weren't you busy tonight?" Her gaze flicked toward the door. "What about your appointment in town?"

"I canceled it. I'll meet with my investors in the morning."

"So you'd like to come inside?"

"I am inside. If I'm invited, I'll stay."

"It's your apartment." She started for the kitchen while he tugged off his parka and placed it on a chair. She glanced over her shoulder. "How's your sister?"

"Sleeping." He followed her. "Since the concussion, she's susceptible to headaches and requires a lot of rest. Now she goes to bed at the time she used to go out partying."

"Thanks to the information the agency provided, I read up on her case."

"Then you know that because she's in her early twenties, the doctor confirmed she should recover quickly. Youth is a great healer."

Chiara looked up just in time to see an unexpected emotion pass across his face. Sadness? Contemplation? She couldn't identify it.

"I'm protective of my little sister," she offered into the silence. "Apparently so are you, and I understand completely."

She took a breath when he didn't respond. "I was brewing tea, although sparkling water sounds … refreshing." She reached for two glasses in the cupboard, then motioned toward the counter. "I brought the last batch of Christmas cookies I baked the other day. Do you want any?"

"Cookies?" He grinned. "Now I'm even happier I canceled my appointment tonight."

Why was he here? From what he'd said, he was beyond busy.

He flooded their glasses with water and brought them into the living room. She trailed with her container of cookies and set them on the coffee table.

They perched on either end of the deep-buttoned sofa, sinking into the smooth leather. She kept her hands on her lap, her feet on the floor.

Sitting on a sofa with a man. She hadn't done anything like that in ages.

"Tell me more about Kansas." He reached for a cookie, closed his eyes and chewed appreciatively.

"Well, I lived there all my life, until I moved to Virginia. Our snowfalls around the holidays are lovely, and that's one of the things I miss most."

"And soon you're flying back."

"Finally."

He was quiet before grabbing another cookie. "These are heavenly."

"Thanks. It's a simple recipe, compliments of my mom's Christmas cookie collection."

"My family never celebrated Christmas."

"So you never attended church services?"

"Very rarely."

"You're a musician. At Christmas, the music is awe-inspiring, especially if there's a full choir and an organist."

He shrugged, and she couldn't tell if he didn't care or if he had learned not to care. And why had she asked him such personal questions, about religion and music?

"We just never attended," he said. "Too swamped with the ranch and my parents traveling far and wide."

"I'll be happy to bake one of my favorite cookie recipes with your sister and bring a little

Christmas cheer into your lives. That is, if you're interested."

The melody from the other room had definitely inspired her.

He gazed at her for an interminable moment and then smiled. "I'm very interested."

A shiver of attraction raced through her. Quickly, she changed the subject. "And yes, to answer your earlier question, I love Kansas."

"I've never been."

"You need to go. People expect *The Wizard Of Oz* and tornadoes, but Kansas is so much more. Our motto is Ad Astra per Aspera."

"To the stars with difficulty." He translated the Latin. "But what does that really mean?"

"Honestly, I don't know." She chuckled. "What about you? What about your work?"

"Besides the ranch and ensuring my sister gets better, I'm developing a computer app."

"I applaud anyone who's skillful with computers. I can turn my laptop on and off. If anything goes wrong, I've got the Geek Squad on speed dial. What's your app about?"

He was quiet. The music coming from the kitchen had changed to a violin rendition of "O Little Town Of Bethlehem."

"It's a dating app," he finally replied.

"A dating app." She caught herself before she

gaped. Certainly, he hadn't made the app for himself. With his good looks and easy charm, he probably had more dates in a month than she'd had in her twenty-five years. "Does your app have a name?"

"Vulcan."

"Vulcan?" She paused. "As in *Star Trek?*"

"In Roman mythology, Vulcan is sometimes referred to as cupid's father."

She quirked an eyebrow.

"Sometimes, not always." He smiled. "So we ran with that idea and our slogan will be 'An outer-space love,' and will feature a cherub aiming a bow and arrow toward the sky."

Really? *Really?* She couldn't imagine any woman subscribing to a dating app with that name and philosophy.

"What about the name Cupid's bow?" she asked.

"I like that." He shrugged. "Too late to change anything now, though."

Wisely, she grabbed her water and took a big gulp, keeping her thoughts to herself. "Oh, well, good luck."

"Thanks, I'll need it." He flashed her a smile, displaying even white teeth. "There's lots of competition in the computer world these days."

She sincerely doubted he needed luck with anything. He was much too self-assured. Competency fairly oozed from his strong shoulders.

"Enough about me." He picked up his glass. "What about you?"

"Most likely, you know more about me than I do, thanks to my agency's profile."

"Tell me anyway."

She wrapped her hands around her glass. "After years of course work and studying, I'm officially a licensed RN."

He chewed another cookie, swallowed a half glass of water. "Officer Bennington said you were exceptionally competent at the accident scene."

"I enjoy helping people. It's what I'm trained for and what I do best."

He shifted closer, lifted his glass to hers and clinked. "Cheers. To Kansas and helping people and Christmas cookies."

"And to your sister's quick recovery and to—to Vulcan."

"Absolutely." He set his glass on the table, then fixed his hands to his knees. "Thanks for a relaxing evening. Unfortunately, work beckons and I should go."

She accompanied him to the door and handed him her coat. "Thank you for the sparkling water."

"You're welcome." He shrugged into his parka. "I'll see you tomorrow."

"Don't you have appointments with investors, and the ranch, and—"

"If you recall," he said, grinning, "I live here. I'll make time. Maybe we can have dinner together."

Wait. No. She wasn't the type of woman to have a casual fling with her employer. She was leaving Virginia soon. Hadn't he listened when she told him about her intent to return to Kansas?

"Why?" she asked hesitantly.

"You do eat, don't you?"

"Yes, but—"

"So, we'll have dinner. Gertrude dines early, and I'm usually done working by seven."

"No, really, I'll be—"

"Chiara." He touched her arm. "You want to bring a little Christmas cheer into my life, remember?"

Vance kept his gaze on the enchanting woman sitting across from him in his living room. Chiara was perched on the edge of a silk-embroidered settee while Gertrude sat in her wheelchair. The two women leaned closer to each other, studying Gertrude's medical record, their serious conversation punctuated by bursts of laughter.

Speaking in a kind voice yet firmly, Chiara paged through the report, confirming all the doctor's instructions. She added at the end, "The doctor will determine when it's safe to begin light physical activity."

"Yes, yes, I know all that." Gertrude waved a hand dismissively. "But I'd do anything to get out of this wheelchair."

"You will. Your equilibrium is still shaky," Vance put in. He was comfortably seated in his wingback chair in front of the cheerful fire in the fireplace. He'd been checking emails on his tablet, but found his attention kept veering to Chiara.

Gertrude slumped back. "I miss seeing Joe and riding Licorice."

"There are two good reasons why you should stay right here in this house while you heal," he said.

Chiara opened her mouth, apparently to dispute him, and he held up a hand. "My sister has trouble setting boundaries, Chiara. One minute she'll be at the stable, the next she'll be riding her horse at a gallop around the widest curve. You've known Gertrude for a half hour. I've known her my entire life."

Chiara smiled at him. "You're right. I'm sorry to intrude."

He smiled back, his gaze shifting to his sister, then Chiara. She set the medical instructions aside and asked Gertrude about the book, *The Horse Whisperer*. Apparently, she'd seen the movie and loved it, although Gertrude was claiming the Robert Redford movie and the book were totally different.

Annoyed his cell phone had pinged a half dozen

times, Vance checked the latest text from one of his tech developers.

I said I'll be at the office by ten, he replied.

He loosened his tie and stretched out his long legs. He intended to stay right where he was for as long as he could, sitting across from Chiara, admiring her lovely face and easy laugh.

The previous evening, he hadn't known what to expect when she showed up at his door with a police officer. He couldn't remember what she wore except for her blood-stained coat.

However, when she'd arrived a half hour ago, he'd caught his breath as he took her lightweight jacket.

"This is not warm enough for December," he'd said.

"All I have," she'd replied, shrugging.

"I'll take your other coat to the dry cleaners today."

"Yes. You told me last night. Thanks." She met his gaze. "Is anything wrong?"

"No. Why?"

"You're staring at me."

"You look lovely." She wore a slim-fitting black skirt and blue turtleneck sweater. That shapely figure. He'd be thinking about her all day while he met with his investors and programmers. Even more captivating than her slender form, her expressive green eyes fascinated him.

His sister had been waiting for Chiara since dawn, her new early-to-bed-early-to-rise schedule prompting her to drink a first cup of coffee with him before he left for the stable to begin chores. When he brought Chiara into the living room, Gertrude had asked her if she'd had breakfast. "We've got coffee and croissants."

"I ate, thanks," Chiara answered. "The loft is certainly well-equipped. Someone thought of everything—right down to bread, milk, and butter."

"All because of Vance. He's a planner," Gertrude said.

Chiara offered him a smile. "I'm a planner too."

"So we have something else in common."

Her smile widened.

She was a beautiful woman, and when she smiled, she was stunning. Her creamy skin glowed, and her curly blond hair framed her heart-shaped face.

Gertrude swept her hand toward the buffet table, where there was a coffee pot and porcelain cups, as well as a selection of croissants. "Coffee?"

"Thank you. I'd love some."

"I'll get it," Vance said. "Cream, sugar?"

"Just black."

Chiara accepted the cup and turned to Gertrude as Vance settled in his wingback chair with his tablet, intending to catch up on tech news while the women talked. But Chiara's first comment caught his attention.

"Tell me about your life before you were confined to a wheelchair."

"You mean last month?"

Chiara grinned. "Go as far back as you're comfortable."

Gertrude clasped her hands. "Brace yourself." She revealed her tumultuous teenage years and the older man she ran away with when she was eighteen. Chiara's expression was accepting, non-judgmental, but Vance was stunned his sister held nothing back.

"And now my excitement every day is trying to decide what to eat for lunch," Gertrude finished.

"All that will change as you get better." Chiara picked up the medical report and began going through Gertrude's injuries and what she needed to do to get better. Now the two women were talking books, Gertrude offering to loan Chiara *The Horse Whisperer* when she was done.

"What are you reading next?" Chiara asked.

Gertrude shrugged. "I've never been much of a reader. I mostly read mysteries. Can you recommend anything?"

"I like mysteries too. Have you read Agatha Christie's short story Christmas collection?"

"No, but I'd be willing to give it a try."

"I used to attend a book club in town with a former classmate." Chiara finished her coffee and set her cup on the side table. "Why don't we create our own book club, and every day we'll discuss the chapters we've read."

"How fun!" Gertrude's smile was one of pure pleasure. "Finally, something to do in this big house until I can get to the stable."

"What's the name of the Agatha Christie book?" Vance interrupted. "When I go to town, I'll stop at the library."

"*The Adventure of the Christmas Pudding,*" Chiara said. "Get two copies."

"You better write it down, Vance. Otherwise you'll forget." Gertrude curved to Chiara, raising her eyebrows. "For such a brilliant man, he overlooks the littlest details. He says he can multitask, although it's been proven humans can't focus on more than one thing at a time."

"I'm right here." Vance's teasing voice roused a grin from both women. "And I can easily multitask."

As proof, he was focusing on Chiara while replying to his sister.

"Nobody can multitask. It's a myth," Gertrude

replied. "But if you're happy being delusional, it's up to you."

Chiara kept her gaze on Gertrude and ignored Vance. "We can bake my mother's sugar cookies too. They're delicious."

"The same cookies I tasted last night?" Vance asked.

"The very same." Chiara's expression grew wistful. "My sister and I bake all sorts of cookies in Kansas."

"I've never been to Kansas," Gertrude said.

"It's wonderful." Chiara's voice had a catch to it, but when she looked at them both, she brightened. "But we weren't talking about Kansas, we were discussing cookies, and we can't have a book club without serving desserts."

"And wine?" Vance suggested.

Chiara regarded him with amusement. "Or tea."

"Wine is better."

For a beat, their laughing gazes held.

"Wine and homemade cookies are the perfect pairing," Gertrude said decidedly, then signaled to Vance to pour them all another round of coffee.

Compliant, he pushed to his feet. His sister's needs always came first.

"Gertrude, do you know if you have all the ingredients for cookies?" Chiara asked. "This recipe calls for several cups of sugar and flour."

"The kitchen is on your left." Gertrude pointed to the foyer. "I'm not much of a cook, but Amanda can show you what's in the cupboards."

"I'll only be a minute." Chiara left for the kitchen.

"So, Vance." His sister gave him a deliberate, knowing smile as he passed her a fresh cup of coffee. "For a busy guy, you certainly slowed your pace this morning."

His own smile was bland. "I wanted to be sure Chiara was a good fit for you."

"And for you?"

Ignoring her, he walked over to the buffet table and chose a strawberry croissant.

Why was Gertrude always so preoccupied with his dating status? She seemed convinced that if she couldn't find happiness and true love, then surely he could. And she might be right ... a few years down the road. Certainly not in the near future. Besides, he desired the kind of love and marriage that would last forever. And children, none of which had happened on his first go 'round.

He took a bite of croissant before turning back to her.

"Vance, you don't have to answer, but I saw the way you look at Chiara. You can't keep your eyes off her."

"Girl talk is so compelling," he joked. He took

another bite of the croissant and glanced toward the foyer. "I'll take Chiara's coat to the dry cleaners today."

"Wow, you certainly mastered the art of changing the subject." When he didn't respond, Gertrude studied him. Her jaw was set, never a good sign. "If you married, your wife would help you with those types of errands."

"You're joking, right? I need a wife to bake me sugar cookies"—he gestured toward the kitchen—"and handle dry-cleaning duties?"

"You're my brother. I saw how happy you were when you were married."

"Yes, for the first five minutes, until I realized Shanna and I weren't suited and she couldn't be trusted."

"All happening years ago." Gertrude leaned forward. "And if it makes any difference, I'm back at Wellington Acres for good. For your own sake, ask someone else to shoulder some of the burdens of running our ranch."

"I can get everything done, and I've learned to rely on no one but myself."

"I'd like to begin dating again." Deeply, Gertrude inhaled. "Joe Brown is—"

Vance shook his head. "No."

As soon as he spoke, he caught the flicker of determination in Gertrude's eyes. He'd also seen the way her expression softened whenever Joe's name was mentioned.

Did he truly have the right to dictate who his sister should or shouldn't date? Of course not. It was just that she had made so many mistakes involving men, and he chose to protect her from making any more.

His practical mind argued that if she was finally settled, he could open himself up again. Somewhere inside, he realized his life had been empty for a long, long time.

Nope. Nope. He didn't have precious minutes to turn into a deep-thinking sort of guy. Days were busy and complicated enough, and he was already stretched in too many directions. He had no mental or emotional capacity left for another responsibility.

In his brief marriage, he'd learned that a woman could be an obligation as opposed to a life-long companion and partner.

Chiara, the primary topic of conversation, reentered the room.

"We're all set, Gertrude," she said. "Amanda showed me the ingredients and we can bake the cookies this afternoon."

Gertrude's eyes gleamed, her grin wide. He'd

seen a similar expression years ago, when she turned twelve and their parents had gifted her with a sleek black horse for her birthday.

He voiced his remembrance aloud.

It was all the prompting Gertrude needed. She swiveled to Chiara and launched into a detailed description of her twelfth birthday, leading up to the excitement of realizing Licorice was truly hers.

Chiara walked over to the picture window, where the winter sun streamed in. She pushed back the heavy draperies, exposing a bright winter morning. In the distance was the stable.

"How many horses do you own?" she asked.

"A dozen, if you count the horses we board." Vance glanced at his wristwatch. He absolutely had to leave for town in five minutes to be on time for his investors meeting. But five minutes was five minutes. "Do you like horses?"

She turned and grinned. "I've never gotten close enough to one to say. Although my sister Emma will be over the moon when I tell her. She'll ask for all the details of each and every horse."

"I'll be tied up the next few days, but by this weekend I should be able to carve out some free time to take you down to the stable."

Another enchanting grin. "I'd like to see the property."

She was so pretty, so engaged in life. Certainly,

she wasn't like the women he'd dated since his marriage ended. He'd been satisfied with brief connections. With Chiara, he wanted more than brief.

Now why had that thought occurred to him?

And why was he staring at her again?

"How old is Emma?" he asked.

A proud smile crossed Chiara's face. "Nine. And she loves new adventures, although she sometimes plunges in headlong without thinking things through."

"Sounds familiar." Vance threw a pointed look at Gertrude.

Gertrude dismissed him with a shrug. "Nine years old is such a fun age," she said to Chiara. "Why doesn't Emma come for a visit while you're here?"

Chiara blinked. "Well, for one thing, she's in Kansas. Plus she has school and—"

"She can fly here on a weekend."

"No really, I couldn't afford—"

"We insist." Gertrude half-rose. "And I wouldn't invite her if I expected you to pay the plane fare."

"I can't accept. I'm sorry."

It struck Vance that Chiara was too proud to consent to anything she considered charity.

"This is a working ranch," he put in. "Emma can help me in the stable."

"That way," Gertrude said, pushing her wheelchair to the window, "she can get to know Licorice and Peppermint and the other horses. And there's an indoor riding ring we hardly ever use. We even have an old sleigh."

At Chiara's uplifted eyebrows, Vance explained, "Years ago, when our grandparents were alive, part of our acreage was a Christmas tree farm. They offered sleigh rides, and they even had a pavilion set up where they served food."

"And yet there's no sign of Christmas anywhere," Chiara said softly.

"No. We've never celebrated Christmas."

"Until now." Gertrude extended her arms and enveloped Chiara in a bear hug. "Thank you for coming," she whispered. "We're going to be good friends, I just know it." She leaned back. "And as your friend, I would like your sister to come visit."

Chiara hesitated and then said she would talk to her parents about it.

Vance smiled and took one more look at his watch. Saying he had to go, he strode into the foyer. Chiara's enthusiasm for a book club and holiday baking, accompanied by her firm recommendation to his sister to adhere to the doctor's orders, gave him a sense of encouragement. Gertrude would experience a day filled with laughter, and he could get back to work with a peace of mind he hadn't felt in quite a while.

And if he'd stayed longer than he'd intended, it was only to be certain Chiara worked out, he rationalized. After all, she was the new caregiver for his sister, the most important person in his life.

But somehow he knew it was more. There was a pull, an appeal that drew him to her. It was more than her friendliness, her sweet charm, her quiet grace. Sure, that was some of it, but the simple truth was, he was attracted to her.

He also appreciated that, just as he was devoted to Gertrude, Chiara's green eyes had glowed with love whenever she mentioned her sister, Emma.

He'd been surprised when Gertrude had extended an invitation for Emma to visit, and even more surprised when Chiara said she'd talk to her parents about it.

It would be wonderful to have a child in the house, Vance thought.

He had always wanted children, although it wasn't in God's plans for him.

He grabbed Chiara's stained coat, started to open the door, and then strode back into the living room at the conclusion of one of Gertrude's long-winded stories, this time about how horseback riding was a true sport and how extensive competition training was.

"What was the name of that library book

again?" he asked. Yes, so okay, his sister was right. He'd forgotten.

Gertrude gave a hoot of laughter.

"It's *A Christmas Carol*," Chiara, said, "and the main character is Ebenezer Scrooge." She winked at him. "Just kidding."

CHAPTER 5

On a late afternoon three days later, the scents of vanilla and spices welcomed Vance as he walked into the kitchen. Chiara had brought small touches of Christmas to the room, trimming the glass sugar bowl and creamer with greenery and red berries. She'd even tied a velvet ribbon to the polished nickel globe hanging from the ceiling.

In fact, there was a touch of Christmas in his home wherever he looked. A fresh pine wreath strung with clear lights covered the entryway door, magically appearing the day after Chiara arrived. Groupings of red candles, circled by preserved leaves, sat on the stone fireplace's mantel. There was also a majestic Christmas tree in the living room that Chiara had picked out, with Gertrude's

Facetiming guidance, at a farm near them. It had been delivered and set up while he was writing computer code in town, and the tree shimmered with silver tinsel and gold and blue bulbs.

And music, always music. At the moment, the Vienna Boys Choir was singing "O Christmas Tree" in German, the music coming from her cell phone propped on a shelf.

The combination of familiar melodies and festive colors, the blends of cloves and cinnamon, filled his heart with a sentiment he couldn't describe.

Chiara and Gertrude sat at the kitchen table, chortling, their heads bent over a printed recipe. "—and you can see where my mother made some alterations," Chiara was saying. Smiling, she glanced up at him. "Hi, Vance."

"Good to see everyone so cheerful," he said.

Their laughter was contagious, and he chuckled along with them. The comfortable warmth of the kitchen made his body relax.

"Chiara, here's your coat." He lifted her cream-colored coat, wrapped in a thin clear-coated plastic dry-cleaners bag. "You'll be pleased to know the blood stains came out."

"Thank you." She gazed across the table at him. "We haven't seen much of you lately. Have you been extra busy?"

Had she missed him? he wondered. He had certainly missed her. He thought about her when he was in meetings, when he was at the stable, when he was in his SUV, his mind always drifting to the same question: How would it feel to kiss her?

She certainly was a temptation, although he knew he should resist. He wasn't ready for a commitment, and Chiara wasn't the sort of woman a man could kiss and walk away from. In his experience, people always let him down. True love didn't exist, at least not for him.

He tugged off his coat. His silk tie and suit jacket came next. It was good to be home.

"I've been tied up in endless meetings," he said. He hung the dry-cleaners bag by the door, then rested his arm on the back of Chiara's chair.

"Always hectic, big brother," Gertrude said. He'd been so preoccupied with Chiara, he'd neglected to say hello to his sister.

"And how are your headaches today, Gertrude?" he asked. "You look well."

"Better and better, thanks. Chiara is keeping me busy between my naps." Gertrude held up a hand. "And before you ask, I'm following the doctor's orders to a tee. Chiara is a diligent nurse."

"Excellent." Vance steepled his fingers and blew out a sigh. The beta testing for his dating app was going well, the ranch might actually turn a profit this month, and his sister was absorbed and happy.

He opened his mouth to ask if the women needed baking assistance, but they were managing well without him—discussing using less sugar, the baking time for chocolate chip cookies, and the benefits of whole wheat versus white flour.

During the next fifteen minutes, he attempted to make small talk but got very little response.

Finally, Gertrude drummed her fingers on the table. "Vance, can't you see we're busy?"

Chiara smiled up at him. "We didn't mean to ignore you. I made wassail."

That smile. He loved her entrancing smile.

"I thought I smelled cinnamon and apples along with all those other wonderful smells," he said.

"Do you want some?" She nodded to a pan simmering on the stove.

"Sure. It's cold in those horse stalls." He rubbed his hands together. The kitchen certainly wasn't cold with the oven blasting, but at least he had her attention.

Getting up, she took a mug from the glass-fronted cabinet and ladled him a steaming cup.

He snatched a handful of cookies from the mound piled high on a gold-speckled platter. "Not that I don't love sugar," he said between mouthfuls, "but what will we do with all these cookies?"

"We'll freeze a couple dozen for Christmas," Chiara said, "and I'll take some back to my apartment. The rest I'll distribute to the homeless shelter when I'm there on Sunday."

She volunteered at a homeless center too. He was impressed, because, well, everything about her was impressive.

"Did you eat dinner yet?" she asked.

"Nothing since breakfast. What about you two?"

"We made tomato soup and toasted cheese sandwiches," Gertrude said.

He touched Chiara's hand. "There's a Christmas-tree-lighting ceremony tonight in the town center. Would you ladies like to accompany me?"

"Vance, we've lived here all our lives and we've never gone to a tree-lighting ceremony," Gertrude said.

"Is that a yes, Gertrude?"

"Actually, it's a no. Amanda and I are watching *A Holiday Engagement* tonight on television. The movie is a romance and I've never seen it. And be honest, Vance." Laughter flickered in her dark eyes. "You would prefer to take only Chiara so you can be alone with her."

He laughed—as usual, his sister was right—but Chiara's alarmed gaze shot to his face.

Trying to keep his voice normal, he said, "When

a man wants a woman's company, there's no reason to pretend otherwise. Chiara, will you join me at the tree-lighting ceremony in town this evening?" He hoped he didn't betray how much it meant to him if she agreed.

Stillness reigned for a beat, cut short by the rhythmic ticking of the wall clock.

"Well, there's one more batch of cookies left to bake," Chiara said. "What time is the tree lighting?"

"Eight o'clock."

She glanced at the clock. "I should get back to the loft. I planned to do some reading."

"Can't your reading wait one more day? I'm sure Agatha Christie won't mind. Besides, the tree-lighting is only once a year."

"When you put it that way ..." A grin broke across her face. "Actually, I've never seen it in all the time I've lived here."

"As I passed by the town square, food trucks were lining up. We can grab a bite to eat there too." He refilled his mug with more wassail and turned to Gertrude. "You'll be okay?"

"I'm twenty-two years old, and Amanda is here." She slid the mound of cookies toward herself and grabbed a few. "You can just leave these here."

* * *

Two hours later, Chiara and Vance were buckled in his SUV with the windows rolled up and the defroster on high. Night fell quickly in December, and the winter air bit through Chiara's freshly cleaned coat. For warmth, she also wore her patent-leather boots and a heavy sweater, and she wished she had thought to wrap a scarf around her neck. On impulse, she had pulled her blonde curls straight up and back, tying her hair at the crown with a red velvet ribbon, the same color as her sweater and boots. After all, it was Christmastime.

Vance wore his usual graphite gray parka and work boots. A white T-shirt and navy sweater peeked from his neckline. He'd gone to the stable beforehand, then showered, changing his stable clothes and mucking boots for a pair of laced-up chukkas and clean pair of jeans.

She glanced at him admiringly. Those dark wash jeans fit his muscular legs to perfection.

He started driving down the long driveway of Wellington Acres. In the distance, a full moon and sprinkling of stars played off the glossy surface of the pond. With temperatures below freezing, the pond was beginning to ice over. Vast fields took on the appearance of rutted brown in the moonlight, the pastures enclosed by visible fencing.

"Do you bring the horses in at night?" she asked.

"It depends on the horse because each is different. Joe and I monitor them every day. If their winter coat isn't coming through as much as we think it ought, then we'll bring them into the stable."

"So some horses stay outside?"

"Yes, and we rug them."

At her questioning glance, he explained, "A horse blanket. It keeps the horse protected from the elements and wind."

"Do horses get cold?"

"If they're in a shelter, they can tolerate temperatures of up to minus forty degrees. Between eighteen and fifty-nine degrees is most comfortable, though."

"You know a lot about horses. And computers. And Gertrude said you're brilliant at finance." Chiara tried to keep her tone matter-of-fact, but he looked so handsome, so well-built and strong, it was hard to keep the awe from her voice. "That's quite a bit of knowledge for one man."

"Thanks," he drawled in teasing amusement. "You're pretty incredible yourself." He paused and studied her for a moment. "You know, exchanging compliments always go better with a—" He slowed the SUV, the headlights sweeping over the expansive pasture land.

Then he put it in park and bent his head.

Surely he wouldn't kiss her before they were even out of his driveway, she thought. Surely she should draw away, not shift closer and raise her head in blatant invitation.

A horse's whinny interrupted them, and they both looked up to see a white horse had trotted close to the fence, not far from Chiara's window.

Vance drew back and grinned at the horse. "Hello, Peppermint."

Chiara turned to peer out the window. "I saw that horse the day I arrived."

"She's an older mare and should be foaling sometime this spring." He shut off the engine. "Do you want to meet her?"

"Sure, although I've never been up close to a horse before."

He came around to open the door for her, then laced his fingers with hers as if it was the most natural thing in the world. Together, their boots crunched on frozen ground as they approached the fence. Overhead, the full moon sailed in a bright clear sky.

The promise of new life, the hope of the holiday, and holding hands with this handsome man who took her breath away filled her with happiness.

"Is it okay to pet a pregnant horse?" she asked as they approached the fence.

Wow, now that was a genius question.

"I wouldn't advise it," Vance said, "unless you want to turn into a pony."

She laughed out loud. There was something about him, the way his grin disarmed her coupled with his wry sense of humor. She didn't understand why her heart fluttered every time he looked at her.

Or maybe she did.

"Peppermint likes to have her ears rubbed," he instructed. "Don't be afraid to stroke her strongly."

The horse held her head high, her ears forward. She nickered softly while Chiara stroked her, then sniffed Vance's coat pocket, investigating.

"She loves peppermints," he explained. He fished a round candy out of his pocket and offered it to the horse. Gently, he stroked her muzzle, whispering to Peppermint as he fed her the candy.

Chiara's heart melted at the sight of his gentleness with the pregnant mare. How could she resist a man who was so kindhearted around animals?

"Thus her name is Peppermint," Vance was saying. "Not the most ingenious name in the world, but it fits." He popped a candy into his mouth, then offered Chiara one, which she accepted.

Back in his SUV, they buckled their seat belts, and he switched on the heated seats.

Chiara snuggled into the warm leather and

glanced at his profile. Well-defined nose and chin, sharp cheekbones, a dark stubble on his jaw. Yes, an extraordinarily attractive man, like a young Clint Eastwood.

As they neared the main road and the metal gate opened, a bald, stocky man was leading a black horse to the stable. He waved as they passed.

"Licorice?" Chiara asked. "Gertrude's horse?"

"Yes."

"She's beautiful. And I know the man." She waved as they passed. "He's Joe Brown."

"Yes, Joe's the ranch manager."

"From what Gertrude has said, he's trustworthy and very dependable."

Gertrude had said plenty more, including how she believed she was in love with Joe. Chiara didn't share that part with Vance.

"My sister's biased opinion." Vance's features tightened. "But yes, Joe is outstanding at what he's paid exceedingly well to do."

Chiara felt a flicker of defensiveness. And although she attempted to overlook the family discord, Joe Brown obviously caused dissension between Gertrude and Vance. She stayed silent, preferring not to get in the middle of a family feud.

"So, how is work going? I mean, computer work," she asked, neatly navigating around the Joe Brown issue.

"I've designed the computer app and algorithms, identified the target group, and developed the prototype. Now the web developers are integrating appropriate analytics tools."

Her gaze widened. "You lost me at 'target group.'"

"Technical stuff." He flicked on his left blinker and eased onto the main highway to Turning Point. "We're well into beta testing. Care to volunteer?"

"No, no. I'm not good at relationships. I don't date much."

"Why would someone like you not date much?"

"What does that mean?" Her tone sharpened. "Someone like me?"

"Someone smart and beautiful and ... Are you dating anyone at all?"

"No, I'm not interested. Okay, I was, which is the reason why I moved here, but it was a huge mistake and I broke it off. I met the guy through an online dating service, by the way."

"What happened to you would never have happened with my app." He grinned. "I came up with the idea because I was tired of hearing about crude photos and distasteful comments. My app is for smart professionals."

"You're very enthusiastic when you talk about it." She offered an encouraging smile. "However, my perception of a dating app is tainted because of what happened to me." She blew out a breath. "However, three years later, I'm finally able to move back to Kansas City."

"Why?" Briefly, he angled toward her. "Are you going back for a Kansas City relationship?"

"I'm going back home. I told you. And I don't date much."

This conversation was a subject she didn't wish to discuss any longer. She switched on the radio, found her favorite oldies station, and experimented with just sitting back and surrendering to the prospect of a delightful evening.

He slowed when they entered the town and eased into a parking space a couple blocks from the square.

"I can drop you off if you don't want to walk," he offered.

"I don't mind. After all those cookies I ate today, a little walking is just the thing."

He parked, got out, and had her door open before she finished unbuckling her seat belt. He had that southern gentleman's character, standing when she entered a room, holding doors, waiting for her to finish speaking while he attentively listened.

"Thanks," she murmured, and stepped outside. The air was brisk, the assurance of snow in every breath she took.

But no. This was Virginia. It hardly ever snowed in Virginia.

Vance took her hand. His fingers were long, his grip firm yet gentle, his palm warm against her skin. It was odd, walking with him like this, like a typical man and woman on a date.

But no, this wasn't a date. It was a tree-lighting ceremony in *his* home town of Turning Point.

Sounds of Christmas rang through the streets. Children giggled and shouted as they raced and twirled; a gathering of teenage carolers sang an impromptu rendition of "The Twelve Days of Christmas." In front of the grocery store, a Salvation Army worker rang his bell, and Vance reached into his wallet to leave a sizable donation.

And the sights—multicolored lights strung along bare tree branches, shop windows adorned in silver stars and colorful garland. Art galleries occupied a side street, selling images of Turning Point at the turn of the century.

And the smells were enticing and irresistible. Hickory logs burned in outdoor wood pits, sweet breads and mince tarts—among many other delectable treats—were being served hot and fresh from a long line of food trucks.

When they approached the town square, the poignant melody of "Silent Night" brought memories of the first time she'd heard the song at a concert in Kansas City. She'd been five years old, and she had cried at the peaceful, soul-touching lyrics.

"The wonder of Christmas," her mother had murmured, taking Chiara's hand.

"Vance, wait. It's my favorite carol." Chiara paused, closing her eyes, inhaling, taking it all in. And tears welled again, just like when she was five. Why had she never perused this enchanting little town and its Yuletide atmosphere? Why had she never been aware of the goodness emanating from the kind residents greeting her with a cheerful smile?

When she opened her eyes, Vance was studying her, her lips, her face.

"This community brings Christmas to life," he said quietly. "I've never taken the time to appreciate it."

He echoed her thoughts, and she agreed. She was appreciating the picturesque town in a whole new way, perhaps because she was seeing it with different eyes and with Vance beside her.

"Should we buy something to eat?" He edged toward a fudge stand displaying creamy chocolate and maple fudge. Nearby, a food truck enticed customers with hamburgers sizzling on an outdoor grill.

"No, I'll wait for a cup of hot chocolate," she said. "What about you?"

"I'll grab hot chocolate and a pretzel farther down."

"You haven't eaten dinner."

A slow flame lit his dark gaze. "I have all I need."

Her heart gave a peculiar lurch. She wanted to tell him she felt the same, that in this moment, all was right in the world. Her thoughts scrambled, and she recognized the telltale warmth on her cheeks, betraying her emotions. Suddenly shy and unable to meet Vance's gaze, she focused on the rustic tavern located across the square, tiny white lights twinkling all around its exterior.

A thin man wearing glasses called out Vance's name.

Vance paused. "And there's one of my brilliant tech developers." He nodded toward the man signaling him, and let go of her hand. "I'll only be a minute."

They'd been holding hands, all this time.

As he walked off, Chiara heard a woman call her name.

She pivoted, delighted to see Adeline, her friend from the nursing agency. Adeline and Chiara were the same age and had shared the challenges of attending school while working. Despite Adeline's unconventional looks—this week, her shaggy hair was dyed a vivid shade of purple—she'd graduated at the top of the class. She was a voracious reader, thus the book club, although the rest of her life was a mystery. Some said she was a transplant from California, others mentioned Canada. At any rate, Adeline loved Turning Point and had declared it was the closest she'd ever come to a storybook town.

"I haven't seen you since we graduated," Adeline said. "Are you still volunteering at the homeless shelter? I'm there every Sunday." She raised her eyebrows, plucked to thin, arching lines, at Vance, who was talking intently with the tech.

"Yes, I missed a few weeks," Chiara said. "I've been busy moving, but I'll volunteer again. I'm working all month at Wellington Acres." She took a step nearer the fudge stand. "It's a ranch a little way out of town."

"The fancy place on the hill with the black metal gate and horse engravings? I always admired that property."

"It's just as beautiful on the inside. My position is live-in, and I'm staying in a loft apartment above the garage. It's a big rent savings for me this month."

"And who's the gorgeous guy you're with?"

"Vance Thatcher. He's my employer."

"Oh really?"

"His sister is my patient. Why are you grinning at me like that?"

"I just don't remember ever holding hands with any of my employers." Adeline shrugged. "Of course, if they were that drop-dead handsome … Oh my. Take a look at him."

That was all she seemed to do, Chiara thought. Look at him, think about him. And yet, he was the textbook example of the wrong man for her. He was her rich boss who lived in Virginia, a state she couldn't wait to get out of.

Or not? Sometimes she thought about staying, but that was ridiculous. Her heart belonged in Kansas.

She noted Adeline was studying her. "Before you ask," she said, "we're just friends."

"Is he single?"

"Yes."

"Uh huh. And last I checked, so are you. Is he the reason you haven't attended book club? We meet there every Friday night at seven o'clock, rain or shine." Adeline pointed to the Turning Point Hotel.

"I told you, I've been busy," Chiara reminded with a laughing look. "So, what are you reading?"

"Currently nothing." Adeline chuckled. "Right now, we're using the book club as an excuse to enjoy a night out with the girls. And there's a good band the hotel has hired called The Crestfallen, so we can indulge in a glass of wine and a whole lot of dancing."

"Sounds fun." Chiara grinned. "For now, I've created my own book club with Vance's sister."

"How old is she?"

"In her twenties. We get along great."

"Chiara, do you still want hot chocolate?" Vance had returned. "The stand is around the bend."

Chiara introduced the two of them, agreed to the hot chocolate, and Vance grabbed her hand and led her away as Chiara called good-bye.

"Don't worry about me, you two," Adeline called after them, giving Chiara a deliberate wink. "I only drink hot chocolate on cold winter nights when there's a tree-lighting ceremony. In the meantime, enjoy your evening."

Chiara could detect a delighted matchmaker from a mile away. Her mother had set up numerous blind dates for her, all for naught. Vance hadn't invited Adeline to join them and Adeline clearly took that as a good sign. She was like every other woman, tickled by the prospect Chiara had met a boyfriend.

Except Vance wasn't Chiara's boyfriend.

And wasn't it ironic he was launching a dating app?

Him, the buttoned-up executive by day, and rancher by night. A man who confused her at every turn because she never knew for certain when he was joking about his feelings and when he was serious.

And her, a woman who'd never experienced true love from a man and felt she was navigating unfamiliar terrain. Especially when her only serious relationship had been with a man she met through an online dating service.

That had been disastrous, and she couldn't see the point of online meet-ups. Wasn't it easier for singles to connect with other singles at social events like this one? When they met face-to-face, people recognized that the other person was a genuine human.

"There's quite a crowd here tonight," Vance was saying. He paid for a pretzel at one of the food trucks and then stacked his plate with four thick slices of maple fudge.

They waited in line for hot chocolate, then wended through the crush of people to a spot where they had a perfect view of the Christmas tree.

They savored and munched and shared, leaning against an ancient oak tree, waiting for the ceremony to begin.

And they talked. About his life in Virginia, about her life in Kansas.

Eventually, the eighteen-foot-tall Christmas

tree was lit amidst jubilant applause and a resident brass band performing "O Christmas Tree."

A gust of cold wind prompted her to shiver, and Vance put his arm around her. She snuggled into his warm hug, gladdened by the steady beating of his heart.

Nearly an hour later, when the ceremony was long over and the crowd had diminished to a trickle, when the band members were loading up their instruments and most of the food vendors were shutting down, they stayed in the square. It had a cozy, hometown atmosphere, a sense of timelessness.

Chiara sighed as she looked around once more. "Beautiful," she murmured.

One arm still firmly wrapped around her shoulders, he bent his head and kissed her forehead. "My thoughts exactly."

Her breath caught at the gentle caress. With effort, she focused on making conversation. "The town is presenting an entire month of holiday festivities," she said.

"They always do." His arm tightened when she stirred. "And a parade."

"I've never seen any of that." She leaned her head back and gazed up at him. "And it's my fault, always making excuses for how busy I am."

"Me too."

She didn't want the magic of the night to end, the flutters in her chest to subside. "Vance, thank you for bringing me here tonight. I loved it."

"So did I." Gentleness and desire smoldered in his dark eyes. Slowly, his lips grazed her temple, and then glided lower. "You are beautiful," he whispered, his soft breath warming her cheek. Both his arms encircled her, and his mouth moved over hers.

She molded closer to his muscular body. His lips tasted of chocolate and maple fudge and peppermint.

And he tasted delicious.

CHAPTER 6

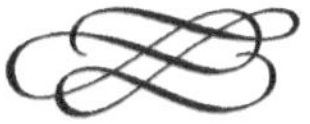

Another week went by, and Vance attended church services with her. The first time in ages, he declared, and she was heartened he was reestablishing a relationship with God.

The pastor's message was simple. God wasn't always going to give you something new. Sometimes the best thing God gave you was something you already had.

So true, she thought.

Vance clasped her hand and locked gazes with her. There was that connection again as if the words of the pastor had really spoken to him, in the same way they had resonated to her.

He seemed always in tune with her, with her thoughts, with her feelings.

Today, he wore a charcoal gray suit and black wool overcoat. Tall and handsome, he sang all the traditional hymns in his bass voice, belting the chorus of "Greensleeves" with enthusiasm. Her heart filled with gratitude, for the man, for God, for the charming town. Sure, she intended to move on, move away, although lately she couldn't remember why.

After service, Vance accompanied her to the homeless shelter on the next block. That was another thing she liked about Turning Point—everything was within walking distance. In Kansas City, where the population was over two million, people drove everywhere.

"Text me if you get done earlier than planned," Vance said as he left her. "In the meantime, I'll miss you." He drew her into a cuddle. His mouth hovered so close, his breath blended with hers.

She hesitated.

"This is the part where you're supposed to tell me you'll miss me too," he said.

"Vance, I'll see you again in less than three hours."

"And?"

She chuckled, knowing she should be truthful. "And I'll miss you."

His eyes glinted with an emotion she couldn't read. "Good."

With seeming reluctance, he released her. She stepped into the shelter, and he walked to his office around the corner.

Sitting in a volunteer planning meeting an hour later, after she distributed the sugar cookies she'd baked, she was thrown a curveball when Adeline slated her as the coordinator for the shelter's annual Christmas party. Complete with Santa Claus, Adeline declared. Which meant they had to find a man willing to play Santa.

After a few minutes of discussion, they decided on designating someone to play one of Santa's elves instead. There was an elf costume in the back room that hadn't been used for years.

Chiara pondered about asking Vance once she looked over the costume and determined it would fit him with minor alterations. However, he was over six feet tall and lean and certainly didn't claim a traditional elf physique. He already sported the hint of a beard, though, and a set of pointy ears, a pointy hat, and padding beneath a green velvet suit could work wonders. In addition, Chiara thought, Wellington Acres could host the shelter's Christmas party in the unused pavilion. She imagined a gingerbread event for the children, using graham crackers and white frosting and colorful candies. Renate, one of the volunteers at the center, had given her the instructions, which were easy enough for everyone to make their own. In addition, Santa's elf could tote a bag of candy canes to give to each child.

And there was a pond at Wellington Acres. Perhaps the kids could ice skate. The weather had turned cold, but as she mulled the idea, she quickly nixed it. Ice skating on a frozen pond could be dangerous if the ice cracked. The pond water was very deep.

"How does the Christmas party sound, Vance?" she asked after explaining the details to him.

He'd picked her up at the shelter, coming inside to introduce himself to the staff, talking and reading with the children, and then assisting with cleanup. To Chiara's and the director's delight, he contributed a substantial donation.

An hour passed before they left.

Dusk had darkened the sky, ever sooner these days as the shortest day of the year approached. Streams of multi-colored Christmas lights stretched across the roofs of homes and businesses.

He held her hand as they crossed the street to the other side of the square.

"I've never hosted a gingerbread house party," Vance said as they stepped up onto the brick sidewalk. "Or really any party."

"But you'll consider it? Someone suggested we

should start putting aside milk containers for the gingerbread houses."

"Good. I drink a lot of milk."

"A pint-size container is best. We'll also need canned frosting and candy and—"

His hand tightened around hers. "If making gingerbread houses brings a mile-wide smile to your face, I'll agree to just about anything."

His words sent little chills of excitement skittering up her spine. She struggled for a sharp, witty response but couldn't think of anything except *thank you.*

They continued their stroll, window-shopping as they progressed. Kiosks selling hot dogs and poinsettias and postcards of the town lined both sides of the square. Conversations from holiday shoppers weaved in between good-natured laughter, and children played near the impressive fountain in the center of the village green.

Never a town with factories, Turning Point had been founded by pioneers in the late 1700's. The colonial charm had been preserved to keep the character intact.

"How goes the development of your algorithms and coding and whatever else you tech guys do?" Chiara asked.

"Encouraging." He gestured to a stately brick

building. "I'd take you to see my office, but several techies are working out last-minute details and I'd rather not disturb them."

Vance fascinated her on so many levels. Not only was he content wearing jeans and work boots while shoveling out a horse stable, he was equally as comfortable in an office sporting a crisp white shirt and silk tie, or honing his computer tech skills.

She paused when they came to a quaint store called Charlie's Unique Gifts.

Chiara peered in the window, noting the local wares ranging from pottery to hand-made jewelry to sparkling scented candles.

"I'd like to stop in for a few minutes and browse," she said.

Vance nodded. "I should buy a gift for Gertrude. I've never bought her a holiday gift before, because we've never celebrated Christmas."

"Are you looking for anything special?" The pony-tailed shopkeeper, wearing jeans and a long-sleeved neon-green T-shirt, welcomed them from behind the cash register. Then he smiled at Chiara, staring appreciatively. "I'm Charlie, gorgeous. Who are you?"

"My name is Chiara."

"Very pleased to meet you, Chiara." He pushed

up the sleeves of his shirt. His right arm displayed a colorful tattoo of the moon and stars.

"You own the store?" Vance asked. "I've never shopped in here before."

"Yes, going on five years," Charlie replied. His gold earring glinted in the fluorescent lighting.

"How about jewelry for her, Vance?" Chiara picked up a flowered necklace. "Although I imagine Gertrude's not a bling type of woman. She's more of a tomboy."

"That she is," Vance agreed, turning to the shop-keeper. "Do you have anything with horses?"

"There's a horse book in the back of the shop." Charlie meandered through the cluttered store to a dusty bin of books, poked through the pile, then pulled out a hardcover book entitled, *How To Think Like A Horse.* "How's this? And we gift wrap at no extra charge."

"My sister doesn't need that book," Vance said. "She probably wrote it."

With a chuckle, Chiara wandered over to a mix-and-match display table. "Vance, look at this." She held up a bronze sculpture of a woman hugging a horse. It was called "Mutual Affection." "It's perfect. Your sister has such a strong bond with Licorice."

Vance agreed and Charlie wrapped the gift in an old-fashioned reindeer-print wrapping paper and tied it with a burlap string. He stamped a gold label on top that read "Charlie's Unique Gifts."

"Advertising," he joked with a half shrug, and handed the wrapped gift to Vance.

As they were leaving the shop, Chiara dawdled over a large Christmas snow globe on a display shelf. The globe portrayed Turning Point's town square, complete with miniaturized shops and the Turning Point Hotel.

Vance watched as she reached for the globe and ran her fingers over the polished edges. "It's heavy!" she exclaimed as she picked it up. Vigorously shaking it, the white particles and silver glitter churned and whirled. "And it's musical." She wound the shimmering gold base and the globe played "Silent Night." She listened, smiling all the while, the melody chiming to the sound of carillon bells. With a reluctant sigh, she placed the globe back on the display stand.

"Your favorite carol," Vance remarked, holding the shop door open for her as they exited. "And I'm surprised Charlie didn't wrap the globe and gift it to you for walking into his store."

She laughed. "Don't be ridiculous. He was just being friendly."

"A little too friendly, if you ask me."

They walked for a while in silence, her hand entwined in his.

"You remembered my favorite carol?" she asked. "Why would you remember something like that about me?"

"You know why."

Right there in the middle of the square, he drew her into his arms and kissed her.

She hesitated for a moment, then wound her hands around his nape. His jet-black hair was thick and silky, his chest warm and hard. "Vance, we shouldn't," she whispered. "We're in full view of the entire town."

"Are we?" He threw a glance over his shoulder, then kissed her again. "No one is concerned with us. They're busy doing last-minute shopping."

She grinned and yielded to the tenderness of his kisses.

Infinite minutes later, he lifted his head. "My app should be ready by next week," he said. "And then I'll have more time to spend with you."

"Then you'll just need to deal with the ranch, and running the estate, and ..." Her voice trailed off. Wow, that hadn't come out right. *Just?* The man practically worked around the clock.

"Thank you for being a perfect nurse," he said. "You've enabled me to concentrate on my app, and I've never seen Gertrude so happy. I feared she was going to go stir-crazy because she can't go to the stable."

"We went soon after I arrived. Didn't she tell you?"

"No." He stepped back. "Was Joe there?"

"Yes, of course. He brought his truck up to the house so Gertrude didn't have to contend with the wheelchair, although she rarely uses it anymore. From what I've observed, she's recovered from the concussion and her ankle is healing nicely."

Vance was silent as he guided her to his SUV, helped her in and then slid into the driver's seat. She felt the heat of his body, the solid strength of his arm as it brushed against hers.

"The weatherman is forecasting a cold front and freezing rain this evening," he said, as he turned his key in the ignition.

So, the conversation about Joe was finished, she thought. "Then it's best we get back before the weather turns," she said aloud.

"I meant to ask how you recognized Joe in the pasture on the night of the tree lighting." Vance kept his gaze on the windshield. His fingers tightened around the steering wheel. "Now I know why."

So the conversation regarding Joe wasn't finished.

Vance seemed entirely put off whenever Joe was mentioned. However, Vance was her employer, so she couldn't not tell him that Gertrude had gone to the stable. And besides, there was nothing to hide. It wasn't like Gertrude and Joe were doing anything wrong. They were simply in love. Sure, there was an age difference, but so what?

She settled into the luxurious leather seat as they headed out of town and didn't respond to his comment about how she'd recognized Joe. Instead, she madly searched for another subject.

"Gertrude booked Emma's flight into Richmond," she finally said. "I haven't seen you long enough to go over all the details."

"That will change, remember?"

She hoped that was true. She hoped to spend as much time with him as possible before returning to Kansas.

"So, is it okay about Emma?" she asked. "I realize you're paying for her flight."

"I'm more than happy to pay and can't wait to meet her. So yes, everything's okay and I'm delighted. I've always wanted children."

She pondered his remark, said casually despite the emotion in his voice. Sometimes, she mused, people could be more open when they didn't actually face each other.

"Emma can stay a week," she continued. "School's out and Christmas vacation started in Kansas."

"Good. Hungry?"

"Sure." *Well, that was easy.*

"I stopped at Pisano's before I picked you up at the shelter. Two large pepperoni and pepper pizzas are in the backseat."

She laughed and swung around. "I thought I smelled something spicy. If the pizza has been sitting a while, though, it will be cold."

"There's a microwave in your apartment. We can eat there. All right?"

"You think of everything."

He shrugged, his grin boyish. "I'm a planner."

"So you said. Just like me." She liked the idea of spending the rest of the day with him. In fact, she liked everything about him.

"Should we stop at the main house and offer one of the pizzas to Gertrude and Amanda?" she suggested. "We can't possibly eat two."

His boyish grin stayed in place. "Of course, we can."

"We? Speak for yourself. Between cookies and pizza, I'm going to gain twenty pounds between now and New Year's."

"You're gorgeous, Chiara, inside and out." His tone softened. "And you're very considerate to think about Gertrude and Amanda, but Gertrude texted me earlier. They decided on a light supper and are watching Christmas romantic movies on the Hallmark channel."

She chuckled. "My favorite channel."

"So, would you prefer to eat pizza with me or watch movies with them?"

What a question. Should she live vicariously through romance movies on television, or experience a real-life romance with a man who made her pulse race every time he smiled at her?

That was easy. She opted for real life.

CHAPTER 7

A half hour later, Vance followed Chiara up the exterior stairs to her apartment.

"Besides the gigantic Christmas tree Gertrude and I decorated for your home a few days ago," she said, "I also splurged on a tree for myself."

"I assume you didn't scrimp on the size, judging by mine," he said wryly. "The one at the house takes up more space than my grand piano."

"A small tree in a vaulted room would look out of place. And did you notice how splendidly it's decorated? All those gold and blue bulbs were Gertrude's idea. She's extraordinarily creative."

"I'm surprised she doesn't sing "O Christmas Tree" every time she passes the tree. She's certainly welcomed the Yuletide spirit."

"It's the music and the cookies and the ornaments."

They had reached the top of the stairs and Vance stopped her from opening the door.

"It's you," he said.

She shifted. "Vance, I've only been here a short while."

He gazed down at her radiant face and kissed her temple, her lips. "It's you."

She looked uncomfortable, and he broke eye contact. Why did she seem to hold back from him when he expressed his affection? He pressed his lips tight and stepped inside with her.

"Remember," she was saying, "mine isn't nearly as large as your eight-foot spruce because—"

He halted in midstep and laughed. A miniature pine perched on the coffee table, trimmed with hot-pink ornaments and gold tinsel.

"Ta-dah!" Not even bothering to take off her coat, she fairly skipped to one corner of the room and switched on tiny white lights strung inside a rustic bird cage. "Gertrude and I found this in an unused room in your house."

He couldn't contain his grin. "You have a flair for bringing your fun style into limited spaces."

"It's an acquired skill from living in cramped apartments. I'm a Christmas lover, so as long as I have the scent of pine and can bask in a holiday glow of lights, I'm good."

"You're more than good, Chiara." She was special and resourceful, imparting a zest for life he'd forgotten amidst all his work. He set the pizza boxes on the kitchen counter and pulled her into his arms.

Her gaze shifted from the miniature tree to him. "Are you complimenting me because I picked the smallest tree in the grocery store?"

Her soft laugh reminded him of shimmering Christmas bells.

"I'm complimenting you because you are exquisite." He lifted her lustrous hair and nuzzled her neck. Her fragrance was light and lemony, reminding him of carefree days and endless weekends.

He couldn't resist her. His lips traveled to her chin, her mouth. He kissed her exhaustively, insistently, and she molded herself to him, pressing nearer.

When the kiss ended, she rested her head against his chest.

"Should we continue, or should we eat our cold pizza?" he whispered.

Her laughing gaze found his. "We probably should take our coats off before we decide what's next."

He preferred kissing her over pizza. Actually, he preferred kissing her over anything, but he kept the thought to himself. He felt like a sixteen-year-old caught in the exhilaration of a first love, unable to stop staring at her.

She beamed up at him, nodding, as if she read his thoughts.

But then she whirled into the kitchen, effectively cooling the ardor between them.

After pizza and sugar cookies, she fixed mugs of hot chocolate and carried them on a tray to the living room. Vance sat on the sofa, appreciating the twinkling lights from the birdcage.

"I love the way everything in here smells," he said.

"Like chlorine bleach?" She laughed as she set the tray on the coffee table. "I cleaned my entire apartment before church this morning."

"I smell pine and chocolate." And lemon from her hair.

She settled beside him, and he brought her nearer. Lazily, he twirled a lock of her curly blonde hair.

"Tell me more about Kansas," he murmured.

She kicked out a breath. "Well, Kansas City was the framework of my childhood. My sanctuary. Whenever life got rough, I talked with my parents and they supported me."

He reflected on his own upbringing. He'd never had a meaningful conversation with his parents. They were always more interested in people and activities outside the home, not in their children.

"How about you?" she asked. "You've lived your entire life right here, in a radius of a few miles. Haven't you ever wished to explore the world?"

"Sure, although the ranch and my sister come first."

"I suppose if I lived here, I wouldn't want to leave, either." Sighing, she looked around the small apartment. "Your gorgeous home reminds me of a castle, and the fifteen-foot-tall entry gate and all that fencing is like a moat keeping intruders out."

Or a fort trapping him inside. A place where he was unable to escape. He was solely responsible for taking care of his headstrong sister as well as maintaining the property's legacy.

He attempted a smile, although he knew it wavered.

"It's the least I could do for my grandparents," he said, "two people I grew to admire. They had died by the time I made my appearance in the world. My father told me his parents worked hard to buy the estate and then to maintain it."

All through his childhood, he'd heard stories about his grandparents' struggles and their commitment to the ranch. And although his parents had preached the "nose to the grindstone" mantra, they hadn't followed suit.

"Your grandparents must have been remarkable," Chiara said.

Her quiet observation made him feel she genuinely cared about him, his story, and Wellington Acres. Having her here, spending so many delightful hours with her, negated much of his frustration toward his parents and his endless responsibilities. She was humorous and fun to be around, but it was more than that. It was her loyalty and kind heart.

"If there's anything I can do to help you with your work ..." Smirking, she put up a hand in warning. "Except I won't sacrifice myself to be your beta dating experiment."

He laughed and brought her closer. He'd never encourage her to use his app, because he didn't want her to date anyone but him. He wanted to have endless conversations with her, long, lazy afternoons like this one, leisurely dinners with stimulating conversation and laughter.

Hold on, his logical mind warned. None of this had been his intention when he hired her.

He stopped his mind from considering logic, preferring to focus on the delight coursing through him whenever he was with her. Curled up together on the sofa, she burrowed nearer as he kissed her.

Along with her other attributes he added affectionate, empathetic, and vivacious. Innately, he knew she'd never bring him down, that she would always support him.

"I love this ranch," he said quietly. *And with Chiara by his side ...*

"I know you do." She smoothed her hand across the stubble on his chin. A fleeting caress, yet so intimate. "And Gertrude loves the ranch too. She's a born horsewoman."

"When she was younger, she pushed against any restrictions to the max," he said. "Finally, at twenty-two, she's settling down. She's even mentioned going back to college and completing her degree." He still remembered with painful clarity the night she ran off with the motorcycle guy, the finality of her shouted good-bye and the slam of the front door.

Chiara leaned back and subjected him to a lengthy scrutiny. "Yes, she mentioned majoring in equestrian studies at a small college a few towns over, the same school you went to. Truly, you should be proud of her."

"Now if only she can keep her head on straight and avoid getting entangled with the next available guy who shows up at our doorstep."

"Like Joe?"

"Exactly. I think—"

Chiara's frown made him pause. "Vance, you may not like this, but Gertrude and Joe get along well, and he's more than just 'the next available guy.' He cares a great deal about her."

Vance thrust a hand through his hair. "A fifteen-year age discrepancy is considerable. At thirty-seven, Joe's five years older than I am. Her daredevil impulses landed her in trouble throughout her adolescence, and she capped them off by quitting college and wasting two years of her life roaming the country with a wannabe rock star."

"She's home now, older and more mature. Let go and trust her to make her own decisions."

"Leaving me to clean up after her latest failure."

Just as he had when his parents practically bankrupted the ranch.

"No. She's an adult and understands there are consequences to her actions, although I wouldn't worry." Her green eyes radiated faith in his sister. "Gertrude is perceptive and exhibits good judgment."

"I appreciate your eternal optimism but—"

"Did you miss her when she took off with the motorcycle guy?" She must have seen the hurt in his expression, because she touched his arm and quickly said, "Oh, Vance, of course you did."

He reached for his hot chocolate, now barely

warm. He drank a mouthful, then set it back down. "I missed her desperately," he finally said.

It had been such a familiar feeling. As a child, he had missed his parents, feeling rejected and abandoned when they disappeared for months, leaving him and Gertrude with a nanny. The same sense of desertion when his wife left him and blown all the wind from his sails. Whenever he opened his heart to someone, they crushed it.

Chiara remained quiet for a full minute, the silence broken by sleet tinkling against the window.

She grasped her mug and sipped. "Vance, Gertrude mentioned you were once married."

"Yes, to a woman named Shanna," he said with a grim smile. "And you were in a failed relationship too."

"But Kevin and I weren't married, and I haven't dated anyone since."

That laid to rest something he'd been wondering. She was selective, and evidently didn't take advantage of men. Surely, with her understated beauty and empathy, there were droves of guys who wanted to date her.

"Do you care to talk about your marriage?" She set her mug on the table and avoided his gaze.

He rubbed his forehead. "Presumably as much as you'd like to reminisce about Kevin."

"Is it okay if I ask you some personal questions?" Despite her wobbly smile, her determination was clear. "Gertrude alluded to your ex-wife, but said the actual story should come from you."

Why not? He spread out his arms, realizing he wanted to be absolutely honest with her. "I'm easy. Ask away."

"Well ..." She nibbled her lower lip. "How long were you married?"

"Slightly over a year."

"What happened?"

"She was unfaithful."

He stated the words flatly. Clearly at a loss for what to say, Chiara hesitated. "There was no chance of saving the marriage by seeing a counselor?"

"No. In hindsight, our marriage began falling apart soon after our wedding vows. We were young, in our early twenties, and I suppose that was part of the reason. And I was so fixated on the ranch, I didn't notice Shanna's disinterest. Of course, the same can be said for me, because I was hardly ever around."

"Vance, I'm sorry. Truly. The loss and the betrayal—"

"Don't be." His arms enveloped her, tightening possessively. "I'm well over it."

Unfaithfulness and busted pride? He'd recovered. Now he understood that for him, love bolted whenever it came within his grasp. Weren't his parents, his ex-wife, his sister, all proof of that? An exit was normal, people came and went.

He drew back. His precious Chiara, so radiant, always with a smile.

No, no, no. He must hold back his emotions. He *would* hold back, because love led to heartache. He could not face picking up the fragments of his shattered heart again.

Better not to become any more involved, no matter how delightful this courtship.

Except it wasn't a courtship, because Chiara openly counted the days until she left Virginia. And not for one minute did he doubt she would take off.

Of course, he would never detain her. But when she looked up at him with her soft green eyes, his practical mind lost the battle to his impractical heart.

He gazed down at her, relishing the exquisite feel of her in his arms.

Chiara, I love you.

The words came to his mind without fanfare, a sudden swelling of his emotions.

Impossible. He'd only known her a short while. Love took time.

Or did it?

Stop overthinking. Since when was there a set time-line for relationships?

He tipped his head back and sighed. A romance when he least expected. But he'd experience it for what it was.

Love.

CHAPTER 8

The next Friday after lunch, Chiara noticed that Gertrude seemed more lighthearted than usual. As she walked from one end of the living room to the other—part of her physical therapy for her ankle—she kept peering out the window and remarking on the unseasonably cold weather.

"Let's get our hair done this afternoon," she finally suggested. "I have a date tonight."

"With Joe?" Chiara looked up from Gertrude's medical file, where she'd been making notes about her patient's progress.

"Who else?" Gertrude's gaze shifted to Chiara. "He's picking me up for dinner. We're trying a new restaurant in a town a few miles away. And before you ask, Vance knows. I may not have always been honest with my brother before, but I am now."

Chiara touched her riotous curls. She had gotten up late that morning, since Vance had been at her apartment until after midnight the night before. He'd brought takeout Chinese, and they'd eaten sesame chicken and fried rice while watching *It's A Wonderful Life* on television. She'd been surprised Vance had never seen the movie which she considered a Christmas classic, and she'd been pleased when he announced it was now one of his favorite movies.

In her hurry to report to the cabin by eight a.m., she had let her hair dry naturally after her hasty shower.

"I haven't been to a salon in ages," she admitted.

Gertrude eyed Chiara's hair. "Platinum-blonde highlights and a trim would bring out your green eyes. And then we'll get our nails polished too. I prefer shiny red nails for the holidays."

Gertrude had welcomed Christmas with a zeal that Chiara had never imagined, perhaps because she'd missed so many Christmases as a child. Not only had Gertrude assigned an Advent wreath to the mantle, she'd also sprayed a basket of pinecones a gleaming silver and arranged them in the foyer. To top off the holiday decor, she'd hung oversized snowflakes from the dining room chandelier and set glass candlesticks with a variety of red candles on the eight-foot-long table.

"Different heights create interest," she'd explained every step to Chiara.

Definitely, Gertrude had a creative edge in addition to her boisterous manner.

"I'll drive you into town for an appointment," Chiara said, in an effort to fulfill her commitment as Gertrude's caregiver. "Although I don't intend to color my hair."

"It's more fun if we go together," Gertrude insisted. "Vance is in Richmond drumming up more investors for his app, and tonight he's hanging out with his computer friends."

Chiara glanced at her watch. "We won't be able to book an appointment on such late notice."

"I phoned the salon this morning." Gertrude's smile was positively mischievous. "And don't use the excuse that you can't afford it, because it's my treat."

Reluctant to dampen Gertrude's enthusiasm, Chiara agreed.

An hour later, the women walked into Cut and Curl, a trendy salon in Turning Point. They settled into side-by-side high-backed chairs.

Sally, Chiara's stylist, fingered the blonde curls. "Do you like the length?"

"Yes, so just a trim, please," Chiara cautioned when Sally brought out her sharp scissors.

"And lighter-blonde highlights around her face," Gertrude chirped.

"I can't."

"It'll be an exciting change," Gertrude urged. "And I've decided on caramel highlights. So nod your head and agree because we're doing this together."

Having little choice, Chiara reluctantly granted her stylist the go-ahead.

While their foil-wrapped hair processed, the women sat in a corner of the salon nibbling chocolate-coated truffles, compliments of the specialty candy shop next door.

"So," Gertrude asked, resting her chin in her hands. "How are things with Vance?"

"He's well. Very well." Chiara took a bite of her truffle, savoring the rich chocolate.

"Uh-huh. I see him every morning," Gertrude said. "I want to know how *you* feel about him."

"I respect him. He's remarkably ambitious." Chiara mustered her sunniest smile.

Still, she would be leaving soon. And because of the ache forming in her chest, she couldn't control the catch in her voice.

Gertrude subjected Chiara to a studied analysis. "You realize he's keen on you."

"We're just great friends. Our relationship will end when I fly back to Kansas. He's never encouraged me to stay."

"And he won't." Gertrude snatched a spare towel to mop a glob of hair dye off her arm. "He has a considerable amount of pride. I suppose it's because people have left him flat—our parents, his wife, and me, although I came back."

"He told me about his wife."

"Then you must've had a lot to talk about."

"He didn't say much. Knowing him, I assume he was a wonderful husband."

"He was. And he's a dutiful brother." Gertrude went for another truffle, sending the towel sliding to the floor. "Vance shows his love in a thousand ways, although he'll never say the words out loud. Look at everything he's sacrificed—shouldering the burdens of the ranch, putting up with my antics. Always remember you can count on him."

It was true, Chiara thought. He was a man of his word, treating people with respect. He was responsible, level-headed, and loyal.

She viewed Gertrude's reflection in the mirror and saw her affection for her brother radiating on her freckled face.

"He'll never say 'I love you,'" Gertrude went on, "because he's closed off that part of himself. He's afraid to connect. But as his sister I know he's a man who loves and loves deeply."

"Our relationship can't develop." Chiara hesitated, trying to remain nonchalant. "My home is in Kansas."

Or was it? More often than not, especially of late, she questioned her decision. And now, the thought of Vance holding back, afraid to utter words of love because he might be hurt again, melted her heart.

* * *

AFTER THEIR TWO-HOUR hair and nail appointment, the women returned to the ranch. The last rays of the sun scattered across endless pastures as the day disappeared into early darkness.

"Ladies, you look stunning!" Amanda exclaimed as they walked in. She called for them to twirl and show off their new hairstyles.

When Chiara had looked in the mirror at the salon's unveiling, she'd done a double-take. Sally had styled her hair into a wavy bob, and the platinum highlights framed her face. Her self-confidence rose the longer she stared, and she felt pretty and rejuvenated.

Gertrude's ebony hair floated in cascading

waves, her caramel highlights creating an ombre effect at the tips of her waterfall braids.

"I assume you two are planning something special tonight," Amanda declared.

"Joe's picking me up at six o'clock." Gertrude glanced at the grandfather clock. "Umm, Chiara, would you like to come with us?"

Cheerfully ignoring the reluctance in Gertrude's voice, Chiara replied that she had other plans. Certainly, she wouldn't intrude on their date. And she could rest and catch up on her reading.

Then she recalled Adeline's book club. It was held every Friday evening, rain or shine, and she had enjoyed it the few times she attended. That sounded much more fun than staying home alone, especially since she didn't expect Vance to return from Richmond until after she'd gone to bed.

Decision made a couple hours later, she donned a black sequined skirt and cozy red turtleneck to match her fingernails. She spent extra time adding a vivid red lip color, along with swipes of mascara to her long lashes.

Self-assured and confident, she shrugged on her jacket, got into her Ford Escort and started to town.

* * *

AT TEN O'CLOCK THAT EVENING, Vance was perched on a bar stool at the Turning Point Hotel with some of the tech geeks who had built his dating app. A local band, The Crestfallen, had just begun their second set. The band featured both a guitarist and keyboardist, and he focused on the keyboard player's ability.

They opened with a Billy Joel classic, and Vance was immediately impressed. He really should hone his piano playing, he thought. He'd taken lessons for nearly ten years and was losing his skills because he hardly ever practiced.

He tapped his foot to the beat and sipped his non-alcoholic beer. After nursing Gertrude through one too many hangovers, he rarely drank anymore.

A rock classic by Journey followed Billy Joel.

No Christmas music tonight, Vance mused, leaning back on his stool.

Earlier, he'd texted Chiara, asking how her day had gone. He was glad she and Gertrude had enjoyed an afternoon at the salon, and encouraged her plan to stay in that night and get some reading done. He made a mental note to bring her to hear the band; they were booked every Friday through New Year's at the hotel. He considered FaceTiming her now so she could listen with him, but he didn't want to interrupt her reading.

Since she had told him she wasn't going out, Vance didn't recognize at first the blonde bombshell sitting with her back to him, chatting and laughing at a table with several other women. When he saw one woman's purple hair and recognized her as Chiara's friend from the tree-lighting ceremony, he took a closer look at the blonde.

She was talking to a man with long hair tied back in a ponytail. She kept shaking her head no as the man gestured to the dance floor. He was persistent, though, and the woman finally stood up, confirming that she was Chiara, dressed in a tight-fitting red turtleneck and a black skirt that skimmed sleekly over her hips, drawing the attention of every man there.

As they stepped onto the dance floor, Vance recognized the guy. Charlie, the owner of Charlie's Unique Gifts. The man with a tattoo of the moon and planets on his arm who had taken a decided interest in Chiara.

Vance debated storming over. What was she doing, dancing with someone else? He watched the way Charlie smiled at her and how she smiled back, appearing to be having a marvelous time.

The tempo shifted to a slower song—"Have I Told You Lately?" by Rod Stewart.

Not only was the keyboardist excellent, Vance granted, but so was the vocalist.

However, the primary target of his thoughts, Chiara Johnson, was dancing way too close to another man.

His Chiara.

Instinctively, he pushed the thought aside. He had no claim on her, although he'd just admitted he was jealous.

He and Chiara were only friends, he told himself. She was an admirable nurse and outstanding in her care for Gertrude. His sister couldn't stop talking about her.

He couldn't stop thinking about her.

But nothing would come of it for she planned to return to her beloved Kansas very, very soon.

Vance shoved to his feet, made excuses to his friends, and paid the tab. If they gave him speculative looks as he stalked out of the hotel, he didn't care.

He just couldn't bear to watch Chiara in another man's arms.

CHAPTER 9

"Vance, she's here!" Chiara called as she and Emma stepped into the foyer. They stamped their boots on the entry rug. Snow was falling, a dusting of white powder that outlined the pine trees along the entrance. "Come out of your study to meet her."

On the drive from the Richmond airport to the ranch, Emma was her chatty self—possibly because the attendants had let her have as many sodas and bags of candy as she wanted.

Emma's flights included one stopover between Kansas City and Richmond. Because the airline classified her as an 'unaccompanied minor,' she required special supervision.

As Chiara hung their coats on the rack in the foyer, Emma peeked into the living room. "Mr.

Vance and Miss Gertrude have a piano *and* horses? They're so lucky!"

"Yes, so it will be hard for you to choose which to do first." Chiara laughed.

"And there's a pond so we can ice skate."

"The weather hasn't been cold enough for the ice to freeze properly. You'll have to wait for when you go back to Kansas."

In a quick mood change, Emma sighed. "I wish you were coming with me."

"Remember I told you I'd return by New Year's to build our gingerbread house? I'm committed here at the ranch until then."

In truth, she could leave sooner. Between her good health, youthfulness, and diligent attention to physical therapy, Gertrude was almost fully healed. So, Chiara had booked herself a ticket back with Emma, because it had become clear that Gertrude didn't need her anymore. She hadn't yet shared the news with Emma, or anyone, for that matter. She was waiting, although she didn't understand why she waited.

Every day Gertrude went down to the stable to see Licorice. And Joe, Chiara presumed. At her doctor's appointment a few days earlier, the doctor's only advice had been that Gertrude stay off horses for another month.

"You've allowed your brain and ankle time to heal," he concluded. "Excellent recovery."

As she reported the doctor's prognosis to Vance when she and Gertrude returned to the ranch, Chiara told him she was uncomfortable accepting her full salary. He insisted he would keep paying her. Trying another tack, she suggested she leave Wellington Acres early, for she obviously wasn't needed anymore. She could fly back to Kansas with Emma and celebrate Christmas with her family, something she'd dreamed about for three years.

Vance was silent at first. She held her breath, half hoping he'd voice an adamant no, that she had signed a contract to be Gertrude's nurse through the end of December and that was that.

He did nothing of the sort. "The decision is yours and I'll pay your salary either way," he flatly stated. "Although your gingerbread house event for the homeless shelter is scheduled on Christmas Eve."

"Yes, but it's in the morning and Emma's flight leaves at four o'clock. I can do both."

Vance shrugged with apparent indifference. "The decision is yours. Although that sounds like a lot to do in one day."

She hesitated, and so did he. She hid her hope behind a facade that she trusted was as imperturbable as his.

Instead of disagreeing, she tapped a finger on her lip. With all the goings-on the day of the event, packing her belongings would be difficult. Better to honor her contract and stay until New Year's, in case she required a reference from him for a future job in Kansas.

Sure, it was too late to turn in the plane ticket. Perhaps Gertrude could use it at a later date to fly out to Kansas to visit Chiara and Emma.

At least, that was what her sensible mind rationalized when she told him her decision. Her heart, however, leapt elatedly when his expression softened and he smiled. She'd be able to spend the last few precious days with him. Perhaps he'd devote more time to her, because his elusiveness this past week had been shattering.

She planned a Christmas feast, intending to remain useful. When she asked Vance whether he preferred ham or turkey, he elected for a turkey dinner with all the trimmings. For a moment, his chilly reserve of the past week had thawed, only to swiftly return.

The object of her musings strode from his study. "So, this is the famous Emma," he teased.

Emma giggled. "Hi, Mr. Vance. I saw your horses as we entered the driveway. Miss Gertrude is visiting Mr. Joe near the stable, in case you're wondering where she is. Do you have any ponies?"

He chuckled. "In a few months, Peppermint is having a foal."

"Is she the white horse?"

"Yes."

"Can I come back to see her pony?"

He grasped her small hands in his large ones. "Emma Johnson, you can visit Wellington Acres any time. That's an open, forever invitation."

A lump rose in Chiara's throat as she pictured Emma enraptured by a playful, newborn foal. The estate would be beautiful in the spring, the sun warming the air, mountain bluebirds hovering near their nests, the little stream she'd discovered rushing with water.

"And Licorice is Miss Gertrude's black horse?" Emma asked.

"Yes, she's owned Licorice since she was twelve years old."

"I'll be twelve in three years and I want a pony." Enthusiastically, Emma jumped up and down, her blue-green eyes sparkling. "Do you think I'll get one?"

Vance knelt to be at Emma's height. "I heard."

Loudly, Emma whispered in his ear, "I told Santa."

Chiara caught Vance's gaze and smiled. Briefly, he nodded and looked away.

What had happened to their easy camaraderie?

Her eyes burned with sharp tears, hurt by his indifference.

Emma balanced on her tiptoes. "Mr. Vance, did you know I flew here by myself? Mom and Dad forced me to have supervision although I didn't need any."

"I'm sure you didn't." He grinned. "So how do you like flying in an airplane?"

"I love it, and I wasn't afraid, even though it was my first time." She swiveled and grabbed Chiara's hand. "C'mon, you promised I could see the horses!"

"Aren't you tired?" she appealed, as Emma towed her toward their coats. "We can go to my garage apartment and unpack."

"Nope, I want to pet the horses."

And so the following days passed in a blur of activity. By the time they all gathered in the dining room for dinner, Gertrude insisting that Chiara and Emma eat with her and not in Chiara's apartment, Chiara was pleasantly worn out. Gertrude and Emma had become fast friends, noisily chatting about horses and how they both planned to tour exotic places. Their mutual zest for adventure and disregard of any hazards created a strong bond between them. Chiara loved the sound of their enthusiastic laughter ringing throughout the house, but the best part of the meals was that Vance joined them. It was the only time she saw him, and she didn't know if he was kept even busier than usual with the launch of his dating app coming ever closer, or if he was avoiding her.

So, she was surprised when, four evenings before the gingerbread house event, Vance invited Chiara to dine at Pointers, a restaurant they'd favored, both agreeing the intimate atmosphere and friendly wait staff were unsurpassed.

She quickly accepted the invitation, looking forward to seeing him alone. She prayed this would lead to a tender reconciliation.

She decided on dressy wool slacks and a red-sequined knit sweater, adding a shimmery cubic zirconia necklace and matching earrings.

Vance held open the door at the restaurant, and she grinned as she walked past the four-foot-high nutcrackers that flanked the entrance. The noble nutcrackers' arms were lifted, directing customers inside. In the dining room, a guitarist nimbly strummed a holiday carol. Chiara's boots clicked against the wide plank floors as she and Vance were led to a table near the central fireplace, where lively flames crackled.

A waiter in pressed black pants and a long-sleeved white shirt filled their water glasses and handed them menus.

"What looks appetizing?" Vance asked, perusing the entrées.

The menu changed nightly, but could be depended on to include pork roast, beef tips, and mashed potatoes smothered in thick brown gravy.

"Everything, as usual." She took a long look at him. His nearness kindled a fire in her belly, a yearning so intense she almost felt faint. He'd been so indulgent with Emma, patient and wonderfully kind. If he broached the subject of his current lack of interest in her, she would fling herself into his arms and beg for …

Beg for what? Forgiveness?

She ached to spend every last minute with him before she left, and he was preventing her from doing that by avoiding her.

Unwilling to think about that, she studied the menu and chose pork roast and a side of macaroni and cheese. Vance ordered steak and scalloped potatoes.

With a sigh and silently counting calories, she closed the menu.

"I'm going to miss this place," she said quietly. As soon as she spoke, she admonished herself. She hadn't intended to voice her thoughts aloud.

Quickly, she glanced at him. Wanting him. Wanting more. He stared at her before she looked away. She knew he'd caught the wistfulness in her sigh.

I'll miss you most, she thought.

He claimed her hand across the table. "You don't have to leave Turning Point, Chiara." His voice was deep, his expression thoughtful. Her senses were alive to everything about him—his strong callused hands, his chiseled features, his impressive frame. She loved how his chestnut-colored cashmere sweater brought out the serious glint in his dark eyes.

"Don't I?" Her throat clogged with an unexpected sob. "Lately, I've seen you only at dinner. You'll hardly miss me."

He let go of her hand. "I assumed you intended to spend your last days here with Charlie."

"Charlie?" She frowned. "Charlie who?"

"The shop owner in town. He's obviously interested in you."

Her mind scrambled for a response. "I haven't seen him since you purchased Gertrude's Christmas gift."

"Haven't you?" His gaze rested momentarily on her face before shifting to his water glass. "What about the other night at the Turning Point Hotel?"

"How would you know? Wait a minute." She pushed her chair back and glared at him. "Were you spying on me while I was at my book club?"

"That's an odd book club. I didn't see a book anywhere in sight."

She narrowed her gaze. "Where were you?"

"I was sitting at the bar with my tech developers."

"I didn't see you." Confused, she shook her head. "Why didn't you come over to my table?"

"You were too busy dancing with Charlie. You know, the guy who wears an earring and is fond of tattoos?" He gave an indifferent shrug.

The full import of his remark gave her pause. He had watched her dance with another man and he'd been jealous. *He'd been jealous.* She swallowed, profoundly touched, and pulled her chair back close to the table. Now she'd figured out why he'd been acting so distant; because he cared. If only he'd admit his feelings.

She tilted her chin and forced him to meet her gaze. "Charlie and I danced twice, and I left soon afterward. And you know what else?" She lay her hand on his arm. "The entire night I thought only about you."

In the flickering firelight, a smile crossed Vance's handsome face. "And I considered Face-Timing you so you could listen to the band with me."

"They were good, weren't they? They're playing every Friday night until New Year's."

Which meant one more Friday before she left for Kansas.

As always, Vance read her thoughts. "And then you fly away."

To avoid looking at him, she scanned the room —the guitarist quietly plucking, the other patrons eating and talking.

The past several nights she'd lain awake, contemplating what to do. She could easily get a full-time nursing position in Richmond. The thriving city was less than an hour commute from Turning Point.

If only the implacably polite man within a hand's grasp would urge her to stay, instead of watching her with an indecipherable expression.

But he didn't, effectively dashing her fantasy, and the meal pushed on.

For dessert, the holiday menu included peppermint chip ice cream and milk and cookies for Santa Claus. They ordered both, cookies for Vance and ice cream for Chiara. The cookies were scrumptious, salted grahams with chunks of candied ginger, served with ice-cold chocolate milk. Chiara opted for hot tea with lemon and a heaping bowl of ice cream, and didn't refuse when Vance offered her a bite of his cookie.

"Do I detect a hint of rum?" she teased.

A smirk tugged at the corners of his mouth. "Rum in salted grahams makes them extra special."

"Uh-huh." She laid down her spoon, realizing she'd devoured her entire helping.

"Should I order another round of desserts?" he joked.

She pressed her lips together and shook her head, too full to answer.

This was a decisive moment. They'd enjoyed dinner at their favorite restaurant, they were alone, and they were poised on the edge of their future.

And the silence between them beat on.

She groped for a subject matter to break the quiet. "Experts say a nine-year-old is on the cusp of adolescence."

"Emma is at a wondrous age," he said. "She's intelligent and fun-loving."

"And chock-full of activity. Thank you for your understanding when she's around the horses. If it were up to her, she'd live at the stable. Every morning after breakfast she races down there, and she's taken a liking to the chestnut mare."

"Ariel?"

"Yes. And Joe's given her a couple riding lessons."

He nodded. "I've seen her. She's got a good seat already."

A rush of pride went through her. "She keeps talking about returning to see the foal."

"She's welcome any time."

"Thanks."

Hypnotic embers in the fireplace cast a reddish radiance, and she inhaled the welcoming smoky scent. Every day at Wellington Acres filled her with contentment. Each hour flew by with alarming swiftness.

On mornings when Vance worked from home, she stole glances at him whenever she passed his study. He was either engrossed in a phone conversation or staring at his computer. She always longed to slip into the room and rub his shoulders, or smooth her hand over his cheek with its ever-present dark stubble.

She had learned this was his isolated world, where he ran the estate and developed his computer app, his ideas far-sighted and perceptive. And the work too often filled up his life.

"I intended to spend more time with Emma," he said.

"You've been buried in work."

"Unfortunately, my last investor meeting resulted in a snag."

"I assumed you were on track for your December thirty-first deadline."

He set his napkin on his lap and cupped his

hands around his glass. "One of the investors voted against the name Vulcan. He thinks women will equate the name with logic and reason and that will deter them from using the app. Women prefer romantic love."

She nodded. "That's because of the *Star Trek*, Mr. Spock inference." Despite the fact she agreed with the investor, she refrained from telling Vance.

"Anyway, I need a name before the launch, so we might be delayed. And of course, it will be years before I see a profit." He shrugged. "Still, I like developing a product that might benefit society."

Typical Vance, constantly thinking of others, although, as his sister had stated, he was unable to express his feelings aloud. Case in point, he hadn't confronted her about dancing with Charlie. He'd simply withdrawn.

"Maybe outer space is too far to fly to meet the perfect partner," she said.

And maybe God had placed everything she was looking for right in front of her. All she had to do was reach out and grasp it.

Imperceptibly, Vance nodded. Surely, he hadn't read her thoughts again.

Whether he was grooming horses in the stable or making small talk with a goat in the pasture, his manner was caring, his voice compassionate. Besides, what woman could resist a guy who loved animals?

Even around Joe, Vance had mellowed. Slowly, he was accepting that Gertrude and Joe cared for each other, and Chiara had encouraged Vance's tolerance.

After a lengthy silence, he finished his last salted graham cookie and said, "You know, these are almost as good as your Christmas cookies."

When her eyebrows raised, he clarified, "Notice I said *almost*."

He signaled for the check, and after he paid they walked to the lobby to retrieve their coats. The entry was deserted as most of the other patrons had left. While they waited for their coats, Chiara remembered one thing they needed to talk about. His elf costume.

"About your elf costume …" she began.

"I'm an elf?"

She plunked her hands on her hips. "Yes, as you well know."

He nodded. "What I know is that you volunteered me and told me about it later. So, I'm one of Santa's helpers?"

She smirked. "That's the plan. And I'm telling the children at the shelter that you're Santa's favorite elf."

He helped her on with her coat, then enveloped

her in his arms. His strong chest was warm and solid beneath her cheek.

"What do you want for Christmas?" he asked softly.

You. The thought came unbidden, and she looked around, half-fearing she'd blurted her wish out loud. She blew out a breath and evaded his stare as well as his question. "Back to your costume. The tailor called and said he's done with the alterations, and you can pick it up anytime."

"Sure." He drew her hand through the crook of his arm, and quickly ushered her to his SUV. Sometime during dinner, it had started to rain. She hadn't even noticed. But then, she had found that when she was with Vance, she noticed only him and nothing else. It was a little disconcerting.

He switched on the heater, and the interior of the SUV quickly warmed. The wipers began their rhythmic flapping in an attempt to chase off the droplets.

"I like the sound of raindrops." She settled back, loving the heated seat. "However, snow for Christmas is better."

"The weatherman forecasts a white Christmas because a cold front is moving in again."

"Emma will be gone by then, although she's loved being here. I reminded her she'll see at least a foot of snow in Kansas. Speaking of Emma, I almost forgot to give this to you." Chiara fished a piece of paper from her purse and handed it to Vance.

At the quizzical lift of his dark eyebrows, she explained, "The note's from Emma. She knows you're one of Santa's elves at the Christmas party and figured you had a direct line to Santa."

He unfolded the paper and read the handwritten note aloud. "'Dear Santa, I have been 80% good this year.'"

He grinned at Chiara. "Eighty percent?"

"An excellent percentage for my sister. Keep reading."

"'Here's my Christmas list: A hair straightener. A piano. And a pony.'"

"Put a check mark by the hair straightener from me. As far as the piano goes … perhaps someday. A pony? Well, that's impossible."

"Why do you say that?" He folded the note and slipped it into his pocket.

"Unlike you, my head isn't in outer space."

He threw her an accusing look, his gaze flat. "What's that supposed to mean?"

"I apologize. I was joking." Their misunderstanding had been resolved, and she wouldn't provoke another disagreement. "It's coming from my own frustration because I can't provide Emma with pianos or ponies."

The twinkle was back. "Well there's an excellent reason why you can't."

"Which is?"

He caught her hands in his and kissed her lightly on the lips. "You're not one of Santa's favorite elves."

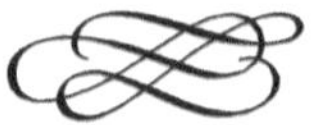

For the next three days, Vance sent Chiara and Emma a little gift. She had mentioned she adored the truffles from the specialty candy shop in town, and two chocolate-coated truffles wrapped in red and green foil waited alongside the Richmond newspaper each morning outside her apartment. Did he know she'd been searching the online classified ads for a nursing position?

Accompanying the truffles was a note.

"From Santa's favorite elf," he wrote in his bold handwriting on stationery embossed with the initials WA—Wellington Acres. "Can't wait to see you tonight."

In any case, this was Vance, showing how much

he cared in the only way he expressed himself, through gifts and thoughtfulness.

Christmas Eve morning dawned cold and clear, the temperatures hovering in the midthirties. Snow was forecasted for later in the evening, and anticipation was in the air for a white Christmas.

They had strung red and green steamers from the ceiling of the outdoor pavilion, and Chiara and Vance had covered oblong tables with green table-cloths. They'd saved thirty milk cartons, the number of children expected, and Emma and Gertrude had rinsed the cartons and let them dry.

Boxes of graham crackers and white canned frosting were set out, and Amanda lined up a half dozen muffin tins filled with assorted candy to decorate the houses.

The party was a great success, and Chiara breathed a satisfied sigh when it ended at noon. The children were on a sugar high, giggling and running in circles while playing tag. Emma made new friends, and had pointed out the horses in the nearest pasture to them. Peppermint was her natural welcoming self, whinnying and letting the little hands pat her.

As parents left with their children, Emma told Chiara she was going to go say good-bye to Licorice.

"Is Gertrude there?" Chiara called after her

sister as Emma headed for the stable with a spring in her step.

"She and Joe are always there," Emma shouted over her shoulder.

True.

"Be back here in fifteen minutes," Chiara said. "You need to finish packing and we're leaving for the airport in an hour."

She turned to Vance as he approached, and was startled when he took her in his arms and kissed her.

She closed her eyes, yielding to his kiss before realizing that not everyone had left yet. She swiftly stepped back. "Vance," she whispered, "there are children here."

"I'm well aware." He yanked off his green pointed hat. "I just handed out a million candy canes."

"Umm, your math is a little off. Thirty children and their mothers attended, not a million. And you were wonderful with everyone."

"Because I'm Santa's favorite elf?"

"Because you're the handsomest elf ever." She ran her fingers along the faux white fur at the neckline of his soft green jacket. "Nice touch with the red pants and striped knee socks, but I'm not crazy about the upturned toes on your green booties. However, at least they match the jacket."

Grinning, he tucked her arm through his and led her to the pavilion. "I have a surprise for you. I was hoping you'd sit on my lap when I handed out candy canes and I planned to give it to you then."

"Another truffle?" She rolled her eyes.

"Miss Johnson, this is a special gift meant only for you."

The heart-touching tenderness in his voice sent a quiver of anticipation up her spine.

"I can't wait." Very lightly, she leaned against him. "Although can we postpone our celebration until later?"

His hand dropped to her waist, and he pulled her nearer. "Tonight is Christmas Eve. My gift can wait a few more hours."

She sensed his reluctance to release her as she playfully danced away. She intended to assist with cleanup while the remaining mothers rounded up their children for the ride back to town.

A while later, when the last child had departed clutching a candy cane and a gingerbread house, Chiara glanced at her watch. Emma had been gone a long time. Vance, who had changed out of his elf costume and into his familiar jeans, parka, and boots, was collapsing one of the tables, and she asked him if he'd seen the girl.

"Didn't she go to the stable to say good-bye to

the horses?" He straightened. "How long has she been gone?"

Chiara calculated the time. "At least thirty minutes. What's taking her so long? I told her to be back here in fifteen minutes." She pulled out her phone and sent Gertrude a text. *Is Emma with you?*

No, Gertrude responded instantly.

Where's Licorice?

With Joe and me. I saw Emma walking toward the pond.

How long ago?

Twenty minutes.

Chiara's phone slipped from her fingers and she quickly retrieved it.

Deep water, barely crusted. The ice wasn't safe.

She started running. Surely Emma was old enough to know better than to venture too close to water that had scarcely iced over.

Vance took off after her. "Chiara, where are you going?" he shouted.

"The pond!"

He grabbed her hand, and she shook him off. He was slowing her down.

"Isn't Emma at the stable?"

Frozen terror. She couldn't breathe, couldn't respond with more than a negative shake of her head. *Not Emma. Please, no.*

"Emma!" she screamed. Blood pounded in her

ears. On the day she arrived at Wellington Acres, Emma had asked to ice skate. If anything happened to her dear sister, she couldn't bear the loss. Why hadn't she kept closer track of the time instead of focusing on Vance?

Her heart skipped several beats when she spotted Emma standing by the pond, gazing longingly at the mirrored surface.

"Emma, what are you doing? Can't you listen to simple instructions?" Chiara knew she was lashing out, but Emma was too adventurous for her own good. "Why must you constantly overstep your boundaries?"

"She's safe." Vance halted beside them, catching his breath, speaking calmly. "See, Chiara? Everything's fine."

Although it wasn't fine because whenever she was with Vance, she noticed only him and forgot about the rest of the world.

"Emma's too young, she doesn't understand the dangers …" Chiara pivoted, facing him. "If she had fallen through the ice, no one would have been there to grab her. She could've died."

He put his hands on her forearms. "But she didn't."

Chiara winced and pulled away. With her arm around Emma's shoulders, she marched the girl to her apartment on legs threatening to collapse beneath her.

She couldn't do this any longer, stay at this ranch where she didn't belong. She needed to be in Kansas with her family where life was familiar and safe. Her decision to stick around until New Year's had been a mistake. Gertrude didn't need her, and her relationship with Vance had reached its end.

Who had she been trying to fool, believing he'd profess his feelings, hoping for more than he could give? Yes, she loved him, but he didn't love her back. The truth had strode quietly beside her and she had refused to acknowledge it, letting her love blind her to reality.

He had followed her and Emma, and she glanced at him, recalling what she had witnessed the day before. She had heard a plinking sound coming from the living room and peeked inside. Emma had sat at the shiny black piano, looking confident, swinging her feet on the piano bench. Both hands on the keys, she had picked out the melody for "Away in a Manger." Vance stood behind her, encouraging, humming as she played, reaching over her shoulder and indicating the next key.

Neither of them had been aware Chiara watched from the doorway.

At the end of the Christmas carol, he applauded

and high-fived Emma, promising to give her a piano lesson whenever she visited.

Remembering that moment, Chiara's chest squeezed. If she never again visited Wellington Acres, Emma would be beyond disappointed. So perhaps … perhaps …

Maybe she and Vance could continue their relationship. If she moved back to Kansas, Vance could fly out for weekend visits. They'd talk nightly on the phone.

No, no. Everyone knew long-distance relationships didn't work. Besides, she hadn't come to Wellington Acres looking for a man. She'd come for a job, and the generous salary had allowed her to pay off her last tuition bill. She should be thankful.

Emma raced up the stairs to the apartment, hightailing it inside to finish packing. Chiara faced Vance on the landing.

"I'll see you when you return from the airport," he said. "Several inches of snow are predicted for later this evening, so drive carefully. Gertrude and Joe will attend midnight church services with us, but that's assuming the roads are plowed."

"Vance, I'm not going."

"To church? I told you—"

She shook her head and stared at him, trying to memorize his handsome features because she'd never see him again. "I'm not attending Christmas Eve celebrations in Turning Point."

"Why not?"

"I've decided to leave this afternoon with Emma. I'd bought an extra plane ticket a while back. I planned to fly back to Kansas." She blew out a sigh. "And then I decided not to."

"Why this change of heart? You never told me …" He paused, then stared at her. "Because of what happened? She's a kid, Chiara, but she's smart and responsible. So she lost track of time. We all do."

And that was the problem. With him, time, place, and emotions became a whirlwind of confusion.

"I need to pack and I'm already late." She turned and stepped inside.

He followed.

For a split-second, he was silent.

"Chiara, you're being irrational." He covered her hand with both of his. "Let's talk about this."

She jerked away and wouldn't meet his gaze for fear of changing her mind.

"We both know we can't be together," she said. "I'll leave the key under the door mat."

She wavered, and then she didn't.

"Good-bye, Vance." With a decided shove, she forced him onto the landing and slammed the door behind him. Then, to be extra sure he couldn't persuade her, she locked it.

* * *

Two hours later, Vance rugged Peppermint and led her into the stall. A cold wind gusted outside, creaking the bare tree branches. Snow had begun to fall, thicker by the minute, hushing the pastures and hugging the distant log home in a snowy blanket.

Chiara would have loved the snowfall. She had said snow was one of the things she missed most about Kansas. And now she was gone.

He had texted her a number of times since her Ford Escort had raced down the driveway.

How are you? Was the first one. He'd cringed as soon as he'd sent it. Did that sound like he expected an answer?

It didn't matter. She hadn't responded.

Are you at the airport? came next.

No response.

I'm waiting. Wow, had that ever come out wrong.

And so on. His one-sided texts continued with no acknowledgement.

He confirmed the time on his watch. She and Emma would have boarded by now.

On his phone, he Googled the next flight to Kansas City and booked the first departure available, frustrated that it was two days later. He'd surprise her, as soon as he found her address. He surmised she'd given it to Gertrude during one of their many cozy conversations.

Done with the plane reservation, he checked his texts again. Nothing from Chiara.

"Can't you send me a courteous reply, so I know you're all right?" he asked the chilled stable. "I won't give up, Chiara."

Didn't she know he loved her?

Unconsciously, he took a step back.

How would she know that? He'd never told her.

He felt the seconds tick by and his heart plummeted. Each tick was another moment without her.

At first when she said she was leaving—when she dumped him—he'd been angry. She hadn't given him a good reason. And then she'd shoved, actually *shoved,* him from her apartment, *his* apartment, before locking the door. Talk about a double-edged sword. For the first time in his life, he'd embraced Christmas, and she had rejected him on Christmas Eve.

Where had they gone wrong? They got along so well together. She understood him, laughed at his jokes. And she was fun, a pleasure to be around, and sweet. So sweet.

I'll be happy to bake one of my favorite cookie recipes with your sister and bring a little Christmas cheer into your lives. That is, if you're interested.

And he had hesitated to tell her. Sure, he'd acknowledged his interest and smiled, but he had never said the words.

I love you.

Because he was afraid.

No, that couldn't be … Yes, it was. His heart couldn't risk another rejection. Ironic, because by protecting his heart, he had lost her, the woman of his heart. And she was all that mattered.

He stood at the entrance to the stable, peering toward his home. Gertrude had switched on the colorful Christmas lights and smoke billowed from the brick chimney. He hadn't told her yet that Chiara had left since the women got along famously, and Gertrude was looking forward to a real Christmas dinner with the ones she loved. A soreness gathered in his lungs, and he breathed in deeply. Already, the ranch was so lonely.

Wishing to escape the sadness, he wandered back into the stable, walking from stall to stall, speaking quietly to the horses. Once a source of such joy, the stable now felt empty and cold.

He remembered the way Chiara curled up to

him when they watched Christmas movies, or shared earnest exchanges over mugs of hot chocolate. Her upturned face, her laughter, how she melted into his arms when he kissed her. Certainly, neither denied their attraction to each other.

He heard the sound of car tires skidding into the driveway as headlights swept across the snow.

He hastened from the stable. Now who would be out driving in—

His heartbeat raced as he recognized the car. He was beside it before Chiara shut the engine.

"Vance?" She pushed the door open and bounded from the car, throwing her arms around his neck. "I'm sorry."

"Why? Is Emma okay?"

"Yes, she's on her way to Kansas and will text me when she lands."

Snow was falling harder, covering Chiara's blonde hair in thick wet flakes. She was here. She'd come back to him.

"Let's get inside." Grabbing her hand, he hurried her into the stable. He pulled her close, inhaling raw air and a lemony scent and the woman he cherished.

She nestled into his embrace. "Vance, I—"

He pressed a finger to her lips. "Chiara, I need to say something, first. Words I haven't spoken in years." He didn't stop to think, or analyze. His feelings were too deep. "I love you."

Her green eyes welled with tears. "And I love you."

"I should've told you long before you left."

"You're telling me now. That's all that matters."

"You didn't answer my texts."

A grin brightened her beautiful face. "Well, for one thing, the roads were slick, and I was gripping the steering wheel with both hands. And Vance, I was so afraid."

"I was afraid too."

"Afraid of what, a snowflake?"

He grinned, then kissed her softly, sweetly. "I was afraid of losing my heart, and losing you," he whispered against her lips. "In fact, I was terrified. Trouble is, I had already lost it to a beautiful nurse from Kansas wearing ruby-red—"

"Don't start quoting from *The Wizard of Oz*," she warned.

"I won't." *Yet.*

He cuddled her, his fingers caressing her damp blonde curls. Still, she shivered in the frigid air. They should return to the house. But first …

Though reluctant to release her, he went into the wash stall. Beneath an assortment of horse hooks was a wire-mounted shelf. A neatly wrapped gift sat on top.

"I have a Christmas gift for you," he said.

"It's not horse shampoo, is it?"

He chuckled. "Nope. I love the scent of your lemon shampoo." He sobered and handed her the large heavy box, gift wrapped in reindeer print and tied with burlap string.

She studied the label on top. "Charlie's Unique Gifts? I thought you didn't like Charlie."

"I never said that. I just didn't like him dancing with you. However, I was forced to patronize his store because of the … uniqueness."

She sat on a bale of hay, untied the string and opened the box. Inside was the snow globe depicting Turning Point's town square. As she wound the base, the sweet, peaceful melody of "Silent Night" chimed softly.

"Vance, it's beautiful," she breathed. "And so thoughtful." She looked up at him. "I'm sorry for what I did, bolting on you like that, not giving you a chance."

"When you didn't respond, I booked the next flight available to Kansas in a couple of days. I was frustrated because I didn't want to miss spending Christmas day with you, so I planned to keep calling the airline."

"Do you know where I live?" She frowned and looked around the stalls as if one of the horses might answer.

"I was working on that."

She gave a sardonic shake of her head, then laughed.

Gazing down at her, he said softly, "I love you, Chiara. I was hiding from my fears. I'm not hiding anymore."

"And I love you. I love you very much."

He tipped up her chin. "Will you marry me?"

Tears glistened and flowed freely down her cheeks. "Yes, yes." Her hands glided around his nape.

Gently, he wiped the wetness away. "I understand you want to return to Kansas, but we'll make it work. Maybe Joe can run the ranch, and I can work on new apps anywhere."

"Vance." She placed her hand on his jaw. "I'm happy here at Wellington Acres with you. I'd like to get married in Kansas, though."

"A spring wedding?"

"After the new foal is born." She tilted her head to the side to regard Peppermint in her stall, then smiled. "I'll ask Gertrude to help me plan the wedding. We'll have to go out to Kansas for a visit first so my parents can meet you."

"I hope they love me as much as I love their daughter." He lowered his head, bringing his lips closer to hers. "Why don't we leave in a couple of days? I booked one ticket, and the airline said there were seats available, so I can book another. Since we're spending Christmas Eve and Christmas Day with Gertrude and Joe, we can spend the rest of the holiday with your family."

She tilted her head so that her lips were within a hairsbreadth of his. "I promised Emma I'd fly back to Kansas for New Year's to build a gingerbread house, anyway, so this will be a wonderful surprise. Especially since I told her I was going with her, then changed my mind."

"How did she take the news?"

"She encouraged me to drive back to the ranch so I could be with you." Chiara laughed. "Besides, she likes being fussed over on the plane as an unaccompanied minor. She was already picking out a soft drink as I left."

Peppermint interrupted with a whinny, then poked her nose through the stall, sniffing in Vance's pocket for candy.

"I only have three left, girl." He pressed a candy into his palm and gave it to her. Then he offered one to Chiara and took the last peppermint for himself.

"There's no place like home, right?" His arms went around Chiara and he winked. "I couldn't resist."

"There's no place like home for the holidays," she modified, then she kissed him, her body softening against his. "Wherever my loved ones are is home to me, because that's where my heart is."

He wholeheartedly agreed, and then he savored the exquisite taste of her sweet peppermint kisses.

THE END

"RECIPE" FOR GINGERBREAD HOUSE

Collect milk cartons ahead of time. (Pint size is recommended)

Rinse the cartons and let them dry.

Ingredients:

Graham crackers (plain or cinnamon)

White canned frosting

Candy (any kind is fine)

Paper plates

Milk cartons

Directions:
Attach the graham crackers to the milk carton house with frosting, then attach the house to the paper plate with frosting. Decorate with candy as desired. Please note: These houses are not meant to last a long time.

Additional tips:
Place the candy in muffin tins for easier visibility.

Use craft sticks to spread the frosting on the houses and when adding candy.

If pint containers are not available, use whipped cream or coffee cream containers. Also, you can use up your old Halloween candy for decorations.

Enjoy this fun craft with your little ones!

A NOTE FROM JOSIE

Dear Friends,

Thank you for reading Sweet Peppermint Kisses. I wanted to write a holiday romance in a picturesque location and set *Sweet Peppermint Kisses* in the fictional small town of Turning Point, Virginia.

The heroine, Chiara Johnson, is a wonderful caregiver. I've always admired the dedication and compassion of anyone in the nursing profession.

The hero, Vance Thatcher, runs a horse ranch. He is responsible and loyal and level-headed. In my research, I also learned a great deal about dating apps!

Set against the backdrop of horses and peppermint candy, it is my hope that this book helped you celebrate the joyous Christmas holiday along with me and my characters.

Sweet Peppermint Kisses is available in ebook, Paperback, Large Print Paperback, Hardcover, and Audiobook.

If you loved this sweet holiday romance as much as I loved writing it, please help other people find *Sweet Peppermint Kisses* by posting your amazing review.

I'd love to meet you in person someday, but in the meantime, all I can offer is a sincere and grateful thank you. Without your support, my books would not be possible.

As I write my next sweet or inspirational romance, remember this: Have you ever tried something you were afraid to try because it mattered so much to you? I did, when I started writing. Take the chance, and just do something you love.

P.S. And remember, "There's no place like home."

My Spotify Play List for Sweet Peppermint Kisses is here.

Love sweet romance Holiday stories? Be sure to check out these book bundles:
Holiday Hearts Volume One
Holiday Hearts Volume Two
Holiday Hearts Book Bundle Volume Three
Holiday Hearts Volume Four

ACKNOWLEDGMENTS

An appreciative thank you to my patient husband, Dave, and our three wonderful children.

ABOUT THE AUTHOR

Josie Riviera is a *USA TODAY* bestselling author of contemporary, inspirational, and historical sweet romances that read like Hallmark movies. She lives in the Charlotte, NC, area with her wonderfully supportive husband. They share their home with an adorable shih tzu, who constantly needs grooming, and live in an old house forever needing renovations.

To receive my Newsletter and your free sweet romance novella ebook as a thank you gift, sign up HERE.

Become a member of my Read and Review VIP Facebook group for exclusive giveaways and ARCs.

ALSO BY JOSIE RIVIERA

Seeking Patience

Seeking Catherine (always Free!)

Seeking Fortune

Seeking Charity

Seeking Rachel

The Seeking Series

Oh Danny Boy

I Love You More

A Snowy White Christmas

A Portuguese Christmas

Holiday Hearts Book Bundle Volume One

Holiday Hearts Book Bundle Volume Two

Holiday Hearts Book Bundle Volume Three

Holiday Hearts Book Bundle Volume Four

Candleglow and Mistletoe

Maeve (Perfect Match)

A Love Song To Cherish

A Christmas To Cherish

A Valentine To Cherish

A Christmas Puppy To Cherish

A Homecoming To Cherish

A Summer To Cherish

Romance Stories To Cherish

Romance Stories To Cherish Volume Two

Cherished Hearts Six Book Volume

Aloha To Love

Sweet Peppermint Kisses

Valentine Hearts Boxed Set

1-800-CUPID

1-800-CHRISTMAS

1-800-IRELAND

1-800-SUMMER

1-800-NEW YEAR

The 1-800-Series Sweet Contemporary Romance Bundle

Irish Hearts Sweet Romance Bundle

Holly's Gift

A Chocolate-Box Christmas

A Chocolate-Box New Years

A Chocolate-Box Valentine

A Chocolate-Box Summer Breeze

A Chocolate-Box Christmas Wish

A Chocolate-Box Irish Wedding

Chocolate-Box Hearts

Chocolate-Box Hearts Volume Two

Chocolate-Box Double Hearts

Recipes From The Heart

Leading Hearts

New Year Hearts

SENIOR HEARTS

Summer Hearts

Christmas in the Air (1-800-Book)

A Very Christian Christmas

The 1-800-Series Volume Two

The 1-800-Series Complete

Most books are available in ebook, audiobook, paperback, Large Print paperback and Hardcover.

Many are FREE on Kindle Unlimited!

I HOPE THESE SWEET
HOLIDAY ROMANCES
WARMED YOUR HEART.

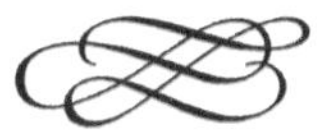

www.ingramcontent.com/pod-product-compliance
Lightning Source LLC
Chambersburg PA
CBHW030142200726
48285CB00004BC/1271